ABOUT SAILOR'S JEWEL

What you don't see can hurt you.

As Rhoe sets out on a trip on the luxurious ocean liner, she expects to spend a pleasant week reading, talking at length to her brother Cyrus, and quietly enjoying herself. When she returns to Albion, she'll be taking up a new and demanding job at the Temple of Healing.

Hugh has been aboard ships half his life, finding his sea legs isn't the problem. But since his father died and his much older half-brother inherited the shipping line, he's not sure where he fits or what his role could be. This trip, he's working to smooth things along for the first class passengers, making sure they have a memorable and delightful voyage.

Of course, the sea has her own mysteries. Something is moving in the deeps, scaring off the pelagic mermaids and other ocean life. Rhoe, Hugh, Cyrus, and others must work together to find out why and bring everyone safely to shore.

Join Rhoe and Hugh for practical conversations, the mysteries of the ocean depths, the glamour of a luxury liner, and of course more than a little magic.

Sailor's Jewel is a romance of 84,000 words set in the magical community of Great Britain in 1901 with a happily-ever-after ending.

SAILOR'S JEWEL

CELIA LAKE

ALSO BY CELIA LAKE

The Mysterious Charm Series

Outcrossing

Goblin Fruit

Magician's Hoard

Wards of the Roses

In The Cards

On The Bias

Seven Sisters

The Mysterious Powers Series

Carry On

The Fossil Door

Eclipse

Charms of Albion

Pastiche

Learn more about the world of Albion and future books at my website, celialake.com.

Sign up for my newsletter to be the first to hear about future books and learn about fascinating bits of research. Happy reading!

ONE

WEDNESDAY, NOVEMBER 6, 1901 ABOARD THE
MOONSTONE

Rhoe had claimed the more comfortable of the chairs in the sitting room. Cyrus was making a full inspection of the space, peering into cupboards and drawers, then out the surprisingly sizable window. These four rooms - two sleeping rooms, the sitting room, the bathing room - would be their home for the next six days, until they landed in Boston.

There was no use rushing her brother. That never ended well. And honestly, she preferred him diligently attentive to his safety - and hers - even if she would far rather get the conversation she knew was coming over with. He would be thorough, and he would talk to her in his own good time. The only immediate question was whether she should go get a book from her trunk, or whether he'd be done in a few minutes.

There was certainly plenty for her to look at. The *Moonstone* was one of the most recently refitted of the Pelagius liners. It was in all ways decidedly better proportioned than the few previous liners Rhoe had travelled on. She had been afraid this trip would be more like those, squeezing along narrow spaces around furniture, or through doors that never quite opened all the way.

That was not the case at all here. The sitting room was more than generously sized, with space for a sofa and two matching chairs with side tables. Their steward had noted that all of the furniture was fully charmed to prevent objects sliding along the surfaces except in the roughest of seas. The bathing room had the latest enhancements in filtering and heating sea water for baths or showers. The heat and cooling were supposed to be just as efficient, though Rhoe assumed they'd care a great deal more about the heat, given it was the beginning of November.

The Pelagius family had risen to prominence in the last century as one of the great shipping families of Albion. Unlike a few of the others, they had made a point of improving their ships with the best comforts - and the best safety record. This was one of the occasional voyages that would be solely magical folk, but she understood the ships were much in demand for the much larger non-magical community. Those travellers might not know why the engines were efficient but quieter, why there were fewer incidents at sea, or why the journey was smoother, but they certainly appreciated the results and rewarded them.

The comforts were nothing to sneeze at either. She knew this must be one of the finest suites, but it was entirely impressive. The furniture here was upholstered in a deep sea-green that would echo the ocean beautifully. Her own room was in shades of a soothing deep blue. And her brother's room was wood panelled with fittings of Council purple, that particular shade of Tyrian purple that had come down through from Phoenicia to Rome to Albion.

She wondered idly if they kept a room decorated just so in case a member of the Council were travelling. You couldn't tell with the Pelagius kin: they had a reputation for doing a given thing for five reasons and never talking about at least three of them.

The fittings were as comfortable as they were beautiful, which was not always the way that went. The bed had been comfortable to sit on, well padded. The chair she was in now was broad, sturdy, and well-sprung, and well-proportioned for her shorter legs. She might not exactly wish to be making this journey, but at least she would be comfortable while she did it.

Finally, Cyrus turned to her. "So, shall we get the tedious part out of the way?"

Rhoe grinned at him. "Obligation before pleasure, as always?"

He sketched a bow and came to settle on the end of the sofa nearest her, tucking one ankle across his knee. She read his actions as quickly as she knew he read hers. Informality, then, and he was making every effort to make it clear he was on her side. "You know Mother and Father don't approve of you taking final vows as a priestess and Healer."

"They have been clear about that. At length. Considerable length." She had been lectured every chance they could get for the preceding six weeks.

"It's not the healing they object to, you know that." Cyrus didn't seem ruffled by it, but Rhoe sighed. Apparently, they would have to at least go through the motions. She did not expect their parents ever to understand, but she had hoped for better from her brother. She was a grown woman, thirty-three, unlikely to marry, and quite capable of making her own choices by every rule and custom of Albion. Healers of her skill and ability were rare: it gave her a tremendous amount of freedom in some ways, while being a narrow path in others. That part didn't trouble her, she'd have taken that road anyway.

"No. They object to the idea of my taking religion seriously. That I might set aside family as my primary concern. The family in general, the idea of marrying or having children in specific." Rhoe shrugged. "And you heard the argument about names. The many, repeated arguments."

"They don't like the idea of you separating from the family." Cyrus spread his hands out. "Smythe-Clive is not the most ancient of family names, but the roots are deep."

"It's the logical inconsistency I object to. If I married, I would pass out of the family and into some other. I am doing that same thing, except I am not going to a family, but to the Temple of Healing. Who will get my best, so long as I am breathing. Which, of course, they've been getting since I apprenticed, so it's not like that should be a shock to anyone who's been paying any attention at all." Rhoe kept her voice even.

Cyrus shook his head. "You know they don't understand it. They're proud of you, having the gift for healing you do. The fact you've helped me more than once hasn't hurt anything. But they think it's something that should be - hoarded is the wrong word. But shared only after thought." That their parents had produced two children so committed to the common good over the family was, admittedly, a puzzle.

"Healing is like wildflowers. You send them out in the world, and they grow and grow, and you have more. Or perhaps like mint, taking over everything it can." Rhoe was very certain of this. Even more certain than she was of the religious commitments she would be making, whether or not her family approved.

"You know I've been busy. Explain the - why you want to make the priestess oaths, not just your Healer's oaths." Cyrus was being fair, at least. Asking to hear her out, rather than assuming he knew all about it.

Rhoe gathered her arguments, feeling the threads of them coil around her hand. "Mother and Father don't understand the structure of the Temple of Healing, fundamentally. There are the Healers, with specialities. The heart, the lungs, the head, all that sort of thing. The surgeons, they usually also train with non-magical doctors. Bones, skin." She waved a hand. "That's only part of healing."

"An important part, but you are right that 'temple' implies you're not just treating the body." Cyrus nodded.

"Inherent in the name, yes. All of us make our oaths to someone. For most people, it's a mild consideration, based on their speciality or focus. But there are also those who have made a particular commitment to a god or goddess. To Christ, to Asclepius, to Apollo, to any number of less well-known powers of healing. There are certain roles at the Temple that only go to people who have made those commitments."

"And you're interested in one of those, then?" Cyrus waved a hand. "You've talked about different treatments you've worked on, over the years. But you haven't seemed to make a specialty of any one of those bits of the body, as it were."

"Always said you were observant." Rhoe snorted, and Cyrus grinned at her before she went on. "I turn out to be, well, a particular kind of generalist. What I really want to do is take charge of the healing baths. That's a role that must be held by a sworn priest or priestess. Usually a priestess."

"That makes a fair bit of sense. And so you - how long have you been thinking about this?"

"How long have I known that's what I wanted to do, or how long have I wanted to swear to Belisama?" Rhoe had known it would come to this question, and she would not prevaricate with her brother. Once he asked half of the question, she had known she would need to tell him the whole answer.

Cyrus blinked several times, the expression he always had when he was rapidly reevaluating a situation. "I gather they have a different answer, then." Oh, she'd got him well and good, she knew him, and she could tell that he was entirely unsure what to make of this now.

"That the baths are where my talents can best be used? Three years. The priestess currently in charge is within a couple of years of retiring to her temple. They pick their successors, it's not a matter of seniority. Omens and whispers from the gods and their conscience, in some proportion. People being people, there are - some choices that get more attention than others, though."

"And if it's not you?" It figured he'd be circling around the much more complicated question.

"Then I will still be working in the baths, helping heal people, body, mind, and soul. All of them. The cup and what it holds, what makes us unique and individual. We need to know both parts." Rhoe was certain of this. She'd been certain since the first time she'd gone to the baths as part of her apprenticeship, down into the spaces under the main temple. Everything was possible, in those candle and charm-lit spaces, in the quiet, where the water washed bodies clean and there was nothing to interfere with the soul's part of the healing.

"You've practised that explanation." Cyrus noted with

amusement. "Well-made." She nodded her head, appreciating the compliment. Cyrus himself was a tremendous public speaker, and she'd learned a great deal from watching him talk people round to his ideas. "And how long have you wanted to devote yourself to Belisama?"

"Since I was seven, and we were at Great-Aunt Imogen's, up by the River Ribble."

"I was mostly concerned with the salmon in it, I remember." Cyrus tilted his head, trying to figure out why her experience had been so different from his. "Was it something specific, there?"

"You were off doing something, looking for frogs or foxes or whatever. I was on the picnic blanket, and Nanny had gone back to the house for more embroidery thread. I fell asleep, and I had a dream. It wasn't the silly things people put in books, with someone who's clearly a goddess telling you to go do something specific."

She glanced at him to make sure he was following. "It was a - there was light, and the sound of someone at a forge, but it was more than that. A village, everyone doing their part, sharing what they did and what they had. I remember going over to the well, and pulling up a bucket, and it was the sweetest water I've ever tasted. It wasn't just the taste, but it made me feel glorious. Beautiful, shining, elegant."

The things she didn't often feel at any other time. Even as a child, she had known she was short, unfashionably shaped, and not conventionally beautiful by any current standard. She was built on a model more of Rubens than the new Edwardian era.

Cyrus nodded again, leaning forward but not interrupting her.

"When I turned around, there was a woman. She didn't say anything. She certainly didn't look like a goddess. She looked a bit like that portrait of Great-great-great-grandmother, the one with her hair down, in the gallery?" Cyrus certainly knew the one. More pastoral than anything else. "I just remember feeling welcome. At ease."

Rhoe shrugged slightly. "Years later, in Ritual class, at school, there was another - something like that. And then another." She wouldn't try to explain those. They didn't go into words at all well. "And my last year at school, I did a project on her, trying to figure out what it meant."

"Decades in the making, then." Cyrus had decided. His voice had the crispness it had once he'd set himself on his chosen course. "Mother and Father wouldn't understand any of that, though I'm sure you've told them enough. I don't understand it either, but I don't need to understand it to back you. Consider this the firm talking to I am supposed to give you, take it as read, and we will have a delightful trip of it, then. You let me know how you want me to play it with them. And here, this week."

"Will you call me Rhoe?" It was the last essential question.

"Is that the name you're taking?" Cyrus leaned forward. "It means - river, or perhaps flowing?"

Rhoe snorted. His Greek was excellent, as always. "It does."

"I have rather a lot of time spent calling you Alexandra," he pointed out. "I may slip, and I apologise in advance. But..." He took a breath, squaring his shoulders. "Rhoe you shall be." It wasn't just about the name, the promise he had just made. It was about everything.

Rhoe reached out a hand for him. "Brother mine." she agreed.

He hesitated. "There's something I should tell you about, before we go out and meet our fellow passengers."

TWO

WEDNESDAY AFTERNOON

Rhoe raised her eyebrow. "Well, that's certainly an ominous way to change the topic." She looked him up and down, trying to decide what it was about.

Cyrus offered a slight smile, so it couldn't be entirely bad. "Council business."

"Oh, well, in that case. What are you permitted to tell me?" There was so much he wasn't. She'd patched him up more than once after something that had left him with his magic tainted with burning ashes and smoke or the sharp tang after a lightning bolt struck far too nearby. He never explained what he'd got into, in those evenings where he turned up at her flat without warning.

He leaned back, steepling his hands. Nothing too difficult, she thought. Or he wouldn't be handling it like this. She couldn't play the games of power and influence like he could, but she certainly knew how to read the room. And her brother in specific. "In the safe is a gem, known as the Sailor's Jewel. A sizable aquamarine." He glanced over as if testing her to see what she made of that tiny amount of information.

Rhoe tumbled that around in her head. "Some people rely on it for poisons." Start with the easy part at least for her. "Please don't."

That made her brother snort and shake his head. "Shan't, no."

"There's a lot of lore about them and ocean travel. Blessings of Poseidon and all that. But this is a perfectly safe liner, excellent record." She tilted her head, rummaging through the bits and pieces she'd heard over the years. "Love. There're some connections to Venus and Aphrodite. I had a fascinating conversation with someone about that once."

A former courtesan, long since married and quite happily, who gave credit in both endeavours to a particular aquamarine piece. "But isn't there also something about scrying? Oracular divination? Some article by, who was it, Phoebus Montague, five years ago?"

Cyrus threw his head back and laughed. "The things that stick in your head. That last one, he talked about this stone. It's used to anchor interactions between different places, but it must be attuned to stones in those other places. So a trip to America, for a stone that's anchored in Boston. And then, sometime after, out to South America, and probably Australia."

"Not somewhere in Africa?"

"Already done, in Alexandria. And Bombay, in India" He shrugged. "That wasn't me. It's not a difficult job. Take it and make the proper introductions to the other stones. Fourth year Ritual classes do harder things."

"Not one of my better skills, so I'm glad it's you. And that's why we don't need to be there terribly long, yes?"

"Exactly. Five days. Three weeks in transit, total, give or take. And then you can go off and - do you have to move to the Temple?"

Rhoe nudged his arm. "That's why I took the flat I did three years ago, you. Nicely convenient to Temple Square, and there's a side door into the garden from the alley off my street."

It made her brother lean back and peer at her. "How long have you been planning that, then?"

She just smiled and shook her head. "If you get it right, I'll tell you." He'd be happier with something to puzzle over, even if it didn't have the sort of high stakes he preferred. "So, how do we handle the social things?"

"That's up to you. You can be my reclusive spinster sister, seen ethereally wafting along the promenade in a veil, or at least a very large hat."

As he'd intended, it was her turn to laugh. He always did know how to do that to her. "I do not waft ethereally anywhere. What's the public excuse for your trip?"

"How about the truth or near enough. You're about to make additional commitments to the Temple of Healing, you won't be able to take time off for a longer trip for a while. We took the chance while we could, with the encouragement of our parents."

Telling the truth had a certain novelty to it. Not that Rhoe lied - it soured her magic, even the little cordial social lies. But she had become even more exquisitely skilled at not telling the whole truth than her family's usual standard. There were quite a few things in her life that weren't anyone else's business, including various things learned from working with patients.

"That will do. And you squiring your younger sister around, then?" She hesitated for a moment. "Someone's going to set their cap for you. More than one someone. Do you want me to be obligingly difficult?"

"Obligingly to me, yes. If you can." Cyrus looked off to his left, out the window to the ocean. They could still see land, but more in a gesture at what land was than any detail. "I know I ought to remarry, certainly Mother and Father wish I would. But not to someone who'd press herself on me for all the wrong reasons." He'd been lucky enough to love his late wife, Tanith. Rhoe would never tell him that was part of why marriage had not appealed. If she couldn't have something like they had, she wasn't sure she wanted to go to the effort.

"Power. Money. Both." Rhoe nodded. "Usual signals?"

Cyrus nodded. "The originals." They'd worked out a series of them, long ago, during her debut, when either of them needed rescuing. His wrist must be doing better, then, he'd had an odd injury last year that meant they'd switched to an alternate set that was more awkward in close quarters. Not that he'd explained how he'd hurt himself. "Shall we, then?" He pushed himself upright.

Rhoe nodded and reclaimed her hat, pinning it in place with a precisely anchored hatpin. Once they were out in the hallway, he offered her his arm and swept her up to the promenade deck.

The other passengers in first class had begun to gather, eyeing each other. The first hours on board - like the first hours in any of the spas or first-class hotels - were a matter of people jostling for status and attention. Or at least the people who cared about those things did. Rhoe, on the other hand, kept an eye out for the people who didn't. They were often vastly more interesting.

She had glanced at the printed passenger list left in their suite by the steward. She recognised the family names, of course. There were a smattering of people she'd been at school with, but no one she knew well.

There were no other Healers, which was a tad unusual, given a hundred and twenty-five or so in first class and several hundred more in second. On one hand, it made her less sure of finding intelligent conversation. On the other hand, she wouldn't have to duck people who were sure they were right about her particular areas of interest. Whenever she made an appearance at social events, the senior Healers always wanted to show off their expertise, and presumed they knew more about her work than she did. She'd begun to make a hobby of spotting their errors and later in the conversation bringing up something that didn't fit with their assumptions. A matter of fact tone and smile tended to leave them blinking.

Looking around, she could spot the usual types quickly. A woman perhaps a dozen years older than Rhoe, wearing widow's blacks, with a young woman beside her. A daughter, Rhoe was fairly sure, on her first trip, from the way she was looking around. What must be a professor and his wife - he was all over tweeds, though it seemed an odd time of year for an academic to be travelling. What had to be newlyweds on honeymoon, the way she was clutching at the man's arm and pointing. The usual set of soberly clad men in business suits, talking earnestly to each other.

As they nodded and smiled at others in passing, they gave everyone a good chance to get a look at them. Most people correctly assumed they were siblings - their faces were too much alike for anything else. Same striking dark hair, same sharp chin and nose, though it looked rather better on Cyrus. Their heights were rather different, though, as she was a good six inches shorter. And, of course, notably more curved, any place a person could be curved.

Cyrus also dressed better, wearing the day robes like they were as comfortable as pyjamas.

She had worn a liberty bodice since she was twenty, when she refused to ever put on a corset again. But even she had to admit that the aesthetic dress she favoured had a tendency to look frumpy compared to the sleekly tailored lines of every other woman visible. They had their puffs of fabric in the places fashion demanded it, but the rest of the silhouette was precisely shaped and limited.

The woman who strolled onto the promenade a moment later made everyone look dowdy. Her blonde hair was up in an elaborate setting with gleaming hair combs, and her dress was a brilliant peacock green that might have been chosen to complement the warm brown of the wood panelling behind her. Rhoe thought her to be in her late twenties.

She was accompanied by an equally elegant Afghan, trotting along beside her, long hair waving. She handed the dog's leash off to an older, mousier woman, who had been trailing behind her, and then turned to beam at the assembled people. Cyrus cleared his throat in Rhoe's ear. "Lady Jenifry Alton. Lady in her own right, inherited an estate in Suffolk. Married to her third husband, but he never travels."

"Any particular concerns?"

"If I were her husband, I'd have some. The previous two died a year or two into the marriage. Both older men, of course. The usual jokes about hearts giving out." Which might be all sorts of things, and they both knew it. Some innocent enough, and others not.

"Remember what I said about aquamarines, then." They watched Lady Jenifry sweep through introductions with several small groups, including a trio of couples who had come up the stairs from the lower deck. Good friends all, she suspected, the way they were already cheerfully enjoying the trip. And the alcohol, judging by the fact their glasses were only a third full.

Lady Jenifry kept her greetings very brief. Then the woman swept off to the next group, as if no one were good enough to hold her attention for long.

By the time she turned in their direction, Rhoe was at least ready. It would be the brief comment to her, the lack of recognition, the slight sniff of dismissal. Lady Jenifry would not be outright rude to her, in case it might put Cyrus off. This was the sort of woman who would want his attention at supper, even if she couldn't induce him to anything more. "Council Member! We are honoured, then."

Cyrus bent to kiss her hand, the proper kiss in the air. "Lady Jenifry. My sister, Healer Rhoe Smythe-Clive." Bless him, he said the new name as smoothly as if he'd used it all her life.

Lady Jenifry sniffed slightly. "A Healer."

Rhoe smiled pleasantly. A fair number of people of that social class of leisure weren't sure what to make of her. Healing was a noble profession, and certainly a necessary one. But there were people - both women and men - who thought that anyone of their social class working for a living was entirely beyond the pale. "A pleasure." she said, cheerfully. "I'm at the Temple of Healing in Trellech."

"Do escort me around, Council Member. I'm sure your sister can spare you for a few teeny minutes?"

"You are travelling on your own, then?" Cyrus did not, exactly, offer his arm yet. "Rhoe, at your pleasure?" That bit of code meant he was fine with it, for the moment, but come rescue him if it went on too long.

She smiled again, genially. "I'm enjoying looking out at

the ocean. Come find me for tea." That would be anywhere from a quarter hour to three quarters from now, and he grinned suddenly, at the range it gave him.

"Oh, my companion." Lady Jenifry waved a hand without looking back at where the mousy woman stood with her dog. And without providing a name. Companions did not count entirely as independent people to women like her, clearly. Cyrus nodded and offered her his arm, escorting her off to the other side of the promenade deck. It left Rhoe alone to take in the rest of the crowd.

Rhoe had been standing there for a minute or two when the professor's wife approached. Rhoe took in the clothes. Her travelling dress was smartly made, but not in the most fashionable of colours. Rather than the more common pale beige or cream, it was a deep green that flattered her darker brown hair. They must have some private income, but she suspected travelling in first class was a particular treat for them. "Pardon, but you were standing on your own, and we can be a little informal, aboard, can't we?" Her husband trailed along after her, looking more out at the ocean than where he was going. "I'm Ilune Merton, this is my husband Ferdinand."

The professor extended his hand. "Ferdinand Merton, professor of oekology." Rhoe let him take her hand, and he surprised her by shaking it rather than kissing it. He nodded at her dress. "I presume you don't necessarily favour the ridiculous social pleasantries? That's why my wife was intrigued."

Perhaps she might find intelligent conversation about her professional fields of interest after all. "Oekology?" she inquired. "People must ask you often, I beg your pardon."

Professor Merton was beaming now, clearly the sort of person who liked making that explanation. "An uncommonly used term, about the relationship between individuals, communities, and the environment." He swept an arm out toward the ocean. "I am particularly interested in coastal populations, of both people and beasts. On sabbatical this term, but we were kept in Albion by our daughter's poor health."

"Oh, I do hope she's recovering, then." Rhoe considered. "I'm a Healer, at the Temple in Trellech. I'd be glad to make some suggestions if it would be a help." That was something she didn't usually say, but there was something in the way he spoke about his daughter that made her more than willing to offer.

"She's in her twenties," Ilune Merton said. "But you must be on holiday? I'd not mind a chance to discuss later, if you don't mind? Make sure we're not missing something? But not right now, surely we all have far more immediate things to tend to?"

Rhoe smiled at that, liking these two a great deal already. There was something delightfully unpretentious about them. Both of them smiled readily and generously, not the tight little social smiles that moved the mouth but not the eyes.

"Your specialty, in healing?" Professor Merton was considering her, thoughtfully.

"When I return to Albion, I'll be making my commitments as a Healer in the sacred baths. I'll be helping to tend the people who use them, and figure out which will suit their needs." It still felt a fragile thing to say, but the only thing left to do before she could begin that work was her oath.

"And up 'til now?" Rhoe was amused, it was a bit like the oral examinations she'd been made to take as part of her training. Coming from the professor, though, it felt engaging, like he was honestly curious.

"A range of positions, but most recently dealing with infectious diseases. Besides the regular work, I was assisting with some research with the alchemists about preventatives and various cleansing potions, to reduce the spread of infection. Most satisfying work."

"Oh, that must have been terrifying. Knowing people had illnesses you might catch."

Rhoe shrugged slightly. "We took excellent precautions, and good charmwork goes a long way. It would be a far better world if we had more ways to prevent more of the worst illnesses through vaccination, though. There are still too many needless deaths."

Ilune Merton seemed about to say something, when a small child - about six - came barrelling through the various people, upsetting a tea table and causing all manner of chaos.

THREE

WEDNESDAY AFTERNOON

Now that they were well underway, Hugh had made the initial circuits of the ship, pausing on each deck to listen to how things were going. The stewards were delivering the luggage and seeing to the unpacking. He'd stopped briefly down in steerage, nodding with approval at how well things were being handled.

Unlike too many other ships he'd been on, the air smelled fresh and clean, and the wood floors had been freshly scrubbed. As he walked through, he could see the single women and single men settling into their larger shared cabins. He also heard the conversations from the berths for married couples and families tucked between the larger spaces.

Working his way up, he'd gone through the second class gallery, stopping in his own room to change into more formal clothing. Brushing his hair back, he made his way up to the promenade deck. Savouring his last few minutes of anonymity, he went first to the bridge, waiting politely at the door for the Captain's attention.

It took only half a minute before one of the bridge crew

alerted the captain. When the man turned around he was all smiles, but Hugh knew this was a delicate moment.

"Master Pelagius, welcome to the *Moonstone*. This is your first trip on her? We're well away and under steam."

Hugh grinned suddenly. "Oh, I did two trips down in the engine room. Father's orders, but that was a good ten years ago, early on in her travels. Before you were captain, certainly. Mostly, I made myself useful and tried not to get in the way." He offered his hand. "What can I do to be of help to you this trip?"

This was the delicate part. His half-brother Ockham was the majority owner of the line, the chosen heir of their father. Hugh was still finding his place in the business, or rather what place he wanted to claim. And more importantly, how that fit with Ockham's plans. Claiming the appropriate amount of authority and influence without overstepping was a constant challenge, and one Hugh struggled with.

That struggle apparently didn't show at the moment. Captain Melcott shook his hand heartily, looking suddenly relieved. "I'm glad to hear you say that."

Hugh waved his hand. "I am here to be charming with our first-class passengers, and help handle any difficulties outside your scope for the others. And learn how things go from this side of things. I've done trips in the purser's office, most recently, or assisting the senior steward."

"We have quite a few notable passengers this trip, so another hand with the social pleasantries would be quite the thing, actually. Nothing too out of the ordinary but there are a lot of them, and several known to stand on their station."

Hugh nodded. "I saw the lists. Council Member Smythe-Clive and his sister, Lady Jenifry Alton, that group from the Scali bank. Professor Merton is quite well respected in his field. And there's the two retired generals."

"The Scali men are easy going enough about anything other than banking. There's a few travelling who Lady Alton might set her sights on for shipboard amusements, at the least. She has a certain reputation." Captain Melcott inclined his head. Hugh appreciated that he provided the information, but assumed Hugh could handle himself. "You're rather like her usual target. Though the Council Member is a widower, and a better social catch, the way she's likely to count it."

"What is her goal, then, do you know?"

"A bit of amusement. But she met her second husband on one of these voyages. People did talk after his death, I heard a bit of a rumour the Guard looked into it, but here she is." The Captain waved a hand. "To be honest, I did my best to avoid that sort of entanglement, even before I was married."

Hugh nodded. "Never know when you'll see someone again, in very different circumstances." He, for one, worried about that kind of unpleasantness a lot. Or the possibilities for blackmail.

Captain Melcott inclined his head in approval and went on. "Two singers - Lily Freeman and Monty Williams. She does rather nicely with art songs, and she's generously agreed to give a concert during the voyage."

"Anyone you expect trouble with?"

"The purser will have the list of those we know to be card sharps. If you're able to, circulating through the saloon after dinner would be a help. Especially once people know who you are."

"Already introduced myself to the bartender and stewards." Hugh was very clear on how that worked. It would let them decide how visible he should be, what would be helpful. "Any concerns about the voyage?"

Melcott turned his head, looking out of the broad windows. "We're out of iceberg season, so we should be all right. We're not going full speed, though. One of the engines has been running a little rough..." He let his voice trail off.

"I know my navigation, but I've no mastery of running a ship this size, Captain. And we've no need to break speed records this trip." The *Moonstone* was recently refitted, in the last year, but her bones were rather older. "Any concerns about anything else?"

"Have you sailed this route recently, sir? Last three years or so?"

Hugh shook his head. "I've mostly been on the routes to India or South Africa. Once to Brazil."

"We've had a few more sightings of creatures, out in the open ocean. Generally nothing of concern, but lights in the distance. Sometimes the mermaids basking on the surface, but that's expected. And not a problem on this voyage, of course."

"Fully magical, passengers and crew. No problems with the Pact, no need for glamours on our end. We've made the proper offerings, I'm sure?"

"And will do again when we hit their territory, quite. There's no need to be rude." Captain Melcott shifted his hands in the rudimentary sign language used by the pelagic mermaids. It was rather different than the much more nuanced one favoured by the coastal merfolk used to talking to humans on a regular basis. "I'll have someone come find you when we're reaching position, if you'd like."

"Any time, even middle of the night. That's precisely the sort of thing I'm supposed to be learning about."

Captain Melcott broke into a broad grin. "Well, we should get along fine then." He didn't say out loud - didn't need to - that he'd been worried Hugh would try to take charge of things he had no business making decisions about. "Right, then. Do dine at my table tonight, wherever you end up on future nights."

Hugh made a slight bow. "An honour. I'll let you get back to it." He withdrew, pleased at how well that had gone. Being the younger half-brother of the owner of the line had a number of challenges. Navigating the changes since his brother had inherited had been tricky, the past two years. But it seemed like the crews were finally settling down into the new expectations.

Making his way down from the bridge, he glanced around the first class public rooms. He wanted a sense for how people were grouping themselves, before the bell sounded to dress for supper. It wouldn't be formal tonight, of course, they'd only just set sail, but the women would want to fix their hair and the gentlemen spruce themselves up.

When everyone assembled in the formal dining room, Hugh made his way to the Captain's table, nodding amiably at the Captain. The table seated eight, and tonight that included Council Member Smythe-Clive, his sister, Lady Alton, the widowed Mistress Wallace and her daughter Thessaly, and the senior of the Scali bankers, Amadeo Scali. He was travelling on his own without his wife or family. He was well into his sixties, but was looking around amiably rather than scowling. That was promising.

"Ladies, good evening. Gentlemen." Hugh bowed slightly, after assisting Lady Alton with her chair. He noticed that Council Member Smythe-Clive had done the same for Mistress Wallace as well as his sister. Hugh took his own seat, as the Captain came to join them. "Captain Melcott, good evening."

"A very good evening to you all." Melcott nodded. "May I introduce Hugh Pelagius, travelling with us to continue learning about the workings of the line. Lady Alton, a pleasure to see you travelling with us again. Healer Smythe-Clive, I don't believe we'd had the pleasure of your company before."

The Healer was a woman not much older than Hugh himself, perhaps mid-thirties. Experienced, certainly. She was dressed in lovely fabrics, but decidedly in the aesthetic mode, in a deep blue that complemented her dark hair. Hugh supposed that must be more practical for a Healer. She smiled. "Do please, call me Rhoe." It was said evenly, but it was a fascinating shift of power, not expecting people to use her earned title. Certainly not standing on ceremony.

It did, at least, lead to a general round of introductions and first names, though he was quite sure no one would drop the 'Lady' when addressing Lady Jenifry.

Rhoe's brother waited until everyone had settled, then added, "And Cyrus or Smythe-Clive, please. Council Member Smythe-Clive is such a mouthful, and this is a family trip, after all."

"I hadn't thought Healers had much opportunity for a long voyage, Rhoe?" That was Euphremia Wallace.

"Oh, we normally don't. Quite difficult to get away, and I always find it terribly difficult to leave my patients in other hands, no matter how competent. But I am moving into new responsibilities at the Temple of Healing. My brother pointed out it's been ages since I've had more than a day or two off at a time." Rhoe was quite amiable about this, her voice even and just slightly amused, like she was constantly on the edge of laughter. He liked that sound.

"And you're going to Boston of all places?" That was Lady Jenifry.

"There's a medical collection I'm interested in looking at. We might go down to New York, too. We've tickets back on the 20th. I'm quite sure we'll find some amusements in the week or so in between."

"That's the *Citrine*, isn't it?" That was Amadeo Scali. "All the ships in the line are named for stones, I gather?"

Huge nodded back. "A tradition, for more than 100 years. We've re-used names by now, of course, a few times. This is the third *Moonstone*, actually."

"Why stones?" That was Cyrus, who was settled into his meal now. "Or rather, I can think of quite a few possible reasons, and I'm curious which apply."

"It does simplify the theme of the decorations, as my aunt says - she's responsible for that kind of thing. You can see the touches in the public rooms here, the glass insets in the windows, and so on, even though the rest of the panelling is darker."

"So yellow accents, for the *Citrine*, then? What are the other ships at the moment?"

"Oh, we've a baker's dozen under steam right now, and three more in dry dock for repairs or refitting. But it does give a nice variation." Hugh ticked off the list, in order of age. "The *Spinel, Chalcedony, Lapis, Emerald, Citrine, Opal, Amber, Garnet, Peridot, Carnelian, Amethyst,* and *Ruby*. The *Topaz, Pearl,* and *Sapphire* are in for repairs and redecoration."

Captain Melcott clapped his hands, amused. "I'm not going to ask how long it took you to learn that - that's in order of launch, that list of names."

Hugh grinned back, broadly. "I actually always found it

easier that way? It makes it easier to keep track of which are due to be refitted or at least fully checked through."

"Do you do much with that end of the business, then?" Amadeo Scali tilted his head, trying to decide how that went into the maths, Hugh suspected.

"That is my business, at the moment - learning how the different moving parts fit together. I've served an apprenticeship in navigation, but my brother's not quite sure yet where I can be best put to use, so we're trying a little of everything." He kept his tone light, amiably responding without bogging down in the complex details.

"You must have made many trips, then. Navigation, really?"

That made it easy to shift into a conversation he'd had dozens of times before. He had a set piece about the basic theories of navigation, along with a few funny stories about the ways various pieces of the art had been developed. It let Captain Melcott settle back and enjoy his meal, just chiming in here and there with stories of his own, and carried them well into the cheese course.

When the meal ended, the men stood to retreat to the smoking room. Smythe-Clive bent over and whispered in his sister's ear.

Hugh wondered for a moment about the two of them. Close in age, and at ease with each other, but he had the suspicion they hadn't spent much time together recently before this trip. They kept checking with each other, silently, about things that would have been obvious if they were more often together. If she wished more wine, how to answer a question, that sort of thing. It piqued his interest, but then Amadeo murmured something in his own ear, a question about the size of the ship, as they walked down the hallway.

FOUR

WEDNESDAY AFTER SUPPER

The smoking room itself was as predictable as always. Hugh extracted himself amiably from Amadeo Scali at the door, promising to come round and chat with him and his brothers and cousins and brothers-in-law in a few minutes. He wanted a chance to get a lay of the room first.

Of course, people grouped up differently than they had at supper. Separated from the women, the men formed groups based on mutual interest. The cards had already come out, and Hugh recognised two of the card sharps from previous voyages. One was leaning back, waiting for hands to be dealt, the other was settling into the game in front of him.

It was the eternal question. The line could not prevent people from gambling, and they didn't exactly want to. For one thing, it was entirely impractical: if it were barred in the public spaces, the games would just move to private suites.

In the saloon, the bartender or one of the stewards could at least come in with a message of some kind. Or perhaps mention a spill on the back of someone's jacket. The steward could take the excuse to get him away from the play for a few minutes until he came to his senses about not betting everything he had.

And on a purely mercantile level, Hugh had seen the books. Gambling was exceptionally good for the income from the bar. His brother did not entirely approve, and Hugh didn't either. What people did with their money wasn't any of their business, as long as the passengers didn't do damage to the ship or each other. But neither Hugh nor Ockham were entirely happy with people destroying their lives on board.

Their father had been rather more about the money involved than the good of once and hopefully future passengers. Ockham had been cautious about making sweeping changes. So one of Hugh's tasks this trip was to observe the gambling, and see if there were ways to moderate it or give those who were losing badly a way out that saved face.

Hugh did a lap around the room slowly, taking his time, pausing here and there to have a word with a steward, or order a drink, or say hello. There were several regular travellers here, men he recognised from previous trips. They were unsure how to place him, since they'd last seen him in the Purser's office. "Hugh Pelagius," and a cheerful hand stretched out for a firm handshake usually sorted that out. The family name was unmistakable.

Eventually, he found himself with the Scali men. There were six of them, two brothers born into the main line of the family, two cousins, two brothers-in-law. They were all comfortably familiar with each other, in the way of people who'd worked together for twenty years with mutual goodwill. Three had their wives along, having after-dinner conversation elsewhere. He found that encouraging, actually. Ockham wanted to do better with the interactions between senior and up-and-coming staff in the Pelagius clan. Hugh was now wondering if the Scali might be willing to do a little consulting on how to handle some of it, perhaps in exchange for some shipping considerations.

Amadeo was clearly senior, and the others deferred to him - but with plenty of teasing. He didn't start out with the easy questions. "So, you're learning about the line, then? Have you been doing that long?" It was asked pleasantly enough, but Hugh had no illusions he could wriggle out from answering it.

Hugh settled back, using all the tricks he'd learned to seem at ease. "You, of all people, must know my family well enough, sir."

It made Amadeo laugh. "Your family, yes. But not you. And I find that curious. I knew you existed, of course. That you've accessed your personal vaults with us from time to time. But not what you've been doing with yourself."

Hugh spread his hands. "I'm quite a bit younger than Ockham, and our sister Meraud." Near enough twenty years. "My mother was Father's second wife, later in life. Father thought - and I agree, now I'm most of the way through it - that there's nothing like learning the line by working your way up. I've the mastery in navigation I mentioned at dinner, but I've done my time in the engine room, with the stewards, the purser's office. Even in the galleys, though no one with any sense should trust me with anything more than the most basic of vegetable chopping."

Amadeo nodded. "We've much the same sort of scheme for our younger folk, working their way through the different positions. It must be a particular challenge, on a ship, so many different skills needed."

"Oh, you don't want to trust me as a carpenter or fitter,

certainly. And I'm more or less capable of putting the right amount of coal into the furnace, if someone else is keeping pace with me." Hugh leaned back, spreading his hands. "But the record keeping, understanding all the pieces of that, decidedly useful. It hasn't been all voyages, of course. I've done my time in the offices, as well. And on the docks, helping oversee and manage some of the refitting projects."

Donato, one of cousins, grinned. "There's a man after our heart. Do your projects come in under budget?"

Hugh laughed. "Mine to know, not mine to tell. But Ockham's been generally pleased with my work."

"Fair enough." Donato considered, then asked, "Are there things you can share, about any future projects? Relevant to our banking work."

Hugh ran the maths and patterns in his head, as well as the question of how annoyed Ockham would be if he showed his hand here. "I was thinking, earlier, that I'd like to consult your family on a few matters, and encourage Ockham to do so. The one that brought it to mind was seeing how you are with each other. We've been wanting to encourage a greater sense of interdependence between arms of the businesses, and you do that so well."

It was earnest and rather open for a business negotiation, but he thought that would do well here. The men facing him watched him, one eyebrow slightly raised, in an unnerving and unified quiet for a good minute, before Amadeo slapped his hand down on the table. "Tell your brother we'll be glad to discuss mutually agreeable terms. That's not something many people notice about us."

Hugh beamed at that. "A pleasure, sirs. I'm quite glad we're on the same trip, then." That led them into a cheerful discussion of the shipping schedule through the rest of the year and into the spring. Then they got off onto the balance of voyages solely for the magical community, versus mixed ships.

"Tell me," Donato said, "How does it work on one of the mixed trips? I've never been on one, our security measures normally make it impossible."

Hugh took a sip of his brandy before answering, partly to gather his thoughts. "The feel of them is quite different. On the staff side, of course, there's a need to keep the two sets separate enough. The Pact does a lot of that, of course. Those used to moving in mixed society know how to hold their tongues about magic, and the Pact reminds anyone who slips."

"Ah, it was not like that in Italy, where we come from, though there are ..." Donato fumbled, clearly searching for the right word. "Agreements there now too. But we Scali, we have been under English law since well before the Pact. The 14th century was not kind, but the 15th, ah, that was much better for us. And since, of course." It made Hugh wonder, all of a sudden, how the great change of the Pact of 1484, in England, might have affected the trade and banking networks of the time. Certainly they'd come through it well.

Hugh nodded. "We have been very pleased you've entrusted us with your shipping, both to the Americas and through the Pacific. Another reason I'm sure my brother would be interested in an ongoing conversation."

Amadeo chuckled. "Never anything for just one reason, it's a waste of time and energy." He gestured. "The mixed trips, how is the public space, then?"

"This would be the non-magical folks. We set up a few of the suites as public space for the magical passengers. There are three, central, on this deck, with a lovely view, and plenty of space. A bar and gaming tables in one, space for the ladies in one, and a general gathering space in one. And then dining space, of course. That is the gymnasium at the moment, quite an elegant one, if you go have a look at it. It's quite easy with glamours and illusions to divert people from those areas of the ship who shouldn't be there."

"Later, later. Now is for drinking, and talking. Do you expect an easy voyage, then?"

Hugh shrugged. "I'm not the one to proclaim on that, and I'll not court bad luck. But the Captain said the trip looked promising. We are not going at full speed, there's no need, and they're still breaking one of the engine repairs in. No problem, of course, but better to ease it up to a greater strain."

"No lurking sea monsters?" That was the junior brother-in-law, Hugh hadn't quite caught the name in the introductions.

"It is a very large ocean, of course. And even those who glimpse a kraken or a leviathan do so only rarely. No one's quite sure of the cause, either. It's not a magical cargo, even one of great power - plenty of ships over the centuries have travelled in perfect safety. It isn't storms, the sightings have been in all kind of weathers. It isn't presence or absence of the smaller creatures, generally. We'll likely see whales, especially once we reach the Canadian coast. And there's a good chance we'll spot some of the pelagic mermaids tomorrow or the day after."

"There's something about the merfolk and the kraken, isn't there?" That was Donato, sounding thoughtful rather than worried.

"If they suddenly disappear, it's a sign there's something else about. That might be a shark, of course, which isn't going to bother us. Most of the ones this far north are fairly small. The largest of them don't go in for boats, as a general rule, and aren't a bother to the merfolk. But there are squid, or other creatures, and we certainly don't know about most of them yet. The sea is a mystery, as it always has been."

Amadaeo lifted his glass. "A mystery." It made a proper toast, and, Hugh felt, a properly respectful one.

"Do you know the sharks then, to look at?" Donato asked.

"Some. The thresher has a very distinctive long tail, if you get a look at it. And the Greenland and basking sharks, those are the two biggest, they are fairly easy to identify. I'm better at spotting the whales. We might get lucky and see a killer whale, I believe the preferred term is."

"Ah, a grampus. We know them well. Fierce, and also showy. The white and black, so stark. You have seen them often?"

"They're a rare treat, along this route - we're a bit far south for them, I gather. Donato, you were sitting at supper with Professor Merton, I saw? He'd be an excellent person to ask, I gather. He's made a study of the ocean and the cities on the coasts. A historian, of course, not a naturalist, but he must know a fair bit about the ocean life. I'll ask Captain Melcott if there's someone on the crew who might give a talk, as well, if there's interest."

There were general nods of agreement, entirely amiable.

"The rest of your evening, do you have plans?" That was Amadeo, eyeing him. "Do you go to the dancing, when it starts?"

They had opened up the ballroom, as the seas were quite calm at the moment, to let people get their sea legs. Hugh nodded. "At least for a little bit."

"Is there a particular lady who has caught your eye?" Amadeo must have caught something in Hugh's expression, and he laughed, warmly. "Ah, you must be polite to them all, I suppose. Squire each around who will be danced with. Bring tea or punch to those who do not dance. It is harder work than the furnace, I suppose."

His easy amusement put Hugh at ease, though he did not forget that these men were weighing and measuring him with every word he spoke. "It's a pleasure, a chance to meet so many people. I enjoy the puzzle, figuring out what we can provide that will give them a pleasant journey."

It made all the men laugh, first Amadeo and Donato, then the others joining in, before Donato clapped him on the back. "An honest answer and a tactful one. Come, join us, at any time. And you may escort my wife for a dance, if she wishes."

Hugh nodded, appreciative of the compliment he'd been paid. The gong went then, indicating that the ballroom was open, and he stood up. "I should see that everything is in order, though I'm sure it is. Later, gentlemen, it's been a pleasure, and I hope for more chances to talk soon."

Rhoe stayed settled in her chair after the men departed. Cyrus had disappeared, not to the smoking, she suspected, but about his own business, while it would not be so obvious he was absent. One of the challenges of a shipboard schedule was that if you were not visible when other people expected you to be, there would be gossip.

"Tell me, dear." That was Euphremia Wallace. "About your family?" It had a delicate hesitation. Lady Jenifry had been about to get up and find some more agreeable prey, but she instead lifted her hand to summon another drink.

"Cyrus is my elder brother by nearly three years. We don't get much chance to see each other, in the ordinary course of things - we're both so terribly busy with our own commitments. Our parents manage the family estates, of course. Not as lords of the land, naturally." She nodded at Lady Jenifry. "But there are tenant farmers, and wool mills, and a lot of sheep. The family holdings are in Devon, down near Exeter."

There was a sniff from Lady Jenifry, who Rhoe knew

well was from somewhere in Suffolk. She couldn't remember precisely where, anymore. All the details of about who held which bit of land had largely fallen out of her head by the time she'd completed her Healer's apprenticeship.

"And you live in Trellech, I suppose, now?"

Rhoe nodded "I have a small set of rooms near the Temple, in a rooming house with several other Healers. Our landlady sees to things like our laundry and meals." It worked out well enough, and sometimes they were even free at the same time for a meal. Mostly, though, it was luncheon or supper snatched in the Healer's dining room between patients. Every so often, she had the occasional meal out when Cyrus or someone else was in Trellech and she could get away. She was looking forward to somewhat more predictable hours, if long ones, when she took up her new duties.

"And he's one of the younger Council Members, isn't he?" Euphremia leaned forward, visibly interested. Rhoe had known that was coming, certainly. Cyrus was far more interesting to other people than she was. Mix that air of mystery with his good looks, charm, and status as a most eligible widower, and it was a surprise anyone talked about anything else.

"He is." There was no use denying that part. He'd won his way through the challenges to claim a seat in a mix of fury and grief and bloody-minded use of ancient magical techniques no one had used in centuries. And a fair bit of luck, as he'd admitted to her privately later. "The autumn of 1889, he was nearly twenty-four."

Lady Jenifry arched an elegant eyebrow. "A widower already, wasn't he?"

Rhoe nodded, keeping her expression pleasant. "We all

miss Tanith a great deal. She was the year after him at Schola, and I was delighted when they married. Their daughter, Gemma, is looking forward to Schola next year, she did brilliantly on her examinations."

As if Gemma, who had all her father's love of knowledge and her mother's quicksilver mind, would do anything else. Rhoe was looking forward to finding something in Boston to bring home for her, she'd been unhappy this trip had to happen during term time at her tutoring house. "He spends his time with Gemma, when she's not at her schooling, or on Council business, with little variation. And occasionally with me." She gestured at the table, to indicate this trip was the last.

"Ah." Lady Jenifry put volumes into that one syllable. She then rose, and made her way, in elegant small steps, off toward the doorway.

Euphremia waited until she was through the door. "You do realise she's gone to find him." She sounded amused for a moment before she sobered.

"I'm so sorry for your loss." Rhoe said promptly. "It's such a bother, having people assume things, isn't it?" Which nicely threaded the needle about whether Euphremia might or might not want to remarry. Or even think about it.

The older woman nodded. "A year ago, but it still feels quite recent. But dear Daniel was insistent Thessaly should have her debut among his people, in New York City, no matter what, and we'll be out of deepest mourning once we arrive."

Rhoe had to admire the precision of that timing. "A new era of your life, as you step off the ship?" she suggested.

Euphremia smiled suddenly at that. "You're very kind, to realise it. And not to judge." She tilted her head. "I suppose that goes with being a Healer?"

"I feel it goes with being a good one, certainly. Listening and understanding that a person has some reason for the choices they make. Trying to understand that works better than insisting I must know better than they do. No matter how that is sometimes frustrating, I admit."

Thessaly had sat quietly throughout all of this, listening. "Is Healer training very long?"

"Seven years is the usual range. We're taking people's lives and magic into our hands. Three years of additional learning after we leave school - usually Schola or Alethorpe - and then four working under a senior Healer. Another two or three some specialities, depending. Surgeons usually take training in the non-magical community, as well, for example. Some people train with apothecaries, to be able to better recommend potions and medicines." Rhoe shrugged. "I didn't specialise, at least not then."

"And now?" Euphremia picked up on it quickly. Rhoe thought she would make a formidable ally, at least for the length of the journey.

"When I get back to Albion, I'll be taking on duties in the sacred baths, under the temple. As a junior, there, of course, learning how things go, but I am looking forward to it a great deal. I am competent, with day to day care, but I've learned the place I want to be is in knitting all of it together. The injuries that wounds and illness bring to the sense of self, not just the body."

"And that is a focus of the baths? I admit, I've never been?" Euphremia frowned. "My late husband thought it - well, I know they go back to the Romans, but he thought it a bit immodest."

"There times set aside for men and for women, separately. Rather a lot of people think like your husband did, and that's fair enough. But we also have private rooms, shrines, dedicated to particular gods and goddesses, tended by those who have made their oaths to them." She gestured. "Do consider coming by when you return to Albion. Drop me a note at the Temple - the attendant at the entrance can do that quickly - and I'd be glad to arrange something."

"Very kind." Euphremia looked her up and down. "It was implied you are not married?"

A rather unusual thing for a woman of her age and station, Rhoe knew. "No, not I. My parents would prefer it, certainly, but I think they've largely given up hope." She had turned down all three of the men they had suggested, and all for excellent reason. One had been imprisoned for embezzlement two years later, another had turned out to be entirely unpleasant. And the third - well, the third was happily married to a school friend of Rhoe's, and they suited each other very well in all the ways Rhoe wouldn't have.

"You didn't wish for your own family?" It was a daringly personal question, and after a moment Euphremia withdrew slightly, moving as if to stand. "I shouldn't have pressed, I do beg your pardon."

Rhoe shook her head. "I'm not offended, just not entirely sure how to reply." She let her own smile linger. "Most people aren't nearly brave enough to ask, you see. So I have all the polite demurrals ready, and not an actual answer."

She was delighted when Euphremia smiled and relaxed, before adding to Thessaly, "You could learn quite a lot from observing how Healer Smythe-Clive does things. That is the proper form of address?"

"For a few weeks more, yes. Then I'll be Healer Belisama. Or, honestly, simply Rhoe or Healer Rhoe."

Euphremia tilted her head. "Not a marriage. Your Healer commitments?"

Rhoe nodded. "The role I am taking on is as much priestess as Healer, and I will be making additional oaths to Belisama. She is not well known to many, but she is light and fire and healing waters. Not unlike Brigid, among the Irish, or some aspects of Minerva."

That explanation, at least, she had down pat, so she tackled the more complex one. "I could marry if I wished, but for much of my life, my hours have been long, unpredictable, and unwieldy. I take Gemma out to tea on Saturday or Sunday afternoons at her tutoring house when I can get free. I see my parents occasionally, catch a meal here or there with Cyrus when we are in the same city at the same time." She shrugged. "It would not be much to offer a husband I liked, and I am not inclined to marry one I do not."

Euphremia snorted at that. "You certainly know your own mind, and I have more sense than to try and argue you out of it, even on such short acquaintance?" She looked off out the door. "Do you need to warn your brother Lady Jenifry is on the prowl? Or can he handle himself?"

"Oh, in a few minutes, when they start up the music, I'll go claim him for a dance or two and rescue him as needed. I suspect I'll have a pleasant time dancing with the Scali men. They have excellent manners and good humour, as a clan."

"You have done this sort of thing before." Euphremia was considering her in a somewhat new light now.

"An ocean trip twice before. This sort of social expectation? Often enough. Over the holidays, when I was not on duty. I regularly go with Cyrus to the Council gatherings, when he needs someone on his arm."

"Where Lady Jenifry would sell her teeth to be there, and does not get invited." That was a delightfully accurate - if catty - comment.

"I like your humour, Euphremia. Shall we wander that way? I think I hear them tuning up."

They made their way aft, toward the large ballroom. Cyrus had indeed reappeared and was doing his best to dodge Lady Jenifry's company. Rhoe glanced over. "That's my cue. I do look forward to more conversation in the days to come." Euphremia waved her off and turned to ask something of one of the stewards, as Rhoe slipped her hand into the crook of Cyrus's elbow. Lady Jenifry had said something about the weather, but paused.

"There are you, brother mine. We're sailing very smoothly, don't you think?" She could match inanity with inanity. "Hello, again, Lady Jenifry. You are going to give me a dance or two, aren't you, Cyrus?"

He spread his other hand as the music started up. "A brother's obligation." Once they were properly in motion, he let out a breath in her ear. "She latched right onto me as soon as she saw me. If you need to find me, look in the funnels and lifeboats. I suspect I'll be taking up residence anywhere she can't track me down."

"That bad?" Rhoe considered, watching her brother as they went through a figure, then another, in one of the dances they could both do without thinking. She was not a stunning dancer, but she made it a point to be competent at anything she did, or to avoid doing it to the best of her ability.

Cyrus gave the little jerk of his chin she knew so well, lifting it for a second as he moved her from one hand to the other. "Not my sort, darling sister. You know how I feel about adultery."

"Never mind the other rumours." Rhoe agreed. "I'll do my best. And at least we're sharing the suite, and you can claim, rightfully, I'm a terribly light sleeper. Even with silencing charms."

"A trait I did not think I'd actually need, but very handy at the moment, yes. You always do know when there's someone moving around near you."

Rhoe grinned up at him. "Healer's sense. Terribly annoying if you want to sleep in on a Saturday, but it has its moments." She considered. "Anyone else likely to be a bother?"

"What was Euphremia like? Or were you talking to someone else while the men were smoking?"

"She's delightful, and I'm looking forward to more conversation, actually. Entirely safe for you to dance with, she loved her husband and is looking forward to a new stage in her life. Especially after she sees Thessaly well-settled. But I suspect she's interested in the freedom of a widow, not more matrimony."

Cyrus relaxed at that. "Ah, excellent. I knew her husband slightly, through one of my clubs, he was a good man. And you? Anyone likely to be a difficulty?"

"I've plenty of practice, and it's not as if people bother me on my own accord." Being unfashionable in half a dozen ways, most of them quite deliberately. "I thought I might see if one of the Scali men might give me a dance? They're usually most pleasant if you're not a threat to their interests."

"I am not, certainly not at the moment, and you even less so. Abandon me to Euphremia when you like, then, and I will squire her around."

That left them amiably disposing of the rest of the dancing, both able to make the proper show of things without dealing with the less pleasant assumptions or attachments.

SIX

THURSDAY MORNING

Hugh was up bright and early to get a walk around the deck in before breakfast and the social duties that would land on his shoulders. It wasn't that he minded them, precisely, but they were constant. He'd ended up being Lady Jenifry's choice of dancing partner last night, as much as social decorum permitted. That was a rather larger number of dances - five - than he'd have preferred. There'd been at most one dance with the other unaccompanied women, and he hadn't managed to dance with several at all.

Ockham had been clear with Hugh about this part of the work, that among the first-class passengers, the reputation rose and fell on how welcome they felt. Whatever Hugh's preferences were among the passengers, they must absolutely not damage the company's reputation.

In theory, it would be easier if he were married. Then, he could at least have an easier time dodging various propositions. As it was, as a single man of entirely marriageable age, it was assumed he would be interested in whatever woman crooked her finger. At least for a tumble. Even if he had been, he knew most of the women who'd asked him simply wanted a story to dine out on and laugh over for months afterwards.

He was coming back along the starboard side when he saw Cyrus Smythe-Clive leaning on the railing. Waiting for him, because the Council Member pushed himself upright and nodded when Hugh walked by to say "Good morning."

"Good morning to you. Beautiful, isn't it? Brisk, but lovely." Cyrus was dressed to be outside in it, coat and scarf and fine gloves that Hugh was sure had additional warming charms as well as a proper lining. That showed sense, at least. Far too many people found themselves out on the deck not dressed for the weather. "Do you have a moment for a word in private?"

"The Captain, surely, if you've a question about the voyage..." Hugh was just as a cautious of offers made by men who wanted privacy as of women who wanted to bed him. If usually for different reasons. He had no interest in bribes to let someone get away with something. He didn't think Smythe-Clive wanted to sneak something through the Customs House to escape import duties or any number of other schemes. But you never knew. Sometimes the most respectable looking people did the worst things.

"I think in this case, I would prefer your advice. If, after we talk, you think I should take it to the Captain, I will gladly do so. Do you have somewhere private?"

Hugh considered. "Your suite, sir?"

Cyrus shook his head. "My sister's still asleep. Or if not asleep, lounging around in bed reading. She knows about this, but I'd rather not disturb her. She gets very little time to enjoy her pleasures in anything other than healing."

"A corner of the deck? I'm afraid I have no office on the ship that would meet your standards." He could not ask this man into the windowless room he'd claimed for storing paperwork. "And the first class suites are all full this trip."

"A corner of the deck would be fine. Somewhere people can't come upon us without warning."

"The bow, then. If you don't mind a ladder." Cyrus shook his head, and so Hugh led him forward, toward the bow. He let Cyrus go first up the ladder so that they could find places to lean against the railings at the bow. "We'll see anyone coming, when they come up the ladder."

Cyrus snorted. "Fair enough. I suppose it encourages an efficient conversation." The wind was a tad brisk.

That had not actually been Hugh's aim, but it was certainly also true. "So, how can I be of help, then?" He leaned against the railing, watching the older man carefully.

"My trip is not solely personal. I have a bit of Council business. I wanted to let someone with appropriate authority know about it, and ask about some specific precautions." Cyrus lifted his hand, forestalling Hugh's rather obvious complaint. "I do not expect you will know all the answers, but I do suspect you will know which other people I should consult."

Hugh smiled at that, and the way that Cyrus somehow put him at ease, despite the seriousness of the request. "That is fair enough, and certainly within my scope. Tell me a bit more about the specifics?" He raised his hand. "Do you need an oath on it?"

Cyrus considered, looking him up and down. "No, I don't think so." That was a rather notable bit of trust. "I know your family." Something on Hugh's face must have given his uncertainty away, and Cyrus added, laughing. "If you hadn't offered, I'd have asked for an oath. But you offered, and I do not think you would risk bluffing me and being found out later. Therefore, logic says, your offer is honest, and we can take it as read."

There was nothing to do with that but laugh, and Hugh did. "Fair enough." He watched Cyrus for a moment. "It's tiring, isn't it? Calculating all the ways someone might go, and navigating them." He had no idea what made him say it, but Cyrus broke into a broad grin.

"Ah, you do understand. I thought so, seeing you at the dancing last night. That's a delicate balance, avoiding being snared by one or the other. I do appreciate you keeping Lady Jenifry busy."

"I'm afraid I have only one self to give in that battle. I might end up fleeing into escorting some of the older widows, to save my sanity, some night." It was far more frank than Hugh would normally be, but Cyrus was the other man she was most likely to target and deserved a fair warning.

"Noted. I noticed you didn't dance with my sister?" Now, however, that pleasant voice had something there, like that lurking darkness below a ship that Hugh had spotted only once or twice, when everything went eerie. He sucked in a breath, doing the best he could to keep steady.

"I meant no insult, of course. The two times I could get free, she already had an escort. Please do convey my compliments, if that would be a help?" It made him feel entirely wrong-footed. Cyrus's sister, now, he wasn't able to read her any better than he could read her brother. Which was to say, only poorly.

Cyrus nodded once. "She's quite able to fend for herself, for all she doesn't usually bother with the more...." He cast around to choose an adjective. "Tedious social circles, shall we say? I simply want her to have an enjoyable trip, so I can tell our parents I trotted out every possible pleasure for her delight."

"Is there a particular reason for that? I could suggest a few options, if - if there's a particular interest?" Hugh still felt out of step in this conversation, the way it had twisted, but that part, he at least knew what to aim for.

"Our parents are unhappy she intends to make a greater commitment to the Temple of Healing. I know perfectly well she will do it, and I've told them so. They are convinced that a reminder of the pleasures of the freedom to travel, of the luxuries she could enjoy." Cyrus shrugged, apparently at peace at this.

"Do her oaths - will they require asceticism, then?" Hugh tried to figure out the difficulty here.

Cyrus immediately burst out laughing. "See, you have grasped in a bare handful of sentences what our parents have not managed in - three years, I think? Her lifetime, in other ways. Her oaths commit her to the temple, to her chosen goddess, but nothing about forsaking all human pleasures. She cannot travel at a whim, but she has not done that since she left school. She might manage a nicer flat, and she'll have a more regular schedule much of the time. But she will take a temple name, and no longer bring direct glory and influence to the family." He shrugged, grinning broadly. "I've been saying for years that if you want obvious power and influence, that's what I'm good for."

Hugh strongly suspected Cyrus was good at quite a deal more than that. "In that case, I will be glad to offer what I can to give her a pleasant trip, not expecting it will change her decision for a moment. I've certainly had many less pleasant tasks in a voyage."

Cyrus laughed, entirely at ease now. "She is a fine

dancer, but she enjoys a good conversation even more. Should you be wondering. I'm sure she'd enjoy a chance to use her skills, but you would rather not have need, so I won't wish for that."

Hugh shook his head. "I'd prefer an easy trip, thank you." Then he took a breath and left it out. "Which brings us to your question, doesn't it? Now you've got a better sense of me."

"Oh, you are sharp. And honest. I like that. A great deal." Hugh was only human. He liked that praise, particularly. He was sure Cyrus didn't give it out unless he meant it, and this was the sort of self-assured, confident man he wanted to be a few years from now. "It's Council business. I am taking a stone to Boston, there are some particular rituals, and I will be bringing it back to Albion when we return."

"On the *Citrine*." Hugh considers. "Security concerns, magical concerns, both, neither?"

"A combination. I'm sure if you knew someone might steal a thing, you'd not have let them on board, but do you know of any particular concerns?" Cyrus's voice had settled into a businesslike tone, clear and even.

Hugh considered. "I'll check with the purser. One or two names I remember hearing a bit of gossip about, though I believe all of them go for the easy targets. I assume you've taken your own appropriate precautions?"

"A safe and such, yes. My sister could work out to open it, if needed, but it would take her a while, and I don't think anyone else would manage inside a month."

"Is it a gem of particular potency?" Hugh wasn't quite sure how to ask about that. His own studies had been heavy on the practical side, not the theory of magic.

"There has been a little concern that it might attract

attention. It's been elsewhere, to Egypt and India, without drawing undue notice, but the Atlantic is a different ocean, isn't she?" Cyrus spoke with respect, and Hugh liked that a great deal. Most people who weren't sailors just saw every ocean as the same. They were much more interested in the ship perching on the top of it than the whole of what it contained.

"She is," Hugh agreed. "And there have been a few unusual sightings the last few months. Nothing that's been a problem, but..." He gestured at the waves. "If there is a problem, what do you intend to do?"

"Ah, that's a good question. I am not, shall we say, inclined to throw the gem overboard. Not approved of by my colleagues, never mind anything else. Is this the sort of thing I should bring to the Captain?"

"It is. When we go inside, we can arrange a time for you to speak to him. He should have a few minutes mid-morning." Hugh was certain of that. He knew the watch schedule like the back of his hand. "I appreciate you checking, and I am sure he will as well. Much easier to manage things when they come up with a little warning."

"And I appreciate your discretion. Will you breakfast with me, or do you have other obligations?" Cyrus considered. "Amadeo mentioned you spent some time with them last night, you made quite a pleasant impression on them."

Again, Hugh leaned into the praise, trying not to let it show. "They're good company, and we have mutual interests. They're a fine lot, though, aren't they? Congenial, friendly, so long as it's not business."

Cyrus laughed, loudly. "Precisely. Well, let's to breakfast, then. What's the easiest way back from here?"

Hugh pushed away from the railing, leading the way

back down the ladder, down, and back inside. He stopped to arrange time to talk to Captain Melcott once he'd seen to his morning duties.

SEVEN

THURSDAY AROUND NOON

Rhoe had spent a leisurely morning in her cabin, reading. She'd woken when her brother went out, but hadn't wanted to face anyone. Instead, she'd taken her time with a simple breakfast of toast and tea - she was rarely hungry first thing in the morning. She'd followed the meal with a great deal of enjoyable time reading without interruption.

By the time he returned, half an hour before the bell for lunch, she had finished one book, and was well into the second. She'd packed half a dozen popular novels she'd failed to read when they had first been published. Now she was having an enjoyable time deciding for herself what she liked and didn't like. Eventually, she'd swap over to some of the professional reading she'd brought with her, but the first full day of a holiday should be given over entirely to pleasure and not duty. Or so people kept trying to tell her.

"Luncheon? It's a pleasant day out, but chilly." Cyrus leaned over the back of the sofa as he came in, and peered at the book. "Popular novels, is it? I found the writing overblown."

"You say that about approximately every popular novel you read, and you still like at least half of them a great deal." Rhoe rummaged for her bookmark.

Cyrus grinned at her. "It's a safe thing to say about books. People can very rarely argue about it, and then they go on to tell you the bits they thought disprove that, and you can have a decent conversation. Or at least a good chance at one."

Rhoe swung her feet down and set the book on the side table. "How was your morning?"

"An excellent chat with Hugh Pelagius, and then Captain Melcott. About the stone." He didn't gesture at it, or even look toward the safe in his room.

"Anything else I should know about that?" She stood, going to the mirror on the wall for a final glance at her hair, to see if it had become too untidy. She didn't particularly care, but other people would. It was simple enough to fix.

"I told Hugh that you could probably figure out how to open the safe, but it would take you a few days. That's all the clue you're getting."

She turned, raising an eyebrow. "I am not solving that puzzle for you simply for your amusement. Make your precautions accordingly."

Cyrus made a mock-bow. "Oh, I have. But I trust we will not need them. Anyone I need to fend off at luncheon? I managed to dodge Lady Jenifry all morning, and that Miss Lytton."

"Unfortunate death of her fiance, three years ago, thoroughly out of mourning and trying to latch onto Thessaly as like to an older sister? Despite her rather - well, her tastes wouldn't flatter Thessaly at all." Pink frills would not suit Thessaly's more classical figure. "What did she want?"

"My flattery and attention, I suspect. The woman flutters, rather a lot. Nothing wrong with that if that's what she wants, but you know how I feel about fluttering."

"And how you feel about the kind of dangerously sleek sort, like Lady Jenifry." Rhoe had known for some years now that if Cyrus ever considered another relationship, it would need to be someone who could match him as a partner. "Come on, escort me to lunch, we'll watch each other's backs."

Cyrus offered his arm, and they made their way back to the dining room. The luncheon itself was quite pleasant. They'd managed a table with the Professor and his wife. He treated them to a dozen tales of various cities, intriguing nuggets of history, and the promise of a longer lecture about the oekology of the Atlantic the next day. It was a table for six, the other two seats being taken up by two older women. They were sisters and widows travelling to see family in America, and were delightfully chatty.

Not only was the conversation excellent, but there was no space for anyone being difficult at Cyrus. When the group broke up, however, one of the women Rhoe hadn't met yet came and swept her up, off toward shipboard games with a chipper "Come along, everyone's playing." Her brother, curse him, melted off into the smoking room, where she couldn't follow, and got out of it.

Twenty minutes later, Rhoe was leaning against the railing. She was nominally watching people balancing eggs on spoons. In reality, she was calculating how many steps she would have to take to sidle out of sight behind a lifeboat, so she could go back to her cabin and find her book. She had no objection to other people playing games. But she knew perfectly well plenty of people considered her slightly ridiculous, and she had no need to give them more reason to. Also, the book was far more interesting.

It was then she heard the voice a little further back along the ship. "Explain it to me, please." It had a definite note of command in it, and she understood better why when the other man spoke.

"It would mean quarantine. The entire ship. I'm sure there's a rash."

Rhoe knew perfectly well a rash might mean any number of other things. She began edging slowly in that direction, in order to hear better over the sound of the wind and the waves. She missed a sentence or two, before she heard the first man say, "Tell me what the usual process is."

The second man cleared his throat. "Isolate the patient. Isolate anyone who's had contact in the last four days. But boarding, and the second class dining room..." His voice trailed off. The implication was very clear. That would mean quarantining at least all of second class, possibly the ship.

"I see the point." There was a long silence. This was where Rhoe cleared her throat, and stepped out past the lifeboat, to see Hugh Pelagius and a man in ship's uniform huddled into a nook of the wall.

"May I be of help, gentlemen?"

The other man blinked at her. He was ginger, around Hugh's age, and newly out of his own apprenticeship, she thought. "There's nothing to worry about at all, madam."

Rhoe snorted. "Any time someone tells me that, I'm sure there's something to inquire about, at least." She gave the brief, sharp nod she had practised and perfected. "Healer Rhoe Smythe-Clive."

Hugh Pelagius, for his part, was rather more welcoming.

"I had the pleasure of dining with Healer Smythe-Clive last night. But this isn't a working holiday for you, surely."

"I am still a Healer, wherever I go." Rhoe spread her hands. "I've experience in a number of areas of healing - I've been assigned to the Temple of Healing, throughout. Most recently in the infectious disease wards."

"Children?" The other man - who must be the doctor, Rhoe realised - asked.

"That's the Temple of Youth, but I've some sense of it. You mentioned a rash?"

"A rash, and she wouldn't let me get close enough to get a proper look. The mother, I mean." He cleared his throat. "Doctor Northton. Trained at the London hospitals, only did the first part of my training at the Temple."

Rhoe nodded. That made sense. A doctor on the liners here would have to be thoroughly familiar with the non-magical methods, since most of the voyages were mixed. They often did much of their training at the London hospitals. "Let us take this one step at a time. A child? Give me the particulars, please. The patient, the circumstances, the symptoms." She settled smoothly into the tone of voice she used with junior Healers, respectful but clear about what needed doing.

"A girl, seven years old. Second-class passenger, travelling with her mother and three brothers to join their father in America. There's a rash up and down her arms, and her legs, I gather." Good, he was finding it reassuring not to be dealing with this on his own. He wasn't fighting for control.

"You haven't been able to examine her directly at all?" Rhoe was focused on the doctor's comments, but she saw Hugh take out a small notebook, and take notes.

"Her mother wouldn't allow me in. Not proper, she said."

Rhoe snorted. "Well. I can help there. And at least I don't have to convince her I'm fully trained. Is there - no, you wouldn't know about a fever."

"Her mother dithered about it. So if there is one, it's not high enough to be obvious."

"All sorts of things might cause a rash. Before we decide it's one of the worse ones, how about I go collect my bag and a few things from my trunk. Then we'll see if she'll be more inclined to talk to me and let me do a proper examination."

"Are you -" Doctor Northton cleared his throat. "We are imposing, ma'am. Healer." Poor man, he'd spent long enough in the non-magical community to get turned around by her being fully trained and more experienced than he was.

"You are not imposing at all. I have my oaths, even on holiday. Come along." She swept off, trusting that the two men would follow her. "My cabin, and then you can show me where we're going." It likely made quite a procession, but she didn't look back. It spoiled the effect. She didn't need to. She could hear them behind her, their footsteps louder than hers.

Back at the cabin, she opened the door, saying "I'll be just a minute." She wanted to change her frock into something that could be safely laundered, if the rash were something contagious. She shrugged off her day dress in the privacy of her quarters, and reached for a simple cotton robe from the hook in the trunk, the sort of thing she'd wear in the country, where it might get grubby. She thought about adding her red Healer's gown over it, but there was no need to worry other passengers.

Next, she drew out her Healer's satchel and removed

those things she was not likely to need. Her potions case, for example. If she needed anything, better they come from the doctor's stores and be signed out by him. She added the Healer's medallion around her neck. Hers was set with the deep spinel she'd worn since she was placed in Fox house at school, now reset in her Healer's medallion of rank. It looked impressive, settled in the centre of her chest, and she hoped it wouldn't take too much convincing of the poor mother that Rhoe knew what she was doing.

She then recoiled her hair and stuck pins into it firmly, finishing with the charm that meant all the loose ends would actually stay put, and washed her hands. She'd do so again, once she was about to see her patient, but there was every reason to do so frequently.

All of that done, she presented herself at the cabin door again, where the men were waiting. "Now, what's the mother's name? And I'm going to want a fresh set of linens, and I assume their cabin has a basin, at least, for hand-washing?"

Doctor Northton opened his mouth, then closed it. Hugh, however, spoke up. "A basin, but no running water, there's a shared bath down the hall. Let me go ahead and find the steward. I assume you might need other things once you've had a look."

Rhoe beamed at him. "Exactly. A set of clean towels and washcloths, at least, but I'm not sure what else yet. Her name, Doctor?"

"Mrs Edgars. Um. Winifred Edgars." He swallowed nervously as Hugh went off down the hallway. "The girl is, um. Doris. Three brothers."

"Winifred and Doris. That will do very nicely. Now, how we do this is you take me down, introduce me as a Healer familiar with all sorts of things coming through the

Healing Temple. We'll see if she'll let me look at Doris. As soon as I can reasonably turn the case over to you, I will do so, but we had best get a proper sense of what's going on first."

"That, yes." Doctor Northton was working on pulling himself together.

"Can I ask what the facilities are for quarantine? Or care in general?" Rhoe kept her voice clear, polite, focused.

"There's a medical cabin, but our facilities for a proper quarantine are limited. A cabin, not allowing people in and out but the facilities are down the hallway in second class." He rubbed his hands together, uncertainly.

"And it would be difficult to ask someone in first class to move out." Rhoe could see the problem. She didn't approve of the problem. If it came to that, she'd offer up their cabin. "There's any number of things it could be. Let's find out what's actually going on."

With that, she gestured for him to show her the way down to the Edgars and their cabin, keeping up with him comfortably.

EIGHT

THURSDAY AFTERNOON

Hugh had managed to catch the senior steward promptly, at least. He was just coming out of the steward's office when he saw Rollis Northton and Healer Rhoe coming down from the first-class cabins. She looked entirely at ease, walking confidently through hallways she'd surely never seen. She walked down the steeper stairs smoothly, as if she were used to managing that kind of pitch without thought.

She was not the sort of woman who the papers would extol as a pillar of feminine beauty. He suspected that was at least partly because photographs would not do her full justice. Standing still, being quiet, she was pleasant to look at, a bit like a Rubens painting, all curves and dark hair. Moving, however, there was a clarity and dance to her movements, like she was certain where each step was going and precisely how it would bring her to her goal. He'd noticed it at supper last night.

She wasn't given to needless movement. That might be the way to put it. She'd been the same way in the glimpses he'd caught of her during the dancing last night. Many people - men as well as women - were prone to the little flourish, an extra kick here, a higher bounce. Rhoe didn't do that, instead her energy went into moving smoothly from step to step, always forward. Like a bird in flight, perhaps, only driven from her legs, not by wings.

Hugh realised he was staring, and moved smartly along to the door, waiting for them to join him. "The steward's fetching some linens, and will be ready for whatever other requests."

"Shall I?" Northton was gathering up his dignity, and Hugh nodded.

"Please do." He stood back to give them room, since his role here was purely in a support role.

"Mrs Edgars, it's Doctor Northton. I've a Healer here."

"Don't want a man in here." The door cracked open slightly, but Hugh couldn't see anyone on the other side. The lights inside were dim.

"I'm a woman, Mrs Edgars, a Healer. Normally I'm at the Temple in Trellech. May I come in? See if I can be of help."

"Let me be seeing you, then." The voice, Mrs Edgars, sounded very put upon, and as if she were sure there was some trick here. Hugh nodded at Northton, and the doctor stepped aside.

Rhoe moved in front of the door and held up her medallion with one hand. "This is my Healer's medallion, Mrs Edgars. I'm sure you've seen one before."

"Make it do the thing." Goodness, the woman was stubborn. Hugh couldn't blame her, and it looked like Rhoe had rather expected this sort of reaction. She gathered herself - it wasn't even moving, more like she drew on roots that went deep down to the bottom of the ocean, and then murmured a word. He could see a faint deep purple glow, reflecting against the gloss of the white paint on the door.

"I swear on my magic I am a duly trained and sworn Healer." Rhoe's voice was steady. It took him a second to realise she'd sworn on her magic. From the few times he'd done that, he'd known the bite it had, the way any oath made on their magic called on the Silence to reinforce it. A brush of whatever you most feared.

He could not imagine feeling that terror, no matter how brief, any time somewhere needed convincing of his skill. He didn't think Mrs Edgars had asked Northton, either. And yet, Rhoe had done it as if it were the most natural and logical thing one could do.

Whatever Mrs Edgars saw, it was convincing, and she opened the door. "Just you, Healer. Ma'am."

"As you wish. If the gentleman may stay at the door, in case I need anything? They won't come inside unless you permit." Rhoe was entirely confident they'd obey, but Hugh certainly wasn't going to argue.

"The door." It was grudging, but it meant the door stayed open. There was a smell of something stale now, but Hugh wasn't entirely sure what. Not fever, he thought. It was a fairly ordinary second-class cabin. There were the two fixed berths on the left. Three boys, all younger, were perched on the upper bunk, watching.

There was a washstand with the folding basin in the centre, under a small porthole that let in a little air. A settee stood on the other side, with a bunk folded up against the cabin wall above. The lights were dim, just a lamp on by the basin, and there was a girl on the settee curled up under a sheet, and reaching to scratch her arms.

"Now, may I see to Doris?" Mrs Edgar nodded, and moved back awkwardly to stand by the basin, hovering.

Rhoe came in immediately, and said, "Hello, Doris. I'm Rhoe, and I'm a Healer. That means I want to see if I can help you stop feeling quite so miserable." The girl blinked at her. "Does the light hurt your eyes, Doris?"

The question made the girl blink at her, and then say "They itch."

Rhoe nodded. "In that case, I'm going to use a light charm, all right? So I can put it right where I want it." She went through the motions, very deliberately, summoning light into her cupped hands. Hugh was certain she didn't need the fuss and little gestures here, but she did it like she was playing a game.

When the light appeared, Doris was distracted in spite of herself, reaching out a hand as if to touch it, when Rhoe set it in front of her. "You can touch it if you like, but it will only go where I put it."

When Doris got a hand out from under the sheets, however, Hugh realised that Rhoe was taking everything relevant in, her gaze focused entirely on her patient. She was ignoring them, certainly, standing in the doorway. She was ignoring Mrs Edgars, and the boys, who were near enough staring at the top of her head. Once Doris had had a chance to poke at the light a few times, she asked, "So, how do you feel, Doris?"

"Itchy. Everything itches. My hands. My eyes. My face. Behind my ears. And my knees." It was a litany of complaints that seemed likely to go on.

"Can I take a look at your arm? By the light?" This time she got a nod of agreement, and she carefully held out her hand. Rhoe looked, leaning in, perhaps nine inches from the smaller arm, and tilted her head, as if to get the best angle of the light.

"That's quite a rash you have there. Can I take your

temperature? Have you ever done that before?" Rhoe's voice was still calm, and she wasn't pulling away. There was a solemn shake of Doris's head, Hugh could just see it moving.

"Well, there's a new thing for you. I'm going to want to put it under your arm, right here." And a gesture to indicate that it would go in the armpit, from the way her arm moved. "And your part is to hold it steady there and not move too much. It will have to stay there for five minutes. While we do that, I'm going to ask you a few questions so we can figure out why you're so itchy. Can you stay still for me like that?"

Another little nod, and Rhoe's voice was relaxed. "Would one of you gentlemen get ready to time for me, and let me know when it's been five minutes from my mark?" She didn't raise her voice, just kept going, as she reached with one hand to open the clasp of her bag, drawing out a roll of fabric. "These are some of the things I use to help people, and see, here's the thermometer." She held it up so everyone in the family could get a look. "Are you ready?"

"It doesn't hurt?" Doris's voice wavered for a moment.

"Oh, no. Not at all. You just need to hold still and not wriggle so it works best. It's all smooth, you'll feel something a little like a stick, that's all." In a matter of half a minute, Doris had been rearranged on the settee, and the thermometer had been applied. Rhoe said, "Start the count, please." as if she were utterly sure she would be obeyed. Hugh already had his watch out and had marked the time. "Counting, Healer."

Rhoe went calmly back to her plan, whatever it was. "Do you remember when you started feeling itchy?" From there, it was a slew of other questions, asking Doris to remember what she'd been doing, going back a full ten days, working their way forward, bit by bit. There was an occasional question about where they lived, or if anyone else there had been sick recently. Other than the grocer's wife having a cold, there was nothing like that.

Rhoe gave her praise freely, and the more she talked, the more Doris opened up, telling stories, until they got to "And what did you do yesterday?"

"We were at Aunty Mabel's and we were out in the garden."

Mrs Edgars spoke, her voice a little nervous. "My sister, near Little Beaulieu."

"That's a nice thing, a garden, even this late in the year. Were you playing out there?"

There was exactly the sort of hesitation every child makes when they have been caught out doing something they weren't supposed to be doing. And the eldest of the boys made it all the more obvious, because he suddenly stuffed his hand in his mouth. There was a very soft "Yes'm."

"Let me guess. You were out in the garden when you were wearing your nice clothes, and your Mum didn't want you to get dirty."

"No'm." It was a very quiet voice now.

Before Mrs Edgars could say anything, Hugh held up a hand, at the exact same time Rhoe said, "Well, I'm very proud of you telling me. That's very important, with a Healer, telling us things, so we can help with the right thing and you can get better. And stop itching. Did you touch any of the plants? On your arms, maybe, or your legs?"

There was another "Yes'm. Here and here." Hugh couldn't see the gestures, but he could guess at them. "Bobby got caught on some briars, and I had to get him out without getting holes in his clothes, and there were other plants all round back there."

"And what were the plants like? Were they very tall, taller than you." Rhoe gestured with her hand above her head and got a giggle.

"No'm. Much shorter."

"And were they purple? Red? Blue?" Each of those got an even more amused snort. "I'm thinking they were.... green!" It was presented a grand joke, to resounding agreement, not only from Doris, but the chorus of her brothers perched on the bunk.

"Now, I'm fairly sure I know what happened, but can you open your mouth really wide for me?" There was peering there, and then a "And can you open your eyes for me, wide as you can? Oh, you're very good. I am sure you can make the best faces at your brothers."

Mrs Edgars was clearly not sure what she thought of someone encouraging that kind of thing. Hugh was sure now that she was very set on being as proper as she could be, for all Rhoe was cheerfully ignoring many of those requirements.

"Now, how long do we have on the thermometer?" Again, she didn't raise her voice.

"Thirty seconds." Hugh kept his voice low to match.

Rhoe nodded. "I'm fairly sure I know what it's going to tell us. I don't think you have a fever at all, you're just not used to being in a cabin like this, where it can get a little stuffy."

She kept going like that, an easy patter, until Hugh coughed. "Time."

Extracting the thermometer took a little more teasing, and then the excitement of moving the light so she could read the narrow line of mercury. "No fever at all! Oh, I'm quite sure what you did now. I think you got into some plants that aren't very good for your skin. And then you were standing in line, at the dock, and it was a nice day yesterday. And so you got more sun than you might have."

She glanced up, and shifted, suddenly more directly, including the adults in the room. "I'm suspecting wild parsnip, but it might be something else. There's no fever, no other symptoms other than some irritation."

"Is it - is it dangerous?" Mrs Edgars had a tremor in her voice now.

"A little unpleasant. We'll see about getting you a salve that will help, much faster than the non-magical options. And if there can be a bath arranged, with some oatmeal, that would be a help to the itching. You'll want to soak, and then put the salve on, and then cover them loosely with bandages. We'll make sure you have all of that." The tone in her voice made it clear she would be doing that if she had to spin thread from flax and weave them first.

Hugh promptly said, "Of course, that's no problem."

It took another few minutes to reassure Mrs Edgars that there was no lasting concern. Then she checked with the boys that they were not having the same problem. They'd had long trousers and sleeves on. Twenty minutes later, Rhoe had extracted herself, and once the door to the cabin was closed, she let out a long breath.

"I see why you were worried, but it truly is something like the wild parsnip. Some sort of irritation of the skin, and the plant makes you sensitive to the sun. Absolutely no fever. Do you have a salve for it? Brightman's Soothing Salve or Hildegard's Ease are the two I'd like best, either of them."

"We've Hildegard's, in quantity, I'm sure. It's used by the crew for windburn."

Hugh coughed once. "Perhaps I should follow up with the steward, and you can take Healer Smythe-Clive along to see what your options are? Thank you very much for your time, and - I do hope we'll see you for supper tonight?"

Rhoe turned on him, a broad smile, like doing her proper work had filled her up with something. "I expect so, yes." It was very cheerful and amiable before she turned back to Northton. "Let's see what you have in your apothecary shelves."

Hugh watched her going down the hallway until they disappeared around a corner. That had been unlike most of his experiences on any ship. He was still trying to decide what to make of it, when the steward cleared his throat, to inquire what would be of use.

NINE

"**Y**ou're not married, of course, Healer Smythe-Clive." Tonight, they were not at the Captain's table. Instead, they had been seated with two women who'd taken to joining Lady Jenifry, whenever the opportunity presented itself.

Elaine and Heloise Adams had both been friends since Schola, and were now in their mid-twenties. Elaine, then Elaine Upton, had married Heloise's brother, who was at home in Albion. Heloise was very much on the prowl for something - an affair, a marriage. She didn't seem much to care which. Rhoe rather thought Elaine might not mind a little shipboard dalliance either.

Her brother, of course, was blithely ignoring every bit of innuendo. She was less sure about Hugh Pelagius, who had ended up at their table a bit after the meal started. He'd escorted an elderly dowager to join them.

Rhoe suspected that Madam Foreby was not nearly as hard of hearing as she'd implied. For the moment, she was amusing herself by staring down the table, peering over her lorgnette at the rest of them. Hugh, however, was also keeping quiet, other than the occasional gestured inquiry to make sure Madam Foreby had everything she needed.

The other two men of their immediate party were two Swiss businessmen. She was quite sure their English was better than they were showing. They'd clearly caught a couple of the cattier comments Elaine had made, but they sensibly were refusing to be drawn into it. They had been speaking to each other in what she knew was Schweizerdeutsch, though she couldn't begin to make out much of their low-voiced commentary.

"No, I'm not. I keep abominable hours, of course, or at least I have. My new position will be a bit more steady, for various reasons, but I fully expect to get called out for emergencies from time to time."

Hugh caught this, and asked, "That's just as true for men who are Healers, isn't it?"

Rhoe snorted. "Married male Healers have someone to run their household for them. If they're not married, it's a housekeeper or their old Nanny or something of the kind. I'm not so lucky. I could live in my childhood home, but that's an annoying trip by portal. I've a set of rooms in a rooming house, and my landlady sees to some things, but I catch meals at the refractory, or wherever I can."

Cyrus said, amiably. "I take you out when we're both free. Though I agree, that's not nearly often enough. I admit, I'm not sure when you'd manage to conduct a love affair, never mind a marriage. You never seem to be free for more than an hour at a time, and that on some arcane schedule even an astronomer wouldn't be able to map out."

Rhoe was amused, but Elaine picked right up. "Well, I suppose some women just aren't fortunate that way. Now, Heloise, she's had all sorts of men simply doting on her."

It took a great deal of restraint not to lean over to Cyrus

and say something to the effect of 'And yet, she's not married either'. Being catty was no good, even just in his ear. She was supposed to be mature and responsible and capable of self-control, even if this particular conversation had been trying her patience for some time now.

Not that Cyrus was helping at all. She knew why. It was impolitic for him to be sharp with people who were being awful in the socially-acceptable ways, after all. He needed to keep to the more or less socially acceptable sort of insult, not the ones that would provoke a duel for someone's honour.

Hugh spoke up then. "I'd think it would be the other way round, Healer, that people would be thanking you for your time taking care of people, not finding fault with it."

It gave Rhoe space to shrug, at least. "Oh, I'm always happier to be doing, certainly. Though I did finish another book this afternoon. Such a pleasure to have a bit of time for reading." That, finally, got them off on that topic. Rhoe had to do a bit of clever talking to avoid making it clear she had been reading a delightfully ridiculous novel instead of something high-minded and improving.

The longer the conversation went on, the more Heloise kept trying to get Cyrus's attention. He continued amiably ignoring it, responding to the sensible parts of the conversation and ignoring the increasingly unsubtle comments. Had Rhoe been inclined to help anyone get into her brother's bed, she'd have told them that bluntness was not the way to go. Her brother not only appreciated subtlety, but she knew that he'd never remotely consider even a passing fancy for someone who would be heavy-handed with Gemma.

When supper finally ended, she excused herself, with a

"I should take my post-prandial walk. I didn't manage one after lunch today. Cyrus?"

"Oh, I'll come with you, certainly." He stood, pulling her chair out behind her as she stood up, entirely smoothly.

Once they were well away from others on the promenade deck, he asked, "Did you actually want to walk?"

"I'd like some fresh air. Even if it's getting a bit chilly." She stretched slightly. "Where were you all afternoon?"

"A bit of physical exercise - one of the Scali's not a bad duelling partner, we'll be doing that every day. Not a bad challenge, and he knows some things I don't."

Rhoe snorted. "It's a peculiar form of getting exercise, but you do like it. I did think I'd go in for the concert. That will be restful, not people talking at me, and refusing to consider the wrongness of their assumptions."

Her brother leaned over to kiss her hair. "I'm sorry it's that sort of trip. I'd hoped it wouldn't be."

"Why you're the optimist in the family and I'm the clear-minded realist, I have no idea. You're the Council Member, you'd think it would be the other way around." She shrugged and gestured back toward their cabin. "I have my books. I got to do a useful bit of healing. Best of all, I heard from Doctor Northton that Doris liked the bath with the funny things in it very much. Oatmeal. Good for itching. And then the salve, which actually smells very nice, it's got rosewater in it. She feels very posh indeed."

Cyrus laughed at that, loudly enough to get a few people looking at them. "No wonder you're in a decent mood, despite people at dinner." He escorted her further along the promenade. "Mind a ladder for a minute?"

"I am dressed for ladders, unlike some people." Elaine and Heloise, for example, who were both quite tightly corseted. Cyrus nodded, then led her over to the ladder. "Careful how you go, there's the railing."

Once she was up on the bow, she turned around, delighted. "How did you know how to get up here? Certainly not on the ordinary sort of tour."

"Pelagius showed me. I'd expected him to be a bit more direct at supper."

"Oh, I don't blame him at all for not putting himself in the lion's mouth. Or the shark's, is that the proper idiom out here?"

"You can ask tomorrow." Cyrus sounded deeply contented, and Rhoe turned in the light from the lanterns, to peer at him, with the dark expanse of the ocean behind him.

"What have you been thinking, then? You sound like a cat with cream."

Cyrus stretched. "A break from the usual routine, and you know how I like that. Gemma's education settled at least as much as it can be before she actually goes to school. Mother and Father off my back about that, about whether I've been too indulgent with her."

"You hadn't said they were still on you about that." Gemma had not gone to the tutoring school their parents had preferred, and Cyrus hadn't heard anything but doubts and complaints about it for two years. Rhoe raised one eyebrow. "What else are they being difficult about? Besides me."

"You." Cyrus agreed. "I was thinking, talking to Pelagius…"

That was a different tone in her voice. "Yes?"

"I know a bit of his history. Younger son, his mother was a second wife much younger than the first. And then his father died, rather suddenly two years ago."

"His father was getting on, wasn't he? And known to have heart troubles."

Cyrus snorted. "More than just physically, though I gather he was a good business man, and not as bad to his employees as many."

"That is not saying a lot, and you know it." Rhoe pointed out. "Why do you bring it up, though?"

"I know that Ockham Pelagius has been making changes, and I was curious about Hugh. He's been working his way up - before his father's death. Engine room, the stewards, the purser. That's sensible training."

Rhoe considered her brother. "And you approve of that, that's not a surprise. But something else, too."

Cyrus shrugged. "I like the man. Still finding his legs, I think, for all he's excellent on a ship, but he thinks, he's tactful, he's interesting. And interested."

"You just like people who listen to you." This was true, and they both knew it.

Cyrus grinned, but he waved a hand again. "This trip's the first time he's been up in first class and doing the more social side, but he handles it like he's been doing it for years."

Rhoe wrinkled her nose up. "Honestly, I think this is the hardest bit. Except maybe actually doing the navigation and decisions at sea. That's a lot of responsibility."

"I know you hate the social obligations. And you've held your tongue. I can't reward you like Gemma, can I?"

"You very well can reward me like Gemma and take me to a bookshop when we get to Boston. Though I'll be looking for different kinds, ta."

Cyrus laughed again, and she was caught once more by the note in his voice. For all there were some tedious parts in the social dance here. She was at least giving him a break. "You were saying about Hugh?"

"Hugh, is it?"

Rhoe shrugged. "He said, at supper yesterday. And I do not need to be suitably manly and reserved about my emotions. He was ..." She wanted to put the right words to it. "He listened, when I intruded, about what I was hearing. He didn't dismiss Northton's right as doctor to make decisions, but he also made it clear I had expertise that would be useful."

"So why couldn't the good doctor spot whatever it was?"

"Well, for one thing, he's mostly worked on ships, and he trained in London. Different skills. Less good at something that happened before the poor girl ever got on board. We're Healers and doctors, not omniscient."

"Did you give him a proper reading list?" Cyrus was leaning back against the railing, now, both arms outstretched. If any of the women saw him now, the unattached prowling ones, they would find him even more pleasing, Rhoe thought. Wind in his hair, a man in his prime at his ease.

"Reading list, and a promise to Hugh to see about doing - or finding someone qualified to do - a set of lectures for their training. Frankly, Northton was so grateful it wasn't going to involve quarantine that he'd agree to anything. Actually, what they really need on board is a good nurse. Older woman, soothing but fierce, that sort of thing. I intend to write that up as a proposal, oh, sometime tomorrow. Women travelling alone do have their worries."

"You always have been good at putting things into proper context, sister mine. And having ideas." He tilted his head. "What can I do to make things easier for you?"

"The more we end up eating with pleasant people, the

happier I'll be?" Rhoe was quite clear on this. "I certainly don't care about the table being balanced, if that's a concern."

"I'll have a word with the maitre d'. Or perhaps Pelagius." Cyrus waved a hand. "And Boston should be many things you enjoy, other than my bit of ritual magic, and I'm sure you can find some distraction. You generally can."

Rhoe snorted. "Generally, yes. All right. We should probably go in and find seats. If you want to make useful, find some way for me to avoid those two. And Miss Lytton and Lady Jenifry."

"I will aim for Mistress Wallace. Or someone else interesting. The Mertons. Brave enough to try the ladder, again?"

"I don't exactly have much choice?" Rhoe shook her head, and climbed back down carefully, after her brother, then slipping her arm into his.

TEN

THURSDAY EVENING

Hugh settled into a chair in the back of the music room just before the concert started. He'd been making a circuit of the public rooms, making sure everything was sorted out for the later evening. There'd been a hint of trouble from one of the card sharps last night, and they wanted to keep a close eye on it. He'd caught one of the Scali men watching him, one of the cousins, and when he wandered over, the man had said, "Cheat?"

Hugh had shrugged. "Some people are lucky out of all proportion."

The cousin had laughed, and said, "And some men, we won't play. Good to know you keep an eye out." Then he'd gone back to his own table, and a moment later Hugh had heard everyone there chuckling. He hadn't looked back, just come along to the music room, smiling as the last few people filled in.

Lily Freeman, the evening's performer, was in that curious middle space in her career. She was no longer singing ingenue parts, but not quite at the full mature power of her vocal talent. She was in her late twenties now, according to her official biography, and she'd had time to learn quite a repertoire.

There were the usual art songs, of course, all the songs that showed off the voice against the piano. But she included everything from a Schubert lied, to a version of a Renaissance motet, to something out of one of the operettas that were currently so popular in the last decade. Her accompanist had a few solo pieces, as well, to give Mistress Freeman a chance to rest her voice and recover. It was very generous of her to do the performance, Hugh knew. On the other hand, she'd have been given a pleasant discount on her ticket in exchange. Their guests would have entertainment, she'd be able to have people flatter her. Everyone won, really.

He kept glancing around the room. It wasn't that anything was wrong, not exactly, but he had begun to feel an itch. It wasn't at the back of his neck, or between his shoulder blades, like some people. Instead there was one particular spot, just below his right shoulder, at the back. Just a small knowledge that something was not quite as it should be.

Hugh thought back through his day, from the early conversation with Cyrus to his sister's assistance. The afternoon had been taken up with all sorts of minor queries that were deeply significant to the people involved. And then supper had been a question of not presenting himself as a target, while wishing the conversation had not been nearly so sharp. He thought Rhoe had handled herself well, but he felt rather sorry that she'd obviously dealt with that sort of thing before, and fairly regularly.

He had to commend her patience, really. She'd never shown the least sign of losing her temper. Perhaps even more remarkably, she'd not given into the temptation to be catty back. He was sure she wasn't a saint, whatever a saint was like. He'd seen a few flashes during the meal, but she'd kept her composure.

Hugh knew perfectly well that it wasn't that Healers were above such things. People in every profession, even the most selfless of them, had their preferences and their foibles. He didn't think she was up on some pedestal doing an impression of a perfect marble statue. For one thing, that had always seemed a very uncomfortable place to be.

If anything, Rhoe seemed rather more earthy. She enjoyed her food, rather than just picking it like many ladies did. She wore the flowing gowns that made it clear she wasn't wearing a fashionable corset, much as Hugh had been trained not to think at all about a lady's underthings. She was obviously fairly strong and energetic. He'd caught a glimpse of her going up to the bow with her brother, and she'd climbed the ladder as nimbly as he had.

More than that, she seemed very solidly herself. The shrouded insults - well, not very shrouded - at supper hadn't really touched her. It was as if she knew they'd happen, but had already dismissed them as irrelevant. She seemed to find them a regretful distraction from other, better, conversations she'd rather be having. Even if they'd smarted, they weren't important.

It was the same sense Hugh had got from her brother. That sense of self. It made him wonder if it was something about their family, or about the two of them. He didn't recall terribly much about the parents. Well-born but not notable, he suspected. He knew Cyrus Smythe-Clive had been young to take a Council seat. He was well-respected, the bits that had been mentioned. And he was a widower with a daughter almost of Schola age. All the things in the Gold Book that tracked the great families, but not terribly useful in actually telling you about a person.

It did make him wonder why Rhoe was not ten years married. Even with her Healer's commitments, women from that sort of family were often married during their apprenticeships. Or at least as soon as the apprenticeship was done, if it were to be a longer betrothal. Hugh's own sister - half-sister - hadn't even apprenticed, and that was just as common among young women of good family.

There were single-minded women - or for that matter women who did not enjoy the company of men - who didn't marry. Hugh had travelled, he'd certainly seen all manner of relationships and personal choices during his time aboard ship. But he didn't think it was entirely that. Somehow, Rhoe had side-stepped the assumptions about how her life should go, taking only the path she chose, even if other people found it unfathomable.

The music caught his ear again, then, a rolling piece of triplets and patterns, like the movement through the waves. It made Hugh consider the journey so far, which had, all things considered, gone fairly smoothly. There had been no signs of ice when he'd checked with the captain before supper, and only one ship in semaphore distance, with no particular warnings or cautions.

As the concert came to a lull for the intermission, Hugh applauded. He stood to stretch, trying to decide which direction to aim for, if he should collect refreshments for someone, and if so who. People had gathered into little groups, leaving Rhoe to herself - Mistress Wallace and the Mertons were on the other side of the room, without an easy route there. He came over and bowed slightly. "Are you enjoying the music, Healer?"

She looked up, her head slightly tilted. "Not all of it is

what I would normally seek out, but she's a well-trained singer. I appreciate excellent training and skill, even when a particular piece is not to my taste."

"That's an interesting way of looking at things." Hugh frowned, trying to figure out how to ask about it without being insulting. "May I sit?"

"Please, yes. My brother's off - well, finding a drink eventually." Rhoe waved her hand toward the doors that opened onto the promenade.

"The question of skill. Is that for professional reasons, or some other cause?" Hugh felt that was clumsy, but it got the idea across.

She laughed. "Both. But I suspect the professional reasons, particularly. Are you sure you're interested? Most people aren't."

"You're very blunt." It came out of his mouth before he could stop himself, and then he covered his lips with his hand. "Pardon."

"No, no." Rhoe laughed again. Something in that had put her much more at ease. "I am. It's one of my abiding flaws, my mother says."

"Never catch a husband that way?" Again, his tongue got ahead of him, but if anything it only pleased her more.

"The older I've become, the more I've found myself favouring Shakespeare's Beatrice. Not that I am so sharp of tongue, but that I have standards, and no interest in someone who does not meet them. And plenty of other things to do with my time than go fishing in the world at large on the off-chance I stumble across someone who does."

Hugh tilted his head. "That's quite unusual."

"I am quite unusual, so that works out well." She settled back in her chair, now watching him thoughtfully, as if she were noting down all his particulars.

"I had - I do beg your pardon for not diverting the conversation sooner at supper." That slipped out of him when he hadn't quite meant to say it. Or rather, he'd meant the apology, but not expected it to come out like that.

Rhoe leaned back in her chair a little. "You throwing yourself on the path would just have made things awful for both of us. It's one thing to do that if it will make things better, but just spreading the awful out, that's not always the thing now, is it?"

Hugh considered. "Still. It was unchivalrous. If that's the appropriate word." He then glanced up, following the line of her own shift in gaze to see that Cyrus was standing in the door to the promenade deck. "Your brother seems to be trying to catch your eye?"

She looked up and said promptly. "Actually, it's you he wants. Would you mind escorting me for a breath of fresh air, perhaps? Make a little show of it?"

Hugh was instantly on the alert. There had been some meaningful exchange there, something that she'd read in her brother's posture or perhaps some small gesture. He'd seen it done, of course, plenty of times before, but they were rather more subtle than most people he'd seen do that. And more usually, it was married couples, not siblings. They seemed to get on unusually well. He could, at least, take a cue when it was that openly presented, so he stood. "Do let me offer my arm, we've time for a quick stroll on the deck before the end of intermission."

They managed to make it to the starboard side of the ship quickly enough. The waning moon was attracting a bit more attention on the other side, and Lady Jenifry was gathering even more.

Once they were out on the deck, Hugh gestured as if to offer Rhoe's arm to her brother, but she ignored that. Cyrus had backed up to the railing, tucking himself into a little nook between benches, and Rhoe led the way, Hugh following rather than escorting now.

"Pelagius." Cyrus's voice was even, but it had a note of something different, on alert. "Over there, nearly at the horizon line. Is that something of concern?"

Hugh immediately looked out where Cyrus indicated. Off toward the western horizon, the direction they were sailing into, but a fair bit north. He let out a low hiss of breath. There was a faint glow, not of light, but of something else.

"Bad? Good? Mythical?" Cyrus's voice was a little more urgent.

"Not bad, precisely. But it suggests there's magic there, and closer to the shipping routes than usual. There are all sorts of possible reasons for it, many of them relatively ordinary?"

"What would the more concerning ones be?"

Hugh glanced up at Cyrus, who suddenly seemed taller. "In your official capacity?"

"Just so." His voice was deeper, too, a resonance that hadn't been there before, or not in the same way. It was a voice that would command, if command were called for.

"There are various creatures in the ocean who cause there to be lights. It might be a reflection of stars, a spill. They do not move, so it's not a ship's flare, in distress. Sometimes that can look like it, especially if there are icebergs in the water, or something else for it to reflect from. The moon's not terribly bright, though, waning as she is." Hugh grimaced. "But it could be something out there."

"A dangerous something?" Cyrus's voice was careful. "I know there are ships along here regularly."

"You're thinking about the stone." Hugh looked out over

the water. "I'll consult with the Captain, of course, and let you know immediately I've done that. We're getting close to the territory lines for the pelagic merfolk. They might tell us something."

"Is that tonight, or tomorrow, do you think?"

Hugh glanced up at the sky, more by habit than anything else. He'd checked the charts before supper. Then he glanced at his watch, to consider how far they'd come since. "I'd want to confirm, but - first thing tomorrow, I think, making the offerings."

"Wake me up, if you would. If it's permitted." Again, that note of command was unmistakable.

Hugh nodded. "Both of you?" He wasn't sure at all, suddenly, what Rhoe made of this.

"I'll wake up if he's moving around, but I'd love to see, if it's not a problem. How many times will I get the chance, after all?"

That curiosity made him smile. "Both of you, then. We might get a crowd, if it's not at the crack of dawn, but I'll make sure we've a place for a private chat after."

"That's quite fair." The music began to start up behind them, and Cyrus turned. "We'd best go back in, not draw too much attention. Sister mine?"

Hugh made a slight bow. "I'll consult with the Captain. If there's anything you should know before the morning, I'll come find you, otherwise, have a good evening, and I hope you sleep well."

ELEVEN

Rhoe woke up with a start quite early the next morning, she was sure. At first, she wasn't sure what had woken her, but then there was a knock on her cabin door. "Mermaids. It's about half-six. Dress warm. Three minutes."

Of course Cyrus was sure she could be up and dressed by then. Most women would have needed ten times that. She slipped out of bed, shivering for a moment as her feet touched the rather chillier floor. Then she pulled on a simple morning frock, this one in a blue-green she had always rather liked. Brushing her hair out quickly, she coiled it and shoved hair pins in, for the artistically drooping sort of look. Finally, she grabbed one of her heavier shawls, with the warming charms woven in properly.

Just at the edge of three minutes, she opened the door to find her brother coming out of his own room, looking surprisingly awake and formal. He had on one of his many sets of Council robes, with the strip of deep purple. "There, shall we?" All brisk and business. "We were about fifteen minutes out when they knocked."

And it would take them a few minutes to get up on deck. "Of course. Do you know how this goes?"

Cyrus shrugged. "I've read the theory, but never had a chance at the practice. Offerings, some conversation, negotiation for safe passage through their territory. Possibly something else, there's discussion about favours."

"Also curses. You know how magic is, two sides of a coin." She nudged him. "Come on."

He laughed, and got the door for her, and they made a little procession down through the stairs, onto the promenade deck. When they came out on deck, there were half a dozen crewmen working to lower a platform with a railing off the side of the ship. Captain Melcott was in full uniform. Hugh was over to one side talking to a woman perhaps Rhoe's age, who clearly knew Hugh well enough to be teasing him.

Rhoe considered and realised this must be the one with Merope's gifts. There was one on every magically owned ship, and quite a few travelling otherwise, criss-crossing the oceans, to make peace in the places they crossed. It wasn't needed every trip, but from everything she'd heard, 'often enough' and no one was quite sure exactly what the acceptable interval between offerings was.

So in practice, ships made offerings every time they could. Every time there was someone who could do them properly. She gathered there were more formal versions and this looked to be on the decidedly formal end. The less formal apparently involved a few flower petals and such that might be tossed subtly over the side.

The woman was dressed in something that wasn't quite a uniform, wasn't quite religious vestments, but that wasn't that different from what Rhoe would wear when she took her oaths. A simple dress, pinned at the shoulders and belted, with a broad cloak over it, of what looked like silk and wool.

"Would you like to come down with us, Healer? We've room for a couple more." Rhoe blinked. Hugh had spoken. Then he added. "This is Nerissa. I was at school with her younger sister." No last name, which was intriguing. Rhoe could not tell if that implied a significant degree of intimacy, or if that were the custom for Merope's Speakers.

Rhoe came over to them and nodded, politely. "May I ask what the proper title is?"

"When I'm being official, Speaker. Which is terribly oralist of people, but they will insist on it. And it's not as if I'm not speaking with my hands, there is that argument." Her fingers moved smoothly as she spoke as if she were indeed doing a simultaneous translation, fluidly and quickly.

"How does this go, then? I'd love to see things more closely, but I'd hate to be rude."

"Hugh has assured me that you'll follow the rules, which are simple. Don't speak unless addressed. Give me time to translate in both directions. And don't make any offerings, either gifts or threats. Hands clasped in front of you or on the railing are both fine. Anything else ask first. We recommend the railing, for balance."

"That, I think I can manage. And the platform..." Rhoe looked at it, a bit dubious.

"The platform gets us down closer to them, about ten feet about the water line. You might get quite wet, if there's an unusually big wave, but that only happens, oh, one time in ten."

"In which case, it's the good brandy all round once everyone's dried off." Hugh said, cheerfully. "Your brother, too, of course, the Captain's seeing to him."

Rhoe nodded. "An honour. And I'll be sure to follow the rules."

"Healers are generally good at that, once they understand why." Nerissa was entirely at ease about this. She took a step or two back, going through a series of gestures that were like dancing. Stretching out her hands, Rhoe suspected, so that there would be no stiffness.

It was one of those things like the moments before a particular magical operation, where everyone was lounging around, and then suddenly, everyone was moving, taking their places. She was guided onto the platform, given a space to hold and watch her brother on one side, Hugh on the other. The Captain and the First Officer had pride of place. Nerissa stood in a little half-circle that stuck even more out over the ocean. She clipped two metal chains onto either side of the belt around her waist, for safety, Rhoe assumed.

Then, slowly, bit by bit, the platform was lowered down, smoothly, past the centre of the ship, along the greatest arc of the curve. They stopped, as Nerissa had said, just ten feet above the water, close enough that she could feel the spray of the ocean on her ankles beneath her skirts. The shawl was quite cosy enough, but she wished she'd thought to put on warmer stockings.

Once the platform had stopped, there was a silence, and then there was a louder call, something that might as well be music, a long trilling call. It wouldn't be out of place as a bird's call, of some kind, or even something like a whale call, she'd heard stories about that. It carried, though, without words, and then a moment later, Nerissa dropped something into the water that floated. It looked a little like the illustrations she'd seen of ancient Egyptians with a cone of some perfume that would melt and disperse. It floated, but it looked fragile, like any big wave might tip it over.

Hugh leaned over and murmured in her ear. "Now we wait. Not very long."

Within a minute or two there were signs of something moving quickly toward them. It was like the dolphins she'd seen along the bow when they were still in the Channel. They were somehow sleek and curved all at once with flashes of something that blended with the waves.

As the shapes drew closer, however, she could see that where the dolphins were silvery these were shades of blue, from pale to darker. They kept moving, more than anything else, with flashes of fins, not only on what her mind kept wanting to call their feet, but along the spine too. Their hands had skin between the fingers, up to the first knuckle. Their hair was, she suspected, not hair the way hers was, but some sort of fin or sensing organ. It too was blue, but shading more darkly down to something like the colour of the depths. All of them were well-padded, roundly curved, a necessity in the cold water, most likely.

Rhoe could count half a dozen, for certain, but she was absolutely sure there were things she was missing. They kept diving over and around each other in patterns that must mean something. Nerissa's hands were flashing in broad patterns, as if her hands were trying to be half a dozen people now.

Some of them, the merfolk, she thought, were men. Others were obviously women, bare-breasted, but in a way that didn't seem sexual, even to the men in the party she knew found such things at least visually appealing. Her brother, for one. He might have no particular desire for intimate connection, but he still appreciated the beauty of the thing. Hugh wasn't staring at them, either. Or rather he was. They were all were, but not like that.

There were dozens of research papers in this. Not just about the communication, Rhoe knew there had been papers on that. But on the human response to them, that was something different. They were decidedly humaniform, like people who walked on dry land, but also entirely their own thing.

Nerissa finished the initial set of whatever it was she was saying, and then she spoke without turning to face anyone. "I have made our formal introduction, the name of the ship, Captain Melcott, our origin and destination. That they are welcome to swim along with us, if they wish. What would you like me to ask them, Captain?"

"My respects, first and foremost. As to questions, last night, we saw lights in the distance, just under the water. I would know, if they are willing, if they know anything about what that is. You can do the measurements, I hope?" Nerissa nodded. "And, at their pleasure, anything about the route ahead, any unusual ice or storm."

Nerissa hesitated, considering how to frame that, Rhoe thought. There was something about the tilt of her head, that Rhoe was sure meant she was thinking hard about how to say something complicated, elegantly. Then her hands were moving again, tracing out points in space. Not just on the horizontal, though, there were little pops and twists of her hands, as if placing things at different points.

She realised suddenly that much of the language must be communal. That what Nerissa was doing was translating into two hands what the merfolk said with half a dozen bodies, the alignments of hands and arms and torsos and tails. Not just where they were in space, but the alignment. Once she knew to watch for that, she could see the flicks of fingers that indicated where the great dorsal fin was, or where the hands must be.

At first, the merfolk were in what seemed to be some sort of neutral position. Still swimming along powerfully, keeping up with the forward movement of the ship without any trouble. Then they'd circle back so they didn't outpace it, making great looping curves. They were always watching Nerissa's hands, but they moved back and forth in formation with each other. It might be, she thought, the equivalent of going "Mmhmm" as someone else spoke, making it clear you were following. She noticed that two of them, in that pattern, regularly went under the water, perhaps keeping an eye out for anything that might be dangerous. Then they'd pop up again on the opposite side of the group.

Nerissa began speaking. "I've conveyed your compliments and respects, Captain, and now I'm asking about the lights." Her hands shifted, angling to demonstrate both the angle that they had been at, and then several shifts that seemed to indicate distances. Not only comparative distance, but something Rhoe thought might be length of time, by some measure that made sense.

There were flashes of fins, and the entire pod of them twisted and curled over and under each other. They realigned distinctly into several different arrangements before four of them disappeared below, gone for a good minute. Nerissa kept watching the water avidly, not turning away. The two remaining on the surface traced in circles, still watchful. Then, all of a sudden, water erupted beneath them, soaking the hem of Rhoe's skirt - and everyone else's feet, she was sure.

Nerissa took a step back, then immediately lurched forward again, pulled by the chains attached to her belt.

Her hands were moving quickly now, this time repeating something in the movements, as if she were confirming them. Rhoe had no idea what it meant, but she knew that kind of echo from her own turns doing the most complex healing magics. She had a great deal of experience running her hands through the proper postures and movements for someone across the room, as they checked in with each other.

"Captain, they say that they feel it is one of the Ones Below, stirring. She is not nearby, not at the moment, but she can travel fast if she chooses." She continued watching. "Often, the Ones Below shift, and go back to the depths. They do not know why she moves. It could be nothing." There was an eloquent shrug of her shoulders. "Ahead, there is nothing of note. The ice is well clear, there are no storms. A ship, a day ahead of us."

Captain Melcott nodded. "That's the *Memory*. Only a day? Can you confirm that? She should be more like a day and a half ahead, at least."

There were more of the quick movements, but this was a much easier conversation. "A day."

There was a nod from the Captain. "Atherton, make sure to inform the watches." The first officer nodded. "Please, you may make the offerings." It was curious how the Captain phrased everything to Nerissa as requests, not orders. The offerings themselves were quite simple, a number of wrapped packages lowered into the water on long poles, things that the merfolk could use. Rhoe wasn't sure what, but at least one looked rather heavy, as if it might have metal in it, or something else.

Then, there was one final twitch of fins and tails. All six of them rose out of the water to halfway down their long tails, before they twisted and dove under the water and didn't come up again for a good minute. As the platform was being pulled back up to the deck, Hugh nodded, using his chin to gesture. "There they are. They'll bask along the boat, now. They'll have given what we gave them to some of their fellows, below the surface."

"What was it?"

"Chain mail, some of it, charmed against rusting. Very useful against sharks or squid."

Which left a question Rhoe wasn't at all sure how to ask, about the Ones Below.

TWELVE

EARLY FRIDAY MORNING

As the platform reached the promenade deck, Hugh turned to offer Rhoe a hand. Her brother was still looking off to the ocean. He'd been quiet, the entire time, but now he nodded once at Hugh, and withdrew a half-dozen steps to wait to have a word with Captain Melcott.

Rhoe got out of the way of the others, then turned, looking off to the ocean herself. Hugh wasn't sure whether to say something, whether he'd be interrupting, but a moment later she turned back and asked. "The Ones Below?"

Explanations it was, then. Or at least as much explanation as anyone had, which wasn't much. "You know some of the legends. The kraken, the leviathan. The great creatures of the deeps. Rarely seen." He wasn't sure how to put this. "That's how the merfolk refer to them, as the Ones Below. I don't think anyone's clear which they mean. Or if it's both, or some we have no tales about, or how far below."

"The sign language, that's the right term for it? That's

fascinating. If Nerissa has time, later, I'd be interested in learning more."

"I'm sure we could figure something out. She's on call, of course, now we're formally in their territory, but that just means having the conversation somewhere she can be found quickly if needed."

Rhoe took a breath and let it out. "Does that happen often?" It was not at all clear what she meant before she clarified. "Either the Ones Below, or her needing to be on call?"

"Being on call is standard procedure. She'll sleep in the watch room, at least tonight and tomorrow." He hesitated. "The other, it depends whose reports you trust."

Rhoe tilted her head and considered. "I gather many of them are not terribly reliable."

"There are all sorts of creatures we don't know about. I'm not simply talking about the magical ones that we know something about, and that non-magical folk do not. The custos dragons, the ginsies. But there are more complex tales. Someone on a trip to Hong Kong told me a story of a beast in China, black and white, told about in stories, but never seen. Or at least only rarely, there are stories about creatures that only turn up for a - what he says was a righteous and benevolent emperor. There's a tale of one being taken to an Emperor - oh, a little before the Pact, I think, in the middle of the 1400s, that they called a zouyu. Only, no one has any idea what one is, even now."

Rhoe nodded. "And there's Richard's white boar, and no one has ever quite been certain how much that is a real beast and how much allegory."

Hugh coughed. "Pardon. You must be cold. May I escort you back to your cabin to change for breakfast?

Would you prefer to take it privately? I could have something brought up?"

Rhoe hesitated. He could see her thinking about what to do. "I'm afraid I'm not up for being pleasantly social over a meal at the moment. Not in public. And you must have things you need to be doing. Perhaps something in the cabin?"

"Do let me escort you, then. And then I will make sure someone brings you a properly restorative breakfast." He offered his arm, and she took it, her shoes squelching slightly as she walked. He had worn better insulated boots, but he added, "And someone to see to drying out your shoes. There's a drying cupboard near the funnels, it will do it in no time."

"I should have dressed better, I admit. But thank you, that was -" She looked up at him, craning her neck to catch his expression. "That's why you're here, isn't it? You find that as magical as you properly should."

Hugh was a little startled that she saw it so clearly, but he nodded without hesitation. "I don't want to captain a ship. It's a bad idea for the owner's family, anyway, there's no way not to play favourites then. Or avoid seeming like you are. But crossing the oceans, seeing different places, the moments like this. It's not normally nearly so elaborate as that. They were really quite conversational. Nerissa will be writing it all up, explaining the nuances."

"Do they travel the same routes, regularly, the translators?"

"Nerissa travels the Atlantic, but sometimes here, along the northern route, sometimes more southerly. She's got some fascinating stories about the Sargasso Sea, a fair bit south of us, and the merfolk there. They, mind, are all something like cousins."

"And more distant cousins to the coastal merfolk. I've never spent much time with them, but one of the Healers I trained with had done a fair bit of time in northern Scotland."

"The mer and the selkies both. I suppose that would be quite the challenge for a Healer, wouldn't it?"

"Like us and entirely not, at the same time, and there are so many ways that might affect healing. Never mind the effects of being in salt water all the time, which, we, of course, do not tolerate well at all."

Hugh hesitated as they arrived at her suite. "I'll send a steward along momentarily. May I see to anything else for you?"

"If you see my brother, let him know I'm here, if you'd be so kind? But please don't go out of your way, he can certainly figure it out on his own. Thank you, Hugh. This was fascinating, in all sorts of ways."

Hugh bowed slightly and waited until she'd gone into the suite. Then he knocked on the steward's room and asked him for a hot breakfast and someone to see to soggy shoes needing proper attention. That done, he stopped in his own cabin to change clothes to something more proper for breakfast in the main dining room. As he went upstairs, he hoped that the most difficult of the single women would still be at their morning toilette - or, frankly, asleep. It wasn't yet half eight in the morning.

On the way to find a table, he was stopped by Heloise Adams, apparently on her own, for the morning. He nodded politely. "Good morning, Miss Adams." He did not, however, invite her to join him at the meal. Either she would or she wouldn't.

She made no immediate move to do so. "Oh, Mister Pelagius." It was, technically, Master Pelagius, he'd earned his medallion for navigation and ocean magics years ago, but very few people got that right. It occurred to him that he suspected Rhoe would, for all she didn't stand at all on ceremony herself. He had got up early, he was wool-gathering and missed a sentence.

"I do beg pardon - I'm afraid I was up rather early."

"I was saying, Elaine won't be up for a bit. It wouldn't do to have you lonely! Do come join me with Miss Lytton, here. Unless..." She tilted her head, the sort of slight pout that he was sure some women - her included - practised in the mirror on a regular basis.

"I'll come by for a moment, of course, but I was hoping for a word with Madam Foreby, or Madam Silas and her sister." He let himself be dragged along, though, without complaining. "Good morning, Miss Lytton. I hope you slept well?"

"Horribly." Her face was pinched, which did not flatter it. It rarely flattered anyone.

"Oh, I'm so sorry to hear that." Hugh made the polite half bow, the slight incline that indicated manners without committing to any particular course of action. "Is there anything I might do to help?"

"I don't suppose you know if they carry a proper dream potion?"

Hugh pulled out the chair for Miss Adams, and then pushed it in, taking a chair at the table for the moment. "To discourage, rather than encourage, I assume?"

"Pliny's Potion of Proper Repose, or Alabaster's Dream Arcanum, yes."

Both of which were entirely useless fake nostrums. "I would be glad to let the ship's doctor know. May I ask, if it's not too personal, what sort of dreams?" He cursed internally, for venturing into that territory in the first place.

He was quite sure both of them would take it as a gesture in the direction of flirtation, no matter what he meant by it.

"Oh, clear aquamarine water, like in some sort of lagoon. Only, there was a sense of something else about it, something rather queer. I don't know that it was proper, at all."

There were half a dozen ways that might be interpreted by someone with more skills at dream interpretation than he had. Or possibly the ability to interpret Miss Lytton. Instead, he inclined his head, about to ask something of Heloise Adams, when she exclaimed, "Why, I had exactly the same dream. A broad lagoon, stretching from here to here, and that sea. It was like the best quality maxixe, my grandmother has a beautiful one. It was cut from a stone from Madagascar, can you imagine?"

Hugh knew those were the particularly blue aquamarines, which was actually a help, giving him a better sense of the colour of the water. More like the Mediterranean in certain seasons, or perhaps the Carribean, rather than the Atlantic's stormier hues.

"Was there anything around the water, land or people or ships?"

"Oh, nothing like boats. No, it was just water all around, no one at all, it was so very tedious." She was definitely pouting now. "It was just there. Not doing anything. Quite rude."

"That does sound not at all restful. Miss Adams, should I see if there's a potion you'd like for tonight? I'll go have a word with Doctor Northton." He could see he was quickly going to get pulled into a litany of boring dream stories, which was to say, stories about dreams that were boring. Also boring stories about dreams.

"Well. I suppose that's kind. Are you sure you won't breakfast with us?" Miss Lytton was so very hopeful.

Hugh shook his head. "Let me go have a word with the doctor, and I'm sure he'll have something for you shortly. Do excuse me, ladies, and have a lovely meal." Making his escape, he ducked down to find the doctor, who was thankfully in the medical office.

Northton looked up from his desk as Hugh knocked, then set several papers aside. "Did you come about this proposal?"

Hugh blinked and shook his head. "No, dreams." He caught himself. "Not mine, other people's. Miss Lytton complains of sleeping very badly, due to an odd dream, and when she described it, Miss Adams said she'd dreamed of the same thing. Nothing directly happened in it, but I got the impression there was some lurking sense of wrongness."

"What sort of dream, then?" Northton relaxed, leaning back in his chair again.

"Clear blue water - about the shade of a maxixe."

The doctor coughed. "Explain, please, for those not familiar? More blue than the famous blue stone of Galveston, or less?"

That was one of the bits of literature every educated person knew, from around the time of the Pact. The joke being that the speaker had never actually seen the famous blue stone, so comparing anything to it was useless.

"Aquamarine, so blue, but not that shade." Hugh spread his hand. "Water all around, something more like a lagoon than an ocean, but that particular colour."

"And more than one person." Northton frowned. "Do you think you might have a word and see how widespread it might have been? To the best of your ability, without causing a fuss."

Hugh nodded. "That's why I came by, so you could have a listen. And I suspect you might want some more potions for a good night's sleep on hand."

"It's easy enough to brew up Felicity's Fellow, we've all the ingredients in quantity. I'll see to that, and you can feel free to let anyone know to stop by or ask their steward to. The others that might be a help, we've less quantity, I'd prefer to save them for particularly notable cases."

"Entirely fair. I'll let the captain know. It might be interesting to see what the crew report."

Northton nodded again. "You think it's an omen, or … something of significance."

"I think it's worth paying attention to." Hugh shrugged. "We'll see what comes of it. It might well be nothing. It often is, this sort of thing."

THIRTEEN

FRIDAY AFTERNOON

Rhoe had thought, initially, that it would be safe enough to go to the lecture after luncheon. She had spent the morning in her cabin, feeling rather baffled at the amount of attention from the steward. She hadn't had a lady's maid since she moved out of her family's home, and she was entirely unused to anyone fussing about her personally.

Whether or not she was comfortable with it, there was a warming pan that stayed warm all morning, to tuck her feet against. There was a cosy blanket. And even better, they understood the difference between making your feet warmer and warming the entire suite. Half the people Rhoe knew, even at the Temple, would have tried for making the entire room stiflingly warm and uncomfortable.

Instead, her toes had warmed up nicely, and her legs, and the rest of her was comfortable in the cooler air of the suite. Even better, she'd finished her book. On the whole it had promised to be just as a good an afternoon.

Instead, Rhoe was twenty minutes into a lecture that was increasingly making her actually angry. She hadn't precisely held out great hopes for it. Anything titled 'The Healing Baths of Albion: Their Greatest Miracles' was, she suspected, not going at the healing waters the way Rhoe did. However, there was a sizable difference between a difference in approach and historical focus, and outright wrongness.

Finally, after another five minutes, she awkwardly excused herself, doing her best - and failing - to slide between two narrowly placed chairs on the way out to the main deck. She was trying to decide what to do with herself when she heard a cautious voice behind her.

"Are you all right?" That was Hugh.

She turned around, leaning against the railing not at all sure what she wanted right now. Oh, to be left alone. To not have someone tell her that academic wrongness didn't matter. To not have to be polite.

He didn't give her time to figure out what to say or not say. "You're not all right. Here. Come this way." Hugh gestured, broadly, off further back in the stern, into an apparently empty room. Some sort of office. "Private, but not very comfortable. It's a little windy to be walking, we shouldn't be bothered for a bit. Do you need a drink?"

Rhoe swallowed several times. If he were that worried, she must look rather worse than she'd wanted. She couldn't think of what to say.

"The way you look, I'm wondering if I should be offering to challenge someone to a duel. Though it occurs to me that your brother would far more likely be successful. And frankly, I suspect you're likely to be more successful than I am, I can't imagine you'd engage in something you weren't reasonably competent in." He then coughed. "Pardon."

The babble had, at least, broken her mood slightly, and

she had to smile. His earnestness in trying to sort things out was fascinating. Honestly it was surprising that he wasn't yet more cynical. She took a breath and let it out. "It's not considered sporting to change the mode of combat from academic rebuttal to the duelling salle. Not any more, at least."

There was an instant where he didn't know what to do, and then he smiled, broadly. "Ah, that sort of problem, then? Can I be a listening ear, and you can tell me all the things that are wrong with the argument? I am not by any means expert on anything - well, near enough anything on land. But I am a willing student."

Rhoe smiled a little. "Perhaps somewhere a little more comfortable, where we can keep an eye on anyone getting close enough to hear?"

"The writing room? I don't think there's actually anyone in there. Everyone's either in the lecture in the lounge or the ballroom - some sort of tournament?"

"They had a bohort puzzle going, I believe. The potential amusements had Cyrus intrigued, at least. Though I think half because he expects to have to extricate someone from their own foolishness."

"There are good protections on that room, thankfully. But that's appreciated. Rather a lot. May I escort you, then, and we'll find a corner and put up some privacy protections?"

Five minutes later, they were indeed ensconced in a corner of the writing room, with a bracingly strong drink for her, and some privacy wards. Whatever his other virtues, she realised that Hugh was rather good at those. Hugh settled into the chair. "Of course, you'd have well-informed opinions about the healing baths. Though - I missed part of it - I thought that she was talking about places other than Trellech?"

"If the Honourable Miss Chumondley were speaking about Trellech, I suspect it would come to duelling. I can't figure out if she intended to, and someone warned her off, or whether she had the good sense to avoid the topic on her own. No, she was talking about Baden-Baden. I believe she was going to get on to Bath."

"Have you ever been there? Baden-Baden, I mean. I haven't. No ocean." He spread his hands, amused.

Rhoe nodded. "I did a Grand Tour. A short one. With Cyrus, before my apprenticeship started. I'd been to the baths in Trellech, once, but we were with an aunt, and Baden-Baden is..." She shrugged. "In Trellech, it's a temple. And it's all magical folk. I can't tell which makes more of a difference, honestly? But Baden-Baden, it was a mixed community, and some of it was all about healing, but other parts were all about status and show. And that's never made sense to me."

"The combination?"

Rhoe nodded. "After all, you're naked in the baths, for one thing. And you'd think that would make a difference. Oh, there are still hairstyles, and whether someone's hands are calloused from work." She shrugged. "There's actually quite a lot of signs of what someone does." This part made her tired. "I don't complain about that. Too much. Anymore. It's tedious, even to me. It wasn't that, which made me upset."

"Oh?" Hugh leaned back a little. They were settled against the window looking out on the deck, so they could see anyone coming near.

"This is - you'll hear me out?" Rhoe suddenly realised

she hadn't explained this to anyone before who didn't already agree with her.

"Of course. I am entirely at your disposal for at least the next hour."

She smiled, took a sip of her drink. "There's a particular attitude I find not only distasteful, but that touches on my oaths. Even with someone who isn't my patient. And that's something of a difficulty, because it is absurdly pervasive."

"That sounds both difficult and an important thing for me to understand." He leaned forward, demonstrating that she entirely had his attention now.

"There is a belief." Rhoe tried to figure out how to put it in useful terms. "That if someone is ill, it is because their thoughts - and in our community, their magic - makes them so. That they are not living in the world correctly, because if they were, there would be no problem with their health. I don't just mean the things that do have an effect we know about. Moderation in food and drink, sufficient vegetables, not too much alcohol." She lifted her glass, self-mocking.

He lifted his, and said, "This seemed to have a medicinal purpose. Surely tension is no good for the heart either? Or the head?"

Rhoe had to laugh. "No, it isn't. And yes, moderation is the word. And the horrible thing is, I agree with some of it. If someone is consistently thinking the worse of everything around them - or the worst of themselves, which is unfortunately pervasive - then yes, there are some consequences of that. Besides, I think, being rather miserable to live through, never mind with."

"You have, I agree, seemed to not do that. You have opinions, and not solely positive ones, but your general outlook has tended to be not optimistic, precisely. That might imply a lack of groundedness? Balanced. I have been thinking for a while, Healer, that you are very rooted. A sure sense of yourself, your capabilities."

Rhoe thought that was perhaps the nicest compliment anyone had given her in a very long time, and smiled. Not that she could explain why to him. She didn't know how to do that and have him take it the right way. Instead, she went on with the safer - certainly less personal - explanation. "Miss Chumondley was arguing that taking the waters required the proper frame of mind. I do not disagree on how one approaches it being relevant. But the idea one can think oneself out of illness is terribly damaging to anyone who remains ill, and terribly damaging to anyone else who happens to hear about the thing."

Hugh leaned back again, now thinking hard. "Dangerous to the person, because they will blame themselves, for something that is not at all their fault. Even in the cases where their actions had something to do with it, blaming them for a lack of healing afterward seems entirely counterproductive. Better to teach pigs to fly. But the others, wait, give me a minute." She rather liked that he would think out loud to her. "Because they will blame someone who remains ill. Is it the same for, oh, an injury? As for someone who has some sort of illness?"

Rhoe lit up at that. "Excellent question." She considered how to explain best. "A lot of people feel that an injury has a steady progression. You break your leg, you have it set, you begin to mend. Over time, it heals. You may need to use crutches or a chair, or canes, but eventually it strengthens again, and you walk normally."

"Except it's not that simple, even with legs." Ah, he was very quick to see that, and it delighted her.

"No. I know someone who lost a leg in the Sudan. He arrived at the Temple in a very poor state early in my apprenticeship. It's been fifteen years, more than that. He still has trouble with it, enough to need a Healer's attention, every year or two. And there are times when there is swelling or irritation or whatever else, that affects the prosthetic, for no apparent reason. He has an orderly rational mind, it is not because he has some rush of odd thoughts about needing to punish himself with pain."

"I suppose some people do. Have those kinds of thoughts." Hugh was continuing to think out loud, and Rhoe nodded to encourage him.

"Some do. And honestly, despair is sometimes an appropriate reaction. Grief, certainly, at what someone's lost. But staying there, that's often miserable. And a further danger to someone."

"And you don't like that at all. That's," Hugh waved a hand. "That's leaving the healing work undone."

It made her smile, that he understood it. "Most people don't see that part, nearly as clearly."

"This ship - any ship of any size. There are the things we do today, because they are necessary today. And there are the things we do to avoid problems in the future. The sea is a cruel mistress, any number of things can go wrong, sometimes stacked on each other in unfathomable ways. If we are not ready to respond, well, that's where the tales of ghost ships and shipwrecks and all manner of other mysteries come from. Doing the thing, properly, completely, that helps. The follow through, if I remember my duelling instructor correctly." He looked at her, leaning forward again, as if something in this conversation had now completely engaged him.

"Cyrus would approve. If you want a topic to lure him, try him on that, on that kind of planning and follow through." Rhoe grinned for a moment, before coming back to the original question. "With something not so clear-cut as an injury, matters are even more complicated. And far too many people have no patience for something that mends only so far. Or not fast enough."

"Where fast enough is overnight, a fair bit of the time." Hugh shook his head. "Father was like that. My brother has a much more rational approach to injuries sustained in the line of duty, thankfully. But it's been an uphill battle to retrain people to report things before they get big. We'd much rather rearrange things for one voyage, and keep someone who is experienced and skilled long-term, than have to invalid them out."

She was about to say something more, then they both heard the noise of people filtering back into the space. He stood, and said, "If we duck this way, we'll avoid them. Look. Would you like a look at more of the ship? The parts passengers rarely see?"

Rhoe thought there was nothing, right now, she would like more.

FOURTEEN

Hugh wasn't sure why he'd made that offer. Certainly, he'd never made it to a passenger before. Though, to be fair, it hadn't come up much. On previous journeys, he'd been working somewhere largely out of sight, not talking to the passengers except when they needed something in his realm. He certainly hadn't socialised with them.

He suspected his brother would have a dozen comments when this particular choice was relayed to him. Which Hugh would do himself. He believed in honesty and giving a full report. Just as the Captain kept a log, he kept a record of his day. His father had insisted on it, but never asked about it. When Ockham had taken over as head of the company, that had all changed. After each trip, they had sat down for hours, going through the trip point by point. What had worked, what hadn't. Then, bit by bit, what Hugh had thought of the other staff, of the way things ran.

It was a change from their father, even if Hugh still wasn't sure what Ockham wanted from him. His brother didn't care much for travel, they both knew that and never talked about it. But being Ockham's eyes on the ships was different from Ockham wanting Hugh's intelligence and thoughts as well. And yet, if Hugh didn't do this, something, in this company, what else was he good for?

He swallowed, realising that time was passing. Rhoe had stood up, while he wasn't paying attention, and he did as well, a bit hurriedly. "This way. You are wearing sensible shoes, I assume?"

"My second most sensible are suitably soled for clambering around." She grinned at him, as if this were an unexpected delight. "My most sensible pair are still in an airing cupboard, I believe. The steward was most attentive, but some things shouldn't be rushed, and drying leather is decidedly one of them."

"True, true." He hesitated. "You don't travel with a maid." It wasn't a question, he knew the passenger list backwards and forwards, and any maid or valet or nursemaid would have been listed by title.

"Cyrus's man gets seasick. And I've never had a lady's maid. What on earth would I do with one? Even if I weren't working most of the time, I obviously don't run to the sort of clothing that requires four hands to get into."

Hugh led her down the deck, aiming for the stairs at the stern. Far less chance of running into other passengers. He drew her down, through the second class drawing room, then along into the hallway where they'd be out of the way this time of day. "Is there anything you'd like to see in particular?"

"You've been on a lot of ships. Tell me what you like about this one. What's interesting. Why." She was looking at him now with a particular sort of intensity. He was suddenly aware that however he answered this question, it would be telling her all sorts of things about how his mind worked. He felt exposed, for a moment, laid bare, but he had offered. He'd had plenty of evidence of how sharp-witted she was, how direct she could be. It was far too late to be complaining about her consistency.

When he opened his mouth to answer, she was just waiting. Then he reached for her hand, another intimacy, and drew her along. "Something you won't see anywhere else." Then it was down, and down again, until the stairs turned narrow and painted with thick white paint, nothing fancy. He forged on, then all of a sudden, they could feel the heat from the coal furnaces.

Hugh turned off, into a side passage, to port, and then to the little observation balcony above the great furnaces. Even here, looking down on the stokers, it was pleasantly warm. Much better than the boiling tropical heat of most ships other than the magical liners.

"The power of magic." It was hard to talk over the noise, the roar of the furnaces, so he let her look. She set her hands on the railings - she'd be all over soot, there wasn't a good solution for that, but it would wash off. She looked out, nodding slightly at the rhythm. The stokers switched in and out, tending four furnaces each, for two or three minutes at a time. Then they retreated to a cooler room with fresh air, before doing it all over again. They laid in plenty of potable water and tea, lashings of tea.

After a good ten minutes watching the men below, she looked up at him, and he gestured her back out into the hallway, then along to the mail room. It would be quiet at this point in the trip, with all the mail going to Boston and other parts of America sorted properly into bags and bundles. He drew her over to the sink at one side. "Wash your hands, do."

"Why that?" As soon as they came to a stop, she was

grinning at him. She washed her hands, attending to that thoroughly. She rubbed them together and hummed a charm that she could clearly do in her sleep, that removed even the last hint of dingy black soot. She held them up for inspection, teasing him now.

"That's the heart of the ship. Not just the ordinary way, what makes us charge through the ocean, but in the sense of - that's how we treat people."

"Not like that on other lines, I know. I've heard enough stories of burns and injuries. And the soot's awful for lungs." Her head was cocked to the side now. "There's a project."

"Our men take a potion that helps. Not enough, I'd be glad of more ideas. But it helps clear the lungs. We pay them well, give them plenty of chances at fresh air. And keep the temperature down." He lifted on his toes a little, trying to decide between explaining it to her, and seeing if she got it without the explanation.

A moment later, she was leaning against the wall, in the kind of unstudied position of a young man at university outside a lecture hall in an artist's print. Except for being rather shorter than a university man, and decidedly more curved. "That's the magic, then." She considered, her eyes half closing in concentration. "Enchantments to keep the heat in, so it makes better use of the amount of coal."

"Exactly." Hugh beamed back at her. "Cheaper for us. Better for the stokers. Safer, in general, since moving large amounts of coal has other dangers. Dust, fire, and so on."

"Huh." She considered. "Protective charms, in general, I'm sure. On the ship, the structures. I don't know their names, but I'm sure there are some."

"And navigation charms and aides. We can all do the reckoning by hand, if we have to, but we've a number of devices to check and crosscheck. Captain Melcott has a little tabletop device that alerts him to the presence of ice."

Again, that consideration then the quick reply. "Doctrine of sympathies, then? Though doing it to a form of an element, that's a trick, isn't it. In terms of theory."

Hugh inclined his head, amused. "I gather it was a Schola man who came up with the idea, and we'll give him due credit."

"You're a Dunwich man, of course."

He bowed, more formally. "Alethorpe, for you?"

Rhoe laughed. It wasn't mocking, instead it was delighted. "Oh, I'm a Schola woman, ta. Not all Healers go to Alethorpe. But I don't know much at all about Dunwich. Not nearly as much as I should."

"Where I have read all the school stories of Schola, and the island. Mind, I always thought the island sounded grand, and you do have mermaids of your own, don't you? Dunwich is a bit too populous for them, we have to go out to the North Sea or north up the coast a bit."

"The island does. I do not personally. If anyone could keep mermaids, and I'm quite sure one shouldn't. Merfolk, the occasional selkie. I'm sure there must be other periodic shape-shifters who prefers the ocean to the land, though I've never met one that I know of." She hesitated for a second. "Half a dozen secret societies, though only one deals with the water much at all."

"Overtly, at least." Hugh knew enough about the Schola societies to be clear that any number of things might simply not be discussed. He leaned his shoulder against the wall, a few feet from her and facing her, matching her pose. "Nothing about the Fatae?"

She shook her head. "Not that I know of. But the nature of secret societies does mean one isn't ever entirely sure."

Then, suddenly, she decided something, and pulled out a watch fob, attached somehow to the bodice of her dress. Three small objects hung from it, charms, nothing even big enough to catch. One was a pearl, one an aquamarine, and one a garnet of Healer's red. "You've heard of Many Are the Waters."

"That that's the name everyone uses, not the actual name. And there's some sort of..." Then it clicked for him. "Sister group at Alethorpe and at Dunwich. Though you admit men, as well."

She made a gesture that was not quite a curtsey, certainly not quite a bow. It had all the trained grace of a woman who'd have been taught dancing and etiquette from the earliest age, making it look entirely natural. "Not our name, no." She extended the watch, unclipping it quickly from the chain. When he looked, he could see it was silver-work, and there was that slight tingle that made him sure that significant magic was at play somehow.

"Focused on healing. On water." She shrugs. "If they hadn't taken me, I'd have figured out my own way. But I'd rather do my work with sisters and brothers who understand the meaning of it." Which was a curious way to put it, really. "Cyrus knows. I've never bothered explaining to our parents. Father was in Dius Fidius, and Cyrus is one of the elite of Animus Mundi."

"Those, I know rather less about. We do have an eye toward others drawn to the water, at Dunwich, of course." Hugh was thinking hard and fast now. She'd given him a great sign of trust. It wasn't that speaking of the societies was forbidden. It just wasn't done, unless one had a reason. Which made him wonder, immediately, what her reasons were.

"Dius Fidius is - well. Before the Pact it was the

landholders, the Lords of the Land, who held the magic in their tight little fists. Some of them more nobly than others. The official line is protecting good faith in private affairs, but you can see how that goes without me telling you. Half the men in first class likely aspired to it." Rhoe shrugged, amiably. "Animus Mundi goes in for ritual magic. In his way, Cyrus is every bit as much a mystic as I am."

"Ritual magic covers an ocean of possibilities." Hugh pointed out.

Rhoe laughed again, and again, it was just joyful and relaxed. "Oh, true. In their case, about the interconnection of the world. How you do a ritual about this thing, and it ripples out. We are very much in sympathy about some things, he and I."

"You seem very close, for siblings, considering." He hesitated, then added. "My half-brother and half-sister are much older. A good twenty years, and eighteen. Different lives, different times, different families." He shrugged. "I get on well enough with them, but we're not easy with each other."

"Where Cyrus and I don't get to see enough of each other for either of our liking, but we make do with what we get." She considered, looking rather amused, up toward the upper decks. "He thinks well of you, for the record. He likes people, he's amiable about them, but he's more generous with his presence than his praise, as a rule."

Hugh blinked, his chin coming up before he could stop himself. He knew she could read all those things in his face, his posture, how much it pleased him to hear that. It took him a long pause to get some self-control back in place. "He's been a pleasure on this trip. You as well, of course. Interesting conversation, and - whatever you both are up to, it's not the usual run of flirting and trying to arrange a marriage."

Rhoe laughed. "Hardly, no." She was about to say something else, when someone came breezing through the mail room, stopped, offered an uncertain salute. "Master Pelagius, sir? Something needs your attention, boat deck, the Steward was looking for you."

Hugh wanted to continue, but duty called. He made a slight bow to Rhoe, and said, "May I escort you to your cabin? The main deck?"

"Cabin, I think. I'll read for a bit before supper."

FIFTEEN

FRIDAY AT SUPPER

"It's such a pleasure to see such an obviously thriving community of merfolk along here. Now, it's not my area of speciality, of course." Professor Merton had settled comfortably into what his wife had teasingly called 'tutorial voice'. But he was an enthusiastic man, and his areas of interest were wide-ranging. More to the point, it was keeping people from being difficult at Cyrus, or at Hugh, or at Rhoe herself, and that was beyond rubies.

"How do you tell if a community is thriving, Professor?" Rhoe leaned forward, curious not just about the content of the answer, but how he'd frame it. He had a knack for gathering disparate details into a larger context.

"Ferdinand, please. We're certainly not in a lecture or tutorial here." He beamed at it, though, obviously flattered, his eyes crinkling up. "Well, how do you know a thriving community where you are?"

"Trellech." Rhoe said, dryly. "Which is not so much thriving as utter chaos twelve hours of the day."

The table laughed, drawing attention from the others around them.

"And I suppose the Temple of Healing is its own community in many ways, but not a place where thriving is always quite the word." Ferdinand was thinking out loud. "An unusual case study, at least."

Cyrus spread his hands. "And Schola's the same, even the village on the island's shifted by the weight of the school, I heard someone put it recently. The pole star's in a slightly different place, as it were."

Ferdinand waved a hand. "Quite, quite. Though that's an interesting way of putting it, aligning oneself. That's one of the things I look at, the organisation of communities. Take Trellech, for example, how it's built out from Portal Square. You have the entrance to the Temple of Healing at the short edge, the rest of the Temple quarter further out."

"And the Ministry sprawling all over the southeast." Cyrus said amiably. "And the crafters close together."

"I gather," Hugh said after a moment. "That's partly so they can mingle in the pubs there, and make connections, between fields. I suppose it probably isn't pubs, at the Temple of Healing?"

"Oh, trust me, Healers enjoy a nice bit of beer or wine as well as the next person." Rhoe lifted her glass. "But if we're talking shop, it's somewhere more private. There's a hall for the Healers, and we all have our favourite nooks in the gardens or wherever we spend time in the complex." She tipped the glass slightly at Ferdinand. "Mind, I suspect the patterns there are fascinating. But we've got off topic."

"Ah, yes. Well, I don't know how many of you spent a while watching the merfolk escorting us. First, it's a good sign that they are. It means their community is not under other threat at the moment."

"It hasn't been the same six all the time, though.

They've been changing out." That was his wife, Ilune, swirling her glass thoughtfully.

"Also a good sign. That means that they've a large enough community to want all the suitable members to come up and interact. You noticed, my dear, that some of them were younger adults. Learning how this particular diplomatic dance goes, though I suppose we don't quite know how they view it."

"That is the trick. The translation only goes so far. I did have a delightful short chat with Mistress Nerissa, when she was not otherwise engaged, this afternoon. She mentioned she's known you some time, Master Pelagius?"

"Hugh, please. And yes, I knew her sister when we were at school, and met Nerissa briefly a handful of times." Rhoe glanced over at him, but Hugh's voice was even and pleasant, even though she had a nagging sense it was more than just that. "All of the Speakers are rather singular. It's hard to talk about a trait they have as a group, other than that precision of language and gift for bridging between languages and cultures. And a love of travel, of course."

"There's a research project for someone, sometime." Ilune was grinning now. "Not you, dearest. There's a sizeable number of Speakers, then? Do they have particular routes they specialise in?"

"Curiously, no, they go all over. Nerissa prefers the Atlantic, usually the northern routes - Albion to New York or Boston, but she'll also sail the southern route. And not with any particular pattern I've noticed. When I ask, she just smiles and lets the mystery remain mysterious."

"A most intriguing point." Ferdinand agreed. "If it were consistently the same route, one might posit a particular set of relationships with the ocean. The merfolk in a particular territory, or something else along the route, but clearly it is not that. Has she gone through the Sargasso Sea, do you know?"

"Oh, yes. And once she's off duty for this trip, you're welcome to ask her yourself. For the time being, she's up by the bridge, just in case she's needed."

Ferdinand nodded, contentedly. "I will certainly do so, if she is agreeable." He then nodded slightly. "My lecture tomorrow, we'll be touching on some of the different areas, and what we know about the depths below each."

Rhoe considered, hesitating for just a second. "There are all sorts of stories, aren't there? About massive creatures that come up only rarely?"

"The stories of sea monsters?" Ferdinand glanced around. "If the other ladies have strong enough nerves."

That made Rhoe smile, that he just assumed her nerves were steady. "Not a topic for your lecture?"

"Not in depth - if you'll forgive the pun. I was going to focus on those sea creatures we might yet see along the way." Ferdinand grinned at her.

Cyrus leaned forward a little. Rhoe had noticed he was a little distracted tonight, and she was starting to wonder why. He was decidedly up to more on this trip than he'd told her. She had been assuming it was Council business, but she was increasingly unsure if that were the entire concern. "The merfolk, obviously. Whales, and there are sharks, of varying kinds. Squid?"

"Squid, though of course, we don't know nearly as much about them as we would like to. And any number of fish. I have an excellent bit, if I do say so myself, about the role of cod in coastal societies."

His wife leaned over to pat him on the hand. "You have gone off on a tangent, dear."

The professor nodded. "As to the myths and stories - I

defer to those far more travelled than I." He nodded at Hugh, who nodded back, without a great deal of certainty. "But the tales we have suggest that there are creatures we know little about. Science suggests that is likely, the oceans are enormous, and there are new types of fish caught regularly unknown to the tidy labels of the naturalist."

Rhoe liked how he could poke fun at himself and his academic peers. It made him delightful to listen to. "But you think there might be something in the old tales?"

"All the maps with 'here be dragons' and sea monsters? I think it's not impossible. There are plenty of things in the ocean we see only rarely. And of course, if there were an occasional wreck due to some great monster of the deep, for many centuries, how would we know about it? Even now, we often have only a general sense of when a ship is overdue, or what might have happened."

"There are some options for that." Hugh said, amiably. "If we can get close enough, there are various forms of signals. At night, light can carry a significant distance, so we might see flares or lantern signals. And this route, as the other major shipping routes are, is relatively busy, between cargo and passenger ships. There's talk of developing methods for communicating beyond the line of sight, but nothing's come of that quite yet."

"I am not sure whether I like the idea or not. Being able to hear of news would be a fine thing, but one does enjoy the chance to get away from it all while in the midst of the ocean." That was one of the older widowed sisters.

Hugh inclined his head to her. "We would appreciate a bit of the news, to know what to expect of the weather and the ice. But I do not think you need worry about being tasked with all sorts of minor letters or communications any time soon."

"Ferdinand, what sort of things might be beneath us? Other than your lecture, tomorrow. The whales and all."

"Oh, there's tales of basically two types, in the classic sense of a great beast below the waves. The kraken and the leviathan. And as is the way of all good stories, the tales differ a bit. Many of the early texts of the leviathan make her out to be a great serpent, writhing in the deeps. You know the symbol of the ouroboros, yes? A great serpent forming a circle by eating its own tail. Lore connects her with Tiamat, and with a great land-dwelling beast in the desert." He considered what to say next.

Ilune said, "The a - oh, what's the name again, dear. The very long name. You know I like that one."

The professor beamed at his wife, and nodded. "If you have heard the stories of sailors landing their ship on a great flat island, that suddenly rises, tipping them into the ocean, that might be an aspidochelone. There are all sorts of other names for it, and a whole line of theory connecting it in allegory to the Devil, if one believes in such." He clearly did not.

"An exceedingly large monster, that one." Rhoe tried to get a sense of how big a thing would need to be that landing even a much smaller ship would make sense.

Hugh leaned over. "I have a book or two in my trunk with some drawings, if you'd like."

She nodded, a little distracted now, but managed a smile at him, as Ferdinand went on. "There are other large monsters of that type, something like a whale. Whaling ships have reported particular unusual behaviour from time to time." He added mostly to Hugh. "The Essex, but others. Or there are tales like the Terrible Dogfish, in the children's story, that Italian one."

Ilune patted his hand again. "Keep going, you know it will bother you if you don't do the full list."

Ferdinand laughed. "I do like a good conversational tangent, and really, the range of stories, and their similarities and differences. The last of the great sea monsters is the kraken. We believe that to be something like an octopus or a squid. A thing with tentacles of some kind, but again, the stories are few, far between, and not well documented. Except for the idea of great tentacles coming out of the water, sometimes sweeping sailors into the waves."

Rhoe glanced over at Hugh, who was suddenly quiet, and she ventured to reach under the table, and touch his hand. He glanced up, then coughed, turning his attention to the table again, but making a quick gesture with his other hand, one of those meant to avert bad luck. "I don't mean to have you repeat your lecture, but perhaps something about something simpler, and less dangerous, to end the meal?" She kept her voice cheerful and bright.

"Ah, in that case, it's dolphins we want. All sorts of lore about dolphins and porpoises to be had. You saw some of them, as we were coming through the Channel, setting off, maybe? They do like following along in the wake of a moving ship, or gambolling around the bow."

The conversation moved along, from there, to go with the tail end of the meal. There were stories about sailors rescued from shipwrecks, about dolphins fighting off sharks, even some theories about magical species of dolphins being tied to the mythical - probably mythical - Atlantis. It left the group in good humour, at least.

When the gentleman retired to the smoking room, Cyrus bent down and whispered in her ear. "Go have a look outside, would you? Keep an eye on things? Where we were this morning. I'll be out in a few."

SIXTEEN

FRIDAY AFTER SUPPER

Hugh had been making the necessary circuits of the smoking room for half an hour, amiably checking in with various passengers, when Cyrus caught his attention. Hugh made his way over to the chair Cyrus had claimed in the corner, not at all certain what to expect. He could see that a number of the lady passengers had taken over a table in the garden room, and were setting up to play cards and gossip.

"I gather my sister saw another side of the ship today. She was rather pleased."

It was impossible to tell if the man were amused or offended by it. Hugh was clear that Rhoe was her own woman, deliberately and definitely, and he wasn't going to act like she wasn't. "It's a pleasure to have someone take an interest. And to pick up on details of the underlying magics that I know must be rather outside her particular expertise."

Cyrus looked him up and down, then slowly, his face cracked into a smile. "Ah, she's clever, yes. Picks up on things faster than convenient, sometimes. Do you have a minute to step outside?"

Hugh was not sure what to make of that. He'd worried, for a moment, when he came over, that he'd done something wrong. That he'd overstepped some invisible line and custom of the Council families that no one had told him about. Whatever was going on, however, didn't seem to be about that.

"How long? I should let the steward know if I'll be more than a minute or two."

"Ten minutes, perhaps twenty?"

Hugh nodded. "Meet you out on the deck, then, in a minute or two." He went off at Cyrus's nod to go let the stewards know where he'd be. When he made his way out to the deck, he saw brother and sister, their heads together, talking. He came to within about five feet, and cleared his throat.

Cyrus turned around. "I've a few concerns. And," He gestured out at the water. "What the merfolk said about the Ones Below. Do you think there's a risk?" His tone was straightforward, asking for information as one might consult any expert.

The only problem was that Hugh was certainly not one. Not about this. "That's a question for others. Nerissa in particular. I know the stories." He judged the moment. "And the numbers. There are ships lost at sea without explanation from time to time. Or rather, where the best explanation we have is some great beast of the sea we don't know how to name properly." He swallowed, then said, "I assume there's a reason you're asking."

"The lights, in the distance, and then what the merfolk said. I admit I have a few concerns."

Hugh frowned, wanting to think through this before he made assumptions. "Not solely about the ship, or you'd be speaking to the Captain."

"Quite." Again, Cyrus's voice was dry. "The stone, of course."

Rhoe turned to look at her brother, and said, her voice sharp now, far sharper than Hugh had heard before. "Spill, brother mine. Now." It had a ring of command to it.

There was a moment where Hugh was sure they were going to have some kind of brittle harsh fight. He'd have to decide what to do about it, if there were anything he could do but duck and get out of the way. At the same time, he was absolutely sure he did not want this woman upset with him, as he was seeing only the faintest edges of an oncoming storm.

Instead, Cyrus lifted his chin, then lowered it. "Swear on the Silence it won't go further? Ah, look, Pelagius, this might take more than twenty minutes. And better done in our suite."

Hugh nodded. "Let me let the steward know. Do we need wine, or anything of the kind?"

Cyrus shrugged. "I'll find our steward. Meet you down there." He offered his arm to his sister, and the two of them went off, promptly, for the stairs down. Hugh found one of the stewards in the smoking room, asked him to pass the word, and then followed.

By the time he knocked on the door, it was ajar, and he could hear voices inside.

"Come." As soon as Hugh opened the door, Cyrus turned, and nodded. "The steward will be back with a bottle and glasses. Sit, do." He gestured at the left end of the sofa, where Rhoe had taken the right end, and disappeared into his bedroom.

Rhoe shifted, turning to face him a bit better as he sat down. "Pardon my brother, he gets all fussy about certain things. Not without reason." She pitched her voice to carry, as if to forestall an argument she was certain was going to emerge from the bedroom. "In this case, I am quite willing to call in an old favour."

"Debt, sister mine. The word is debt." Cyrus emerged, carrying a small box carved of deep black wood, almost certainly ebony. Dye or stain didn't achieve that velvety black. He was relaxed about it, this sparring, though.

So was she, turning to Hugh and saying conspiratorially. "I was right about something, what, five years ago. Seven. Where does the time go? And I've been right since."

Cyrus waved a hand. "And she won't let me live it down. It is a good thing you're usually busy for the Council parties. It is very difficult to look like a respected mature man of power when your little sister shows you up on the regular."

This was a kind of banter that Hugh had no experience of. He kept looking from one to the other, like a game of tennis. Finally, he ventured, "If she is right, then I'd think asking her advice in advance would be the sensible thing."

Rhoe broke into a broad grin, and Cyrus laughed again, that amiable laugh, before the steward knocked with the wine. Once that was settled, Cyrus locked the door, and came back to the sofa and chairs. "Rhoe swears on her magic regularly, and so do I. I suspect you do not?" He made it half a question and half a statement.

Hugh shook his head. "Not in the ordinary way of things. Is there anything particular you wish me to swear to?"

"Only that you will not speak of what I share in this conversation. Not with anyone other than the Captain or a necessary official of the ship, in order to take appropriate protective measures."

Hugh opened his mouth, then closed it again. "The Silence's idea of necessary, then?"

Cyrus chuckled, and fairly clearly relaxed. "You are nearly as sharp on the uptake as Rhoe. Exactly, yes."

That was quite a compliment, given what he'd said earlier. Hugh swallowed, and nodded. "On my magic, by the Silence, I swear I will not speak of what I learn in this conversation with anyone other than those here or the Captain or a necessary officer of the ship. And that only in order to take appropriate protective measures for the ship, her crew and passengers, and cargo." He felt the bite of the magic as he spoke. It wasn't drowning, for him, but the feeling of being all alone, bobbing in an endless sea, knowing there was no hope.

The two of them echoed, in nearly the same words, before Cyrus leaned to pour the wine, handing his sister a glass first, then one to Hugh. "Nicely done. Not so many can make a proper ritual statement without preparation."

"Dunwich drills a certain amount of sense on that topic into us. It's more relevant for trade and making contracts, of course, but I've found it useful." He hesitated. "I'm gathering you have some expertise in ritual magics?" He wasn't sure how to bring up that Rhoe had mentioned his membership in Animus Mundi.

Rhoe broke out laughing, and Cyrus spread out his hand. "She wins. Again. As usual. She was sure you'd ask about it."

Hugh was not at all sure he liked being the topic of a bet between them. Or what it meant that they discussed him in private. Even if it seemed largely positive. He cleared his throat, and said, "The stone?"

Cyrus grinned. "To answer your question, yes, that's one of my particular areas of interest. It's not the only reason I'm the one on this trip, but it helped. This is the stone, of course." He didn't move to open the box, but rested one hand on it. Hugh glanced from his hand to his face, then back to the box. He felt like he was in a dream, having shown up for some exam he was entirely unprepared for.

He heard Rhoe's voice, before he could figure out what to say. "Explain, Cyrus," Again, she wasn't upset, but she was being clear. Direct. Insistent, definitely. It wasn't painful, it was more like someone diving precisely into water, the beautiful arc of a body cutting through the waves.

Cyrus let out a breath, and said, "Do you have to do that?" a little plaintively. "All right, all right. The stone is, as I said, a link between stones in four places. Continents, not countries, if you see the distinction."

"One by one? Which is it connected to, then?"

"Alexandria, Bombay, now Boston, and they're still deciding on somewhere in South America. And somewhere in Australia or New Zealand."

"Boston, not New York?" Hugh was distracted, trying to figure out the relevant pattern.

"Age of the city is a consideration, and how organic the city is, in terms of growth. They considered South Africa, but most of the port infrastructure is fairly modern. Not that that's not true of Boston, by Alexandria's standards, but you work with what you have."

"Mmm, quite. Do you know the contenders in South America?"

"They were talking about Santos a few years ago - this is a project some years in the execution. But then there was the plague outbreak through there two years ago." Cyrus flicked his fingers. "The two top choices right now are Callao in Peru, and Valparaíso in Chile. Now we are down to what might be described as questions of flavour and favour."

Hugh nodded, distracted now, by what kinds of criteria might matter more or less. He came back to the conversation when he heard Rhoe saying, "Now explain why you're worried."

"I am not - precisely - worried. But I do want to consider appropriate steps. There has been some concern that the longer distance, over water, might attract attention. The trip to Alexandria was mostly along coastline, they crossed to hug the African coast quite early on. And the Indian Ocean has a different character. Or maybe they just got lucky."

"There are some stories of great monsters of the deep, there's something in Pliny, besides of course the various references in the Odyssey." Hugh considered. "But not so likely nearer to shore, no."

Rhoe snorted. "You two can lay out maps and have a chat about that. Later. The stone, Cyrus."

"The stone." Cyrus spread his hands. "I am concerned it might be bringing some amount of attention. We were, originally, that's why they sent me, as - what was the phrase, 'younger and more able to adapt on the fly'."

Hugh started talking at the same time Rhoe said something, and then immediately stopped. "I beg pardon."

It made her laugh, including him with it. "In this case, I suspect we wanted to say the same thing, namely that that's the sort of thing to tell people before the voyage, not when you're halfway through. With concerns."

Hugh nodded. Though, honestly, he wasn't sure what anyone with authority would have said. Ockham would have agreed to whatever the Council said was needed, he wasn't stupid. He knew how much of their business depended on the Council's good will. How many favours were tallied on their side of the ledger that they could call due. He drew himself up, and said, "What are the actual concerns, so I can direct you to the appropriate people?" It sounded prim and sharp.

"I argued for discussing this in advance, like sensible people. I was overruled. But for the record, I appreciate the position it puts you in - and us." He glanced at Rhoe. "Which is why I was not entirely fond of Mother and Father insisting on this trip."

"Given that you will be next to the jewel, I will be next to you, and we are in a ship bobbing around in a very large and very deep ocean." Rhoe sucked in her breath. "What's the fear, then?"

"Bluntly, that it is a potent enough magical talisman to draw the attention of something wishing that power. Drawn to that power. Perhaps unconsciously. Like a shark in the water, from miles away, so the stories go."

Hugh let out a hiss of breath. "There's tales. What do you plan to do if - we can scarcely put you in a life boat and let you drift, if there's trouble."

"I hope not, anyway. This is, this is a necessary thing. To stabilise long distance communication, in case of urgent need. For the good of all nations. And there is no other way to get it from point to point."

"Had you, perhaps, considered taking it down to South America by land, or must it go by sea?"

"I had argued for that, but ... " Cyrus shook his head. "It must go back to the mother stone each time."

Hugh nodded. "Do you have ideas, then?"

Cyrus nodded. "I am a talented ritualist. And, as my peers say, much more flexible in my way of thinking, able to put something together much faster than most of them."

"Not Alexander." Rhoe pointed out.

"Very few people are Alexander. Which is probably a good thing." He didn't explain who Alexander was, and Hugh didn't ask. He also didn't immediately place the name. "At any rate, he is busy with other things, so you get me. Though I did consult him. I do have some ideas, on how to create a cage, around the jewel, that diffuses the magic as it were. Spreads it out."

"And the ship itself is magical, so if you could muffle it in that, I suppose that might work." Hugh stood. "I'll need to talk to the Captain, and to Nerissa. Do forgive me." He made a little bow to Rhoe. "Good evening."

Cyrus nodded. "I'll be glad to speak with them, if they wish."

Hugh nodded, and stood. He heard them start talking again, quietly, as soon as he was closing the door behind him. He went upstairs, steeling himself for a very difficult conversation.

Rhoe felt her brother had been entirely unforthcoming about too many things. He did tend to prefer to ask forgiveness rather than permission, he always had. And to be fair, with their parents, that had generally been the better strategy. Half the time they didn't notice a thing had gone wrong in the first place.

This however was a rather different situation, and she had said so, at length. Cyrus had tried to console her by finally showing her the gem. He'd opened that deep black case to reveal a pristine lining of pure white velvet, and a stunning pale blue-green stone that almost seemed to pulse with power. She'd told him to close it up, and then come up on deck to clear her head, not even sure what to say about it.

She'd begun in the writing room, but within a few minutes it had begun to seem stifling. It wasn't just the temperature - though the rooms were kept somewhat warmer than she preferred. It was hearing all the snippets of people worrying over nothing more than the latest fashion, or the smallest scandal of the highest social circles.

In the end, she found herself out on the deck, nearer the bow, looking out over the waves to the north. There were, again, those little faint hints of light on the horizon, like impossible fireflies.

It was only then that she realised what she didn't hear. There was the usual rush of the wind, and the waves against the bow of the ship. But she didn't hear the little pattern of shifts and movements of the merfolk. Not any more. She went further down the ship, to where they'd been, and looked down, and there was nothing, just the usual waves.

Their absence seemed startling. Important. She didn't know whether she should tell someone, whether one of the crew would notice. As she was trying to decide how to find a steward, she heard a cough beside her, and turned to see Nerissa, bundled up in a wool cape.

"They've been gone an hour." Her voice was very quiet, but Rhoe could now hear a lilt, there, something up in the north of Scotland, she suspected, the islands. Nerissa's poise might have been a little unsettling to most others, but Rhoe was finding it fascinating. She was still, unless she were deliberately moving, as if even small gestures communicated things.

"Hugh's had a word, then?" It seemed ridiculous to say, but it was what she could think of. "And he's right to be worried? My brother?"

"I wish he'd told us beforehand. I suppose that's rude, but I don't care. The Council can be awfully high-handed." She lifted her hand, and it was one of those deliberate movements again. Rhoe supposed that if you used your hands, your arms, to talk, you would learn to be careful of chance movements, the concern you might say something you hadn't intended.

"Oh, I agree entirely about the high-handedness." Rhoe hesitated, not sure about going on.

Nerissa shook her head once sharply. "I don't blame your brother, entirely. Still fairly junior, isn't he? Even if he's skilled as he claims, which I'm willing to grant for the moment."

"He is very good at what he does." Rhoe took a breath. "Look, what can I tell you that might be a help? I didn't know about the implications of the stone until tonight. I thought it was a more routine courier trip, the sort of thing one doesn't trust to the cargo hold or other people's hands."

Nerissa let out an entirely bemused puff of breath. "I expect so. Are you warm enough out here? I'd rather not go inside."

Rhoe glanced toward the various public rooms, and ventured, "They have no idea what to make of you, do they? You don't fit at all into their tidy little categories."

"Remarkably few people do. I have a habit of observing them, from up on the bridge. The way people ebb and flow, the currents that carry them. Not many people fight the current they're in."

"You're told that it's not safe to fight it. At least I was." Rhoe looked out toward the ocean.

"But you do." Nerissa's voice was clear, precise. Not cold, but very deliberate, everything she said was honed.

Rhoe turned, feeling caught out and suddenly vulnerable. "I do what I think needs doing. With the skills I have. My parents, I admit, would rather I'd been married off a decade ago, and doing something appropriately decorous. If I had to be involved in healing, a little light tending to decoratively ill children, perhaps. Ill children are almost never decorative, for the record."

"And instead, you've been firmly in the thick of it at the

Temple of Healing. I've never been, too far inland for me to feel comfortable."

That made Rhoe consider. "You don't have webbing on your hands, I'd have noticed." She frowned, then considered the other woman's dress. "I suspect you don't see the fluttering birds in all their colours, do you?" There was something about the eyes, the way the pupils responded differently to light, that gave her the clue.

"My oldest sister's the selkie. She inherited our mother's skin. I'm..." Nerissa shrugged. "I'm one of Merope's Speakers. But you are right about the colour. I don't see yellows, and," She blinked a few times. "Are you wearing blue? That's the sort of thing that might also be blue-green where I can't tell."

Rhoe had to smile at that. "I am actually wearing blue-green. It's a change from Healer's red. About as much of a change as one can reasonably get, honestly." She looked Nerissa up and down, now quite curious.

Nerissa snorted. "And now you have a dozen - well, probably more like three dozen - questions you're entirely too polite to ask. Because you actually see me as a person, not as an interesting scientific achievement."

"At least three dozen. But I do think that while the scientific age has a number of virtues, the way it looks at people who are different is decidedly not one. May I ask if it's a problem, as a general rule?"

Nerissa leaned back against the railing. "When I'm working, rarely. It's good luck to have one of the Speakers on a ship. We can't help with a storm blowing up, or an iceberg, but we can often give warning that one is coming, or closer than it should be."

"Women? I mean, are you all women?" Rhoe was sorting through what she knew of the lore.

"Oh, we have men, as well. Like the merfolk, you saw earlier. And people where it's honestly rather difficult to tell without asking unless you're being really quite rude."

Rhoe nodded, amused by the phrasing. "All right. So the crew's not a bother, you don't normally socialise with the passengers. What do you do when you're not on call? When we're closer to shore, or what have you."

Nerissa shrugged. "Honestly? Read novels. Write letters. I keep a detailed journal of natural history, what's in harbour when we are. Birds and fish and seals and whales, and all of that. I make jewellery, too. A little tricky if the seas are rough, but it's portable and easy to pack up." She made it sound entirely normal, to go back and forth across the ocean with a trunk or two holding all her worldly possessions.

"Not a bad life, if you like the ocean. And occasionally go up to, Hugh said Scotland, yes?"

"The Orkneys. Beautiful, if spare." Nerissa turned, not exactly cutting off the conversation, but setting it back on track.

Rhoe coughed. "Yes. The stone. What can I tell you? Since you seem to be both a person of good sense, and someone who has a solid idea of the possible concerns."

"Captain Melcott's a good sailor, but he's not strongly magical. He has respect, but not skill, when it comes to the seafolk, and he knows his limits. Which, honestly, is much easier to deal with than many of the other options. His crew look up to him, most of them know him well and trust him. And I know Hugh well enough to know his strengths and priorities, or ask about them. Which leaves you and your brother."

"As the ones who might put a wrench into things." Rhoe considered, leaning against the railing and looking out to the ocean. "Is it plausible that a single, densely magical stone is attracting something down there? Something large?"

"Possible, yes. But the merfolk might have moved on for all sorts of other reasons. Sharks, orcas."

Rhoe frowned. "Will they be safe? Safe enough?"

"That's not what most people ask." Nerissa turned to her, suddenly intense. "You ask about them? Not about yourself?"

Rhoe gestured at the waves. "It's their ocean. Their home. Not ours. We're just bobbing along on the top."

Nerissa looked out toward the ocean. "What kind of Healer are you?"

It was a question Rhoe had been asked before, but never quite in that tone of voice. "When I go home, I'll be doing something different."

There was a long silence, as if Nerissa were still waiting for a proper answer. When it became clear the other woman would just keep waiting, Rhoe shrugged slightly. "I'm going to be making my oaths to Belisama. As one of the priestesses who keep the sacred baths."

"Beneath the Temple, underground." Nerissa shivered. "Too much rock. Far too much rock. Tell me about what that involves? What's different than it was?"

"I've been a Healer at the Temple since my apprenticeship - and largely there during it, though I've spent time a few other places for a month or two at once. Infectious disease, most recently, but other things." Rhoe shrugged. "I'm not well-suited to maternity wards, but the rest of it I can do well enough."

Nerissa looked her up and down. "No desire that way, or something else?"

Rhoe considered. "No particular inclinations that way. Never having been particularly inclined to marriage. But it's more - Tanith was my friend, before she married Cyrus. She died having their daughter, something no Healer could have stopped, short of a miracle. It makes it hard to be around the easy births, and terrifying to be around the difficult ones. I'm fearless about much of my healing, but - that one hasn't mended yet."

Nerissa tilted her head. "You seem the sort who would tackle it head on."

"If I had personal cause, I'd consider it. But I keep abominable hours, or I have until now. I love my work, I leave books all over the place, and I forget other people exist unless they're the patients I'm responsible for. Or the nurses I'm working with."

Nerissa peered at her. In someone else, Rhoe would have called it bird-like, but it wasn't. It was more like the darting of a fish, something curious to see in a mammal. As if that fish had come across something entirely new, and was trying to determine if it were threat, food, shelter, or something else.

Rhoe shrugged, trying to figure out how to put the next bit into words. "The baths will be different, but I'm not sure how, yet. You never are, until you go across the threshold." This part, at least, she knew how it went. Or rather, what parts she had no idea about yet, and wouldn't until she made her oaths and started doing the work. Then she added, "Besides, a fair half the men who have expressed interest just want the social whirl and the chance to brush shoulders with power and prestige. The ones who actually have it, I often don't care for what they do with it."

"And your brother is different?" Nerissa's voice was now very careful.

"My brother is going to get yelled at, as soon as I have all my arguments in order. For not giving me fair warning, for doing things that might interfere with the ship, at the very least. But I love him, and he does generally try to do the right thing. He just thinks that being brilliant will always get him out of trouble."

"And you know it won't." Nerissa clucked her tongue, once.

"I've known plenty of people who thought that who couldn't be mended. So - I worry. But he's a grown man, my older brother. There's only so much of that a person can do. Like you and your sister, I'm guessing."

"Sisters." Nerissa's voice was simultaneously put-upon and exceedingly fond. "I do know. All right. Let me think about the stone, and will you get your brother to talk to me, if I ask?"

Rhoe snorted. "I'm his little sister. That means I have plenty of ways to get him to do what I ask. When called for."

At that moment, the doors from the salon opened, and people poured out for a breath of fresh air. Nerissa melted away, and Rhoe was left to make her way through the chattering people to a quieter spot.

EIGHTEEN

SATURDAY MORNING

The next morning, Hugh came out on deck for his usual walk after breakfast, and then stopped, looking off toward the north. There were fish rising, flitting back and forth, as if something were agitating them. He leaned on the railing, watching, caught between how beautiful they were and the nagging feeling that something was not quite right.

He was still standing there a minute later when he heard someone clear his throat. Hugh looked up to see Captain Melcott, who gestured at the bridge. "I saw you out here. Do you have a moment?"

"Of course, Captain." He gestured at the fish. "Is this a problem?"

"We're not sure. But that's one of the things I wanted to talk to you about. Keep your ears open for anything unusual, would you, and let me know twice a day? Around luncheon and after supper? If I'm not on duty, leave notes with the Chief Officer?"

"Captain." Hugh was glad to agree. "Do you have a particular concern?"

"There's a ship from another line - non-magical, the SS *Memory*. We wouldn't normally hear anything, while we're underway, but more than one of us has a worry. When we feel like that..." He shrugged. "Magic. Comes in all forms, and more than one of us has a touch of foresight. It's handy in our line of work."

"Any other concerns?" Hugh kept his voice relaxed and even.

"I don't particularly care for the Council's approach here, but it's not as if it's the first time they've blithely gone full steam ahead without consulting anyone. And Smythe-Clive is known to be a sound man, sensible. Not going off half-cocked like some of them like to, given the excuse. Young, to be Council, but thoroughly one of the right sort, isn't that how they put it?"

Hugh considered all the implications of that sentence, and the weighing of a man by whether he was the right sort. He couldn't blame Captain Melcott for that. It was how the world worked. "I've enjoyed my conversation with him." It was a non-committal sort of phrasing.

"What does Nerissa say, do you know?" The change in subject was abrupt.

"I've not seen her this morning. I know the merfolk left last night, and she went back to her cabin, didn't she?"

"No sense making her nap on the cot, with all the noise from the bridge, if we won't need her urgently. Her cabin's not that far, on this ship. There are the traditions, and there are times when she's earned a decent bed and a door between her and the rest of our blather."

Before Hugh could ask anything further, there was a call from one of the ship's officers, and Captain Melcott nodded once. "Pardon. See you at luncheon if my duties permit."

Hugh found himself alone outside the bridge, and then made his way back down to take a walk around the deck. It took him some time to fully make a circuit, as the purser pulled him into his office to talk through a few matters. Hugh did not need to make any decisions - the man knew his work and did it well - but the purser clearly wanted to make sure he was not missing anything. It was pleasant to be a help by being present and listening, honestly.

By the time he continued on his walk, it was well past breakfast, coming up on half ten. He did not expect to hear anything immediately. But once he came around to the port side and the glassed in seating area, he couldn't help overhearing two of the women talking as he ducked in to get out of the wind. It was Elaine and Heloise Adams.

"It was just so very calm, and very blue. Most queer." Heloise sounded very put out. "Why does one's mind hold on to the strangest things? If it were a frock, it would be a very showy sort of colour."

"It wouldn't flatter you at all, dear," Elaine agreed. Then she looked up, beaming at Hugh. "Oh, Master Pelagius, do you have a moment? Heloise mentioned that you were at breakfast yesterday when dear Georgiana Lytton was talking about that odd dream she had."

"I do remember, of course." He nodded pleasantly, but remained standing, at just enough distance it would be awkward for either of the women to reach out to touch him. "I hope she slept better last night?"

"Well, that's the oddest thing. Whatever the doctor gave her - he's rather young, isn't he, but a pleasant manner? He listened very well, I thought. He didn't have either of her usual dream potions, but whatever he gave her must have worked a treat, she said she slept wonderfully."

Likely because it was an actually effective potion, not a

bit of alcohol and flavouring, brushed with a flicker of magic. "I'm very glad." And Hugh was glad. He suspected that Miss Lytton was more pleasant when she had had enough sleep. Most people were. "What, may I ask, was odd?"

"Well, last night, I had the same dream!" Heloise sounded both delighted and offended, as if a second-hand dream was a social faux pas. "Well, perhaps not quite the same. The aquamarine water, but it was as if there was some sort of light under the water, as well as the sun above. It was a clear day, and, oh, afternoon, early afternoon? The sun was quite strong. Bad for the complexion, of course." She was the sort of woman to stay to shade and parasols. Not that that was a concern today, as there were more than enough clouds to mask the early winter sun.

"Did you see anything besides the water? Any people around?" Hugh felt he didn't even know what questions to ask.

"Oh, not that I saw. No one, you know, important." Heloise waved a hand. "Maybe some servants."

Hugh tried not to frown, and turned his head to cough, instead of risking a more open failure. "And how did you sleep, Mistress Adams?" He turned to Elaine.

She pursed her lips. "It's so difficult sleeping on shipboard. I kept thinking I was hearing someone on the other side of the wall, some sort of horrible argument. The Winters. But of course, your sound charms must be better than that?" She asked it artlessly. "And they've been together quite some time, and seemed so happy earlier."

That at least told him which direction might be a problem. The Winters were part of that knot - two couples who'd been together some time, two single friends - who had seemed very at ease last time he'd seen them. But he realised suddenly they hadn't been at supper last night, or if they had been, he'd missed them entirely.

Hugh bowed slightly. "I'll be glad to go check that for you, if you don't mind us entering your cabin for a few moments while you're up here. I believe I saw the Winters up at breakfast early. I'll check with them."

After making his cordial exit, Hugh worked his way around to speak to the Winters. He murmured that the staff would appreciate the chance to tend to a minor issue in their cabin. If they'd be willing to stay up on deck for the next hour or so, he'd be glad to arrange a seat at the Captain's table in the next day or three. They were delighted, at least overtly. Mrs Winters, however, looked rather pinched around the eyes, as if she had a headache. Her husband was rather sallow. Hugh didn't think it was seasickness. They'd been on the voyage long enough for most of that to pass, and the seas were fairly calm.

When Hugh left them, he went straight to find the first class steward, to track down the staff responsible for both Master and Mistress Winters, and Elaine and Heloise Adams.

"Did you notice anything out of the ordinary last night? Or this morning?" The stewardess shook her head. "Mistress Winters has a maid. She's pressing some linens in our workroom. Should I fetch her, sir?"

Hugh hesitated for a moment. It would be tipping his hand, but he thought he saw a way to ask the maid about what she might have heard. He'd have to go delicately, and he hoped he was up to the challenge. "Please, Miss Grant." There, he'd placed her name. Amelia Grant.

When Miss Grant came back three minutes later, Hugh was the picture of confidence. Outwardly, at least. The maid was in her mid-twenties, a bit younger than Mistress

Winters, with auburn hair tucked firmly under a cap, as if it might attract too much attention otherwise. She wore a smartly fitted dress of a deep blue, with a lace apron over it. A woman of some status in her household, and possibly wearing a cast-off dress from her mistress.

"You are Miss Edgewood, yes?"

The woman nodded, rather than bobbing a curtsey as a younger or less certain woman might have. "You wished to speak with me, sir?"

"I am Hugh Pelagius. My family owns the ship, and I am on this voyage to help ease things along for our passengers. I had a chance to speak with your mistress and her husband upstairs. I was concerned that they might be unwell and unwilling to admit it. Of course, I wouldn't dream of asking you to overstep their confidence...."

Miss Edgewood hesitated. Hugh was sure there was something there now. He cleared his throat. "Perhaps Miss Grant could bring a cup of tea."

Miss Grant picked up on his intention quickly. "You were about to pin up the ironing, weren't you, Miss Edgewood? I'd be glad to see to that for you, you were run off your feet this morning."

Put like that, Miss Edgewood did not argue. Hugh steered her to a chair, pulling it out for her. "Here we go. Your mistress will not be back down for quite a bit. I made arrangements so we could make sure nothing was amiss here."

"That was kindly done, sir." Miss Edgewood waited until there was tea in front of her, picking it up carefully. As Hugh had hoped, it was restorative. "She was very upset last night, sir. And Master Winters. They're usually such a lovely couple, so caring."

"Was it an argument, something that happened? Or was

it, oh, a run of tears?"

Miss Edgewood pursed her lips, thinking. "There was an argument, sir, but it wasn't an ordinary one. Mistress Winters was a bit uneasy all evening. She near burst into tears one moment, for no reason I could see, and ten minutes later, she was laughing. But with an edge to it. And then she was playing cards with her friends, and she lost. She's a good player, but she's a good loser, as a rule. And this time it was all sharp edges. That was the argument, I think, Master Winters asked about it."

Hugh nodded. "We had a concern about noise leaking through between the rooms. I've someone checking the charms on the other side of the wall, and we'll do the same here in a moment. I hope that will be a help, but I'd be glad to send along, oh, a soothing flower arrangement, and perhaps a bottle of something? Would that make things worse?"

"Oh, that would be kind, sir. She's not slept well, the past two nights, I know that. She hates taking potions, but..." Miss Edgewood hesitated. "Do you know, sir, if the doctor would have something that I could use, a salve or something of the kind? Nothing strong, nothing she'd refuse to take if she knew."

Hugh suspected that a maid using such a thing was not at all proper, but it was also obvious she was worried about her mistress. Not just the way one might expect, concerned about ongoing employment. "Why don't I walk you along to the doctor, and we'll see what he can come up with. Perhaps your mistress might be willing to take something if he has a word. A calmative, a nervine."

"Maybe, sir." That seemed to end the conversation, and Hugh let her finish her tea before escorting her along to Doctor Northton's office.

NINETEEN
SATURDAY MORNING

Rhoe turned away from the railing to look up. She hadn't felt this way last night, but now there was some sort of faint tremolo. It was much like the sense she had when looking at a person that something was not quite right, even though there was no obvious injury. She supposed, in that sense, that the ship, the community of the ship, was like a person, all the different organs doing their part, and the passengers flitting around, largely irrelevant to the function of the whole.

The passengers, mind, seemed not to be noticing. It was about eleven in the morning by the ship's clock, and everyone was at their morning pursuits. Rhoe had dodged away from the current deck games, coming to find a quieter corner, but was entirely too restless to find a lounge chair and read, even if it weren't a little chilly to be sitting still.

When she looked back the other way, she was surprised to see Hugh had come up next to her from the other side. He cleared his throat. "Pardon. I didn't mean to startle you. Are you all right? I saw you looking out the ocean."

Rhoe shrugged, turning back to look out. "I spent a

while talking to Nerissa last night, and I couldn't help thinking about some of it." She gestured at the bridge. "Do you know if there's any particular reason there are more uniforms than usual up there? Or is it more?"

She hadn't realised until she said it, what she'd noticed, but there was rather more navy blue visible on the spaces around the bridge, people coming and going, now that she'd put it into words. And she certainly knew the signs of people preparing for something, even if they weren't sure what for. She'd seen it when there was some larger accident, waiting for patients to be brought into the Temple, when every hand was needed.

Hugh glanced up, and then back at her, and she could see his studied and careful outward relaxation. He opened his mouth, then considered, and closed it. "If I told you everything was fine, it was normal, you'd know I was lying."

"Please don't." It came out of her mouth immediately.

Hugh shook his head. "I'm not that much of a fool." He looked back up, past her shoulder. "The captain's a bit concerned."

"Is that like saying one is a bit concerned, this leg is no longer attached, or like saying one is a bit concerned, we're running out of tea?"

That provoked a snort. "Not quite the leg, yet. But I suppose it depends on whether you mean this tin is out of tea, or whether the shops are out, and there is no tea to be had for love or money." Then he sobered. "You can feel it, then? The sense of something?"

"I was thinking it's like at the Temple, when we know something's gone wrong - an accident somewhere, say - but not yet what happened or how many we'll need to see to, or what sorts of needs."

"That's," Hugh looked around. "That's probably not

wrong. I'd say there was a storm blowing in, but that's not it." The sky was clear, as far as she could see. Then he changed the subject, or so it seemed. "What did you think, talking to Nerissa last night? She mentioned you'd had a care for the merfolk, their safety."

Rhoe hesitated. "Look, if I posit the idea that the stone might be unbalancing things, much as any great magic sometimes unbalances the smaller magics around it, or draws attention. Draws the soul, one of my teachers would have said, and Cyrus would argue with that translation, but there you are." She gathered her thoughts. No use starting to babble. "If we posit the stone has an effect, as the only thing we know of such weight on board."

"That we know of." Hugh agreed. "There might be any number of things in the hold. There was a mummy, a few trips ago, that - well, there is a reason the crews aren't overtly as worried as they might be."

Rhoe considered the possible implications of that, felt there was likely a gothic novel idea in there, and moved forward without dwelling on that particular problem. "That we know of." She gestured at the space where the hold was. "And if it were the stone, it is not likely Cyrus could be persuaded to toss it into the sea."

"I'm honestly not sure that would help." Hugh said, quietly. "There'd be the lingering trace here. That might be enough. Tell me what you were thinking about the merfolk." Again, a change of subject.

It took a moment for Rhoe to find words. "We came into their territory, carrying something that should not, perhaps, be carried. Positing that the stone has some effect. There are containers, that would insulate. Absorb magic so it could be released safely on land, within them. I did point all of this out to Cyrus last night, and he admits he did not think through the implications nearly as clearly as I expect of him, his usual standard of attention. But they..." She gestured at the ocean, expansively. "They live here. If there's danger coming to us, there's a reason for us to have to deal with it. Not them."

"That is not the way people usually see it. You do realise the threat?"

Rhoe nodded. "You had mentioned, the ways ships disappear, and no one knows why. And in this case it's not like being in a lifeboat would be better. Decidedly worse. Unless one, I don't know, threw the gem one way, and went very quickly the other."

"And your brother seems unlikely to do that. Even if, as I said, it might do good, and I rather think it wouldn't, if it comes to that."

Rhoe shook her head. "He made his oaths. And he'll keep them. Would the Captain put him overboard? Or try to?"

Hugh looked her up and down. "Again, not the question people would ask." There was a quick glance up to the bridge. "I don't know. Truly. But that often doesn't end well, for anyone. Even in cases of murder or mutiny, you don't leave someone in the ocean. You wouldn't leave a Council Member. Fabricate a man falling overboard, maybe, but not leave him in a lifeboat."

It was exceedingly pragmatic, and Rhoe let out a breath she hadn't realised she was holding. "And me?"

"You had no idea about the stone, and as far as I can tell, you are very useful for lecturing your brother on what he should have thought about rather earlier in the process. And he seems likely to listen to you." It was half a question.

"He does listen." She knew her voice was smug, but she'd earned that smugness, every bit of it.

"Frankly, if it does come to any kind of fight, anything from below... your brother might well be useful. I've seen him at the duelling practises."

"He's a ritualist, not a duellist. For all he's been making a show of things with the Scali brothers. I don't know if you've seen him at it with them."

"I have. It's certainly not distracting the society ladies from commenting about his grace and fast reflexes. But I would not, in general, take their gossip as the measure of the man, for all I am no duellist at all."

That made Rhoe throw her head back and laugh. "Exactly so. Cyrus would be the first to say, he is not in the top rank of duellists. He knows this because he knows many of them, does practice bouts with them. He's not bad, but not in their league. The ritualists - there are better ritualists out there, but he's gaining on them every year, and everyone knows it. Much of ritual magic, the perfection of it, is experience and practice."

"Most things, surely. But no, I see that. And with so many ritual magics, one must have a particular timing or location, or what have you. I don't suppose there's a chance he's studied anything about the ocean." Hugh suddenly sounded less sure.

Rhoe thought back to the books she'd seen in his bedroom, stacked on the shelf by his desk. "He certainly brought some references. Bromley's *Atlantica* and Theodoric's *Depths and Echoes,* or whatever it's properly called in Latin. More about the stone magics, and there might be something there. I could have a word, if you liked? Or simply go look at his books."

"He leaves things out?" Hugh considered the implications of magical volumes.

"Goodness, no. Those are all in a properly warded

trunk, unless they're being used. But it's a blood lock, and," She held up her hands. "I am entirely competent to draw a drop of a blood from my own hand as needed. A charm I use regularly. I am not him, but we are full siblings, and he hasn't locked it against me. So."

Hugh pursed his lips. She could tell he was thinking fiercely about something. "May I ask your own skills, then? Since it might be relevant?"

Rhoe rocked back onto her heels slightly, taking up the stance she'd had trained into her during her apprenticeship, balanced on her feet, for any of the suddenly demanded opinions of a case. It was reflex, now, much like the way Cyrus shifted to brace his feet for a duel at times. "A full apprenticeship as a Healer includes a number of things. One must be able to harm in order to heal, is one way it's put. If we don't know how the curses, the hexes, the damaging cantrips are cast, how can we unpick them?"

"Is that the usual run of your work? You said you'd been doing infectious disease."

"Largely, yes. We can't cure it with magic, but we're far more effective at stabilising someone so their body can survive the fevers or the other symptoms. More to the point, we can be much more effective about quarantine, and avoiding carrying infection from the patient to others, with a bit of magic. Much of that is the nurses, but the Healer's role is..." She'd rarely had to put this into words for someone without a Healer's training.

He nodded encouragingly, without interrupting her.

"I'd say the Healer's role is reminding the patient of the proper pattern. The pattern for them, not some idealised pattern." She gestured at the ship. "You have an idealised concept of how a voyage should go, yes? But each voyage is unique. The weather, the crew, the way they respond to the captain, if any of the passengers are particularly difficult?"

Hugh laughed, his eyes twinkling. "Just so. Some of which can be measured, but some of which is more about the experience. More a piece of music than a series of maths equations."

"Exactly. We want people to be their own proper piece of music. Whatever that is for them. The best of a Healer's work is figuring that out."

She felt suddenly shy, having said that. Hugh was quiet, looking at the ocean for so long she almost wondered if she should leave him alone. Then he cleared his throat. "And your new work? That is more directly finding that song, helping someone find it, than the disease wards." This time, it certainly wasn't a question, it was a clear, reasoned statement.

Rhoe could only nod, not at all sure what to do with the fact he'd seen it that clearly and that quickly.

"Which explains why you are attuned to the ship as you would be - as you would be if you were one of the crew." He considered. "A way Doctor Northton isn't. Not yet, at least."

"He does know his medicine." She felt called to defend him. He wasn't a bad doctor - but he was a doctor, not a Healer, and that made more of a difference than it should, sometimes. "But his training isn't mine, and his work isn't mine. I can afford the luxury of patterns and songs, and fitting them back together. He has many patients to see, and many times what is wrong is indeed more - mechanical. If that's the proper word. It needs skill and training, but it's," She gestured at the waves. "At the surface, not the depths below."

"In which there are many things, quite a few of them

delightful. I keep hoping we'll see whales through here. Quite likely right whales, as we come along close to Boston, we're not yet entirely too late for them, before they move south."

"I know there are many kinds of whales, but not much about how to tell them apart. Certainly not from the water level."

That made him laugh again. "If someone calls out we've seen one, you come find me, and I'll tell you all I know, then, how's that?"

She smiled. "I'd like that."

TWENTY
SATURDAY AFTER LUNCH

J ust after luncheon, Hugh found himself on deck again, looking out toward the ocean behind them, back toward the east. The sun had moved enough to the west that it had begun to cast shadows that way, making it easier to see the dips and flows of the ocean.

There were birds in the air above, swooping and diving, but they were too far away for him to identify them accurately, either by colouration or by sound. They seemed to be making much of something a mile or so off, perhaps fish near the surface. He liked hearing them, the way the cries carried. It reminded him of how full of life the ocean was, even though he couldn't see most of it.

Hugh continued scanning the horizon line. He had just begun to make out the shape of something, the occasional curve of a fin, above the waves, then a tail as something dove under the surface again. Whales, he was sure of that, but he couldn't see enough, yet, to be sure of what they were. Not an killer whale. This was bigger, and also decidedly grey.

Hugh was startled when he heard a voice by his shoulder, Professor Ferdinand Merton. "You saw them, then? I don't suppose there are binoculars to borrow, perhaps? Mine were somehow packed in the trunk that went to the hold for the voyage. Most tedious." He didn't seem terribly upset, instead more wistful.

"Oh." Hugh hadn't considered that. "I can fetch mine, give me a moment?" At the older man's nod, he turned, going back to his own cabin and finding the pair of binoculars he kept at the top of his own trunk. By the time he came back, the professor had been joined by his wife, but most of the passengers were engaged in some sort of tournament up closer to the bow.

He held out the binoculars. "Here, sir. Professor."

"You needn't be formal, you're scarcely one of my students. I'm certainly not assigning marks or making you sit exams. Though, if you hang about, I'll be glad to tell you about what we're seeing." He took a good minute to look out at the waves, then he handed the binoculars back. "If you look out there, when you can see tails. That's a small pod of sperm whales. If there were whalers out here, they'd consider it an exceptional catch." He waved his hand. "I believe this is not a prime whaling route?"

Hugh shook his head. "It's rare for us to see whales. More common to the north, especially in around Greenland and Iceland, early in the trip, or near the Canadian and New England coast. Here? It's chance, and a large ocean. I'd been told, in the past, they didn't care for the noise of the engines."

"No, they likely wouldn't. And intelligent whales - and there are theories they're intelligent - would surely come to recognise ships as a threat. What was it caught your eye, originally?"

"There was a spout, I think. And then a tail, one of them diving. They're not at all near us, though?"

Professor Merton snorted. "You know as well as I do the distances are deceptive. But no, I'd say that's at least a mile, possibly nearer two or three. It's a clear day, the waves are relatively calm."

"Will they come closer, do you think?" Hugh wasn't sure if he wanted more people to see them, or if he wished to tuck them away, like something private. Which was a ridiculous desire with something so large.

Professor Merton laughed, warmly, then he sobered. "I'm not sure. As you say, seeing them at all is unusual. There might be some reason they're here. Some change in the ocean beneath. I do wish we had more idea of what happened in the depths. It is very like judging a book by its cover, and having no idea of all the words on the pages themselves."

At that moment, Hugh heard a voice behind him. "Good afternoon." He turned to see Rhoe standing there, sensibly wrapped in a cape, against the wind.

He glanced at the Professor, but before he could say anything, Ilune Merton held out her hand. "Can she borrow your binoculars, Hugh? Do say yes."

Put like that, Hugh could scarcely refuse. Not that he particularly wanted to. He held the binoculars out. "We're discussing the whales there - you can just see them blowing, or the tip of their tails, without. Have a look? Professor Merton has confirmed they're sperm whales."

The three of them stood in silence as Rhoe adjusted the binoculars, then leaned forward, as if trying to see them clearer. Hugh let her look for a good minute before asking Ferdinand, "They dive for quite some time, don't they?"

"They do. And from here, I can see there is a small pod, but it could be five or ten, or nearer forty. No way of telling, this far away. Too far to see the differences in the tails."

Rhoe lowered the binoculars and offered them back to Hugh. He took them, his fingers brushing hers for a moment, before he looped the strap around his neck to leave his hands free. "The tails?" he asked.

Ferdinand nodded. "The tails have distinctive marks, if you look closely. And quickly, I admit I don't have much of the skill, but I've talked to a few people who've developed it."

Rhoe nodded. "I know that spermaceti, their oil was preferred for lamp in the hospitals where charm lights can't be used - clean burning. And of course, too many women believe in whalebone corseting." She shook her head. "They seem so majestic, there."

"Majestic and sometimes dangerous. Not often to ships, but there is not much in the ocean that they fear. Or that can damage them. At least not that we know."

It was then that there was a shift. All of them caught it, some sound that carried, or even was felt, more than heard, like drumbeats against skin. Hugh raised the binoculars again, peering out, then recoiled. "There's something else there." He pulled the strap off his neck, and immediately handed them to Ferdinand. "I'm not sure what."

Only, he thought his first thought might be right. It had looked like some large tentacle, something long. He had seen it extend above the waves for a moment before slipping from view again. He could not tell how close it was to the whales, or even if he were right.

Ferdinand looked, straining, then he shook his head. "Something has agitated them, certainly. That noise. That's been reported before, no one is entirely sure what it is. And you can see there, the spouts, they're more active."

"I should let the captain know." Hugh let out a breath. "I'll be back in a few moments. May I take the binoculars?"

Ferdinand handed them over, promptly, and Hugh headed for the bridge, as quickly as he could. He waited outside until one of the bridge crew gave him permission to enter, rehearsing what to say in his head.

"Captain Melcott." Hugh's voice was crisp. "We were watching some whales off the starboard stern, about two miles off. A pod of sperm whales, but also something else, possibly a tentacle. I can give you the bearing."

"A squid, surely." That was the Chief Officer. "Nothing we want to be too close to, but no particular risk, a ship of this size, and we're moving away from them."

Hugh was not sure it was that simple. "You'd asked I report anything I heard," he said, to Captain Melcott. He'd made a full report about the dreams, as he'd heard about them.

The Captain, at least, was frowning slightly. "We'll keep a watch, see what else there might be. I had noticed the fish this morning, that often suggests there are squid feeding. I'd not have expected them to be so active on our route, but..." He shrugged. "It is not entirely unheard of." Then he nodded, once, a clear dismissal. "Let me know if you notice anything else out of the ordinary, even if it seems small, as soon as you have a chance. But without causing alarm with the passengers."

Hugh nodded, then glanced around. There were several people with charts out, checking angles. "Is there another concern, Captain?"

One of the officers glanced over, and Captain Melcott waved a hand at him, granting permission. "We are a little worried we've not seen signs of the SS *Memory* yet. We should have caught her up, by now, or near enough, if she stayed on heading. We're checking the likely positions, if she got blown off course. There's some clusters of seaweed, that suggests there have been winds, along the surface. Nothing indicative of a recent wreck or a problem, but we keep an eye out."

Hugh nodded. "Thank you for the explanation." He then made his way to the door. "I'll let you know of anything else, Captain." With that he went out, back down the exterior stairs, to the deck. The professor and his wife had moved on, but Rhoe was still standing there, looking out at the ocean. He looked through the binoculars again and then handed them over to her, coughing to get her attention.

She took them, then looked out across the ocean, silently, for a good minute or two, then handed them back. "A squid, Ferdinand said."

Hugh cleared his throat, unsure what to say.

Rhoe looked at him. "You don't think it's just a squid."

Put like that, bluntly like that, he shook his head. "Something feels off. Like a storm coming in. It's not just the sounds - it's something in the pressure of the air."

"What did the captain say?" She handed the binoculars back.

"He thanked me for letting him know, told me not to worry the passengers with anything, and to tell him if I noticed anything else out of the ordinary. I don't know. I've seen whales before, though not sperm whales, and not at this point in this ocean." He looked out at the ocean again, then back at her. "I am no expert here, and I find myself suddenly desperately wanting one."

"And the ones we have, at least the ones more of an expert, do not seem worried. Though I gather the professor is not so concerned with the open ocean as with the coastal cities, and they seem quite different things to me."

"Exactly." That she had seen this, as clearly as he did,

reassured him. Then he realised she'd said 'we'. That he was not alone in this.

"Which brings us to options." Rhoe let out a breath, then went on, thinking out loud. "This might be nothing more than nature red in tooth and claw, the law of the sea."

"It might. In which case we will look very foolish for fussing, I suppose."

Rhoe shrugged. "I don't mind looking foolish, if it's about having a care for the well-being of those around me. Even if they don't realise it. Perhaps especially when they don't realise it." She sounded like that was a feature of her life, quite often, and he supposed it might be.

"How would you handle it, then?" he asked, "Given that we do not have expert knowledge to draw on."

"I think," she said, her voice now decisive. "I will have a chat with my brother. Promptly. He may not be able to tell if the stone is drawing anything to us, never mind what it might be drawing, but he has some skill at scrying if I can talk him into doing it."

Something about her tone broke through Hugh's worries. "I would, I suspect, not be a help with that. You can use more personal weapons if I am not there."

"Exactly. And he owes me, several ways around. It is, what. Half-one now? You keep a look out, and be somewhere I can find you when I'm done getting more information out of him."

"An hour? Two hours? I do not know how long this sort of thing might properly take in your competent hands."

To his delight, she laughed and then grinned at him, her eyes crinkling up in pleasure. "Smaller than a breadbox, as the game goes. Likely under an hour, unless the scrying takes a while, but almost certainly under two. You might wander the public spaces and see if you hear any gossip.

Things people have seen, odd dreams, anything between the two."

"Fair enough." He took a step back to make a little formal bow. "Until we meet again."

She hesitated, just for a moment, reaching to touch his hand. "I am glad you're worried too, as odd as that is to say. It would be far worse to be worried alone, and to think I was making it up."

Before he could say anything in reply, she had stepped back, pulling her cape around her, and had set off for the staircase to go below.

TWENTY-ONE
SATURDAY AFTERNOON

Rhoe closed the door firmly behind her. Her brother was not upstairs, nor was he in evidence in the sitting room. The door to his bedroom was cracked open, however. "Cyrus, we need to talk. Now." If the door had been closed, she'd have knocked. Or something. But this was both urgent and important.

He came out half a minute later, rubbing his hands together as if he'd been writing intently. She could see the ink stains on his fingers. "Yes?" He didn't sound irritated, but he did sound distracted. On the other hand, he hadn't just told her to come in, he'd come out. Which naturally made her more than a little suspicious of what he was up to.

She looked him up and down. Informal working robes, he'd changed since luncheon. "You're researching something." Her eyes narrowed, waiting to see what he did.

Cyrus spread his hands. "I can never fool you. I'm not sure I want to. Yes, I was researching. I am a tad stuck, however. What did you want to talk about?"

"Tell me about the gem. Not the superficial things, how blue it is, or where it came from. Or the polite story about what it does. All those are true enough, I suppose, but they're not the beating heart of it."

Cyrus snorted. "I can tell you want to know, you always work around to blood metaphors when you're serious about something." He let out a breath. "I shouldn't talk it through with you. I'm going to." He held up his hand before she could object. "Healer's confidence?" He asked it, rather than demanding it.

Rhoe considered that, then shook her head. "If it's what I think it is, it affects everyone on this ship. I can't keep that secret." Quite literally, she was certain her Healer's oath would hit her with the full force of the power of the Pact if she tried to go against it.

Cyrus turned away to look out the windows for a moment. "What brought you down here?"

"I was up on deck after luncheon. There are sperm whales, perhaps a mile away. Faint, in the distance. But I am also certain I saw something else. A tentacle." She hesitated for a moment, then sat down, grabbing a piece of paper off the desk and a stub of pencil from her pocket. She sketched quickly. She was no artist, but it got the point across, the sense of proportion. The waves, all along the horizon, the faint bump of the whale's body, the tentacle rising higher.

Cyrus came over as she finished, and she held it out to him. She could tell, the moment he actually looked at it, from how he rocked back on his heels. "You're sure." She nodded, just once.

Her brother looked down at the paper, then back over his shoulder at the desk in his bedroom. "I won't make you swear an oath, though whatever discretion you can offer is appreciated. But we need to talk, yes." He retreated, coming back with the ebony box and three books, one of which had several loose sheets of paper stuffed into it.

Rhoe waited for him to sit down before she raised an eyebrow inquiringly.

"You're right that the gem is more complex than I'd implied. It has a long history. There's lore about it having been associated with a temple to Poseidon, or possibly Neptune, passed down through one of the First Families when they came to Albion. At some point, it was cut down and faceted. There are three known pieces, one still in the family, one thought to be in Cyprus, and this one. Donated to the Council in 1806."

"And no one's done anything with it since?" Rhoe considered this. None of this was her particular area of expertise, but she could tell when things had not been tended to sufficiently.

Cyrus had the good grace to look abashed. "I might have said something about that, when I was told. Knowing what you'd say. That living things need to be tended like living things, not stuck in a box and ignored until convenient."

"You would think that people would understand this who had horses and hounds, at least. Though most of them, that's why they have stablemen and kennel masters." Rhoe shook her head. "So why is it being trotted out now?"

"Two reasons." Cyrus leaned back in his chair. "First, it is a perfect specimen to connect those points we wish to connect, to allow rapid communication. They must be port cities, they must have a solid and sustainable magical community, they must have regular ocean traffic."

"Boston for the age, you said." She added, "And where in Albion? You'd mentioned the others before."

"London. For the age and the quick portal connections." He shrugged. "And Trellech is no port."

"No. Many other virtues, but not a port. Actually, that probably is a virtue, there being fewer infectious disease routes."

When she looked up, Cyrus was eyeing her patiently, and she waved a hand. "Go on. This stone, being matched to stones in other places. Is it dedicated, still, as a stone to Poseidon? Or Neptune? Or anyone?"

He had the good grace to look sheepish. "No one knows. Not who knows about it, anyway."

"And who precisely did you ask?"

"Council Oath, remember? I shouldn't be telling you." He hesitated. "Though my oath isn't pressing on me. So there must be some reason why telling you is all right. I suspect it needs a law-speaker to sort it out."

"Do you have one of those on tap?" It came out a bit archly.

He grinned at her for just a moment. "The Council has more than a few resources. An excellent little black book is just one of them."

Rhoe shook her head. "You needn't rub it in. So. Your oath is not pressing on you, about telling me. What do you know about the stone more recently?"

Cyrus looked down and away now. That was telling, in and of itself. "You'll understand. They wouldn't. The Council."

"The gods, then." She and Cyrus had gone round and round about this, more than once. There were a few among the Council who had their own religious views, from what he'd said, but none of them talked much about it. If it had not been so fiendishly annoying, she'd have found it a fascinating research study. From her point of view, they were perhaps the people who needed some external light or depth or whatever it was their gods brought them, more than anyone else.

"The gods. I don't know. I've had odd dreams. Not the ones people were talking about, a brilliant blue sea, a lagoon. Something older and darker. Being on a cliff, looking out to sea, a great temple behind me, the waves below. Seeing ships coming in. It wasn't Athens, the landscape was wrong for it."

"I'd need a reference." The comment came out automatically. "Posit a temple, to Poseidon, for the moment. There were quite a few, the Greeks being seafaring."

"Classically Greek, I think. All the white marble, a great temple. But much of it was brightly painted, curiously." He shook his head, and she could tell from his eyes how it had affected him. That might be why his oath wasn't pressing on him. The gods were greater than the Fatae, as such things were counted. If all of this were, at least in part, something to do with a stone dedicated to Poseidon two millennia ago or so, that was well outside the terms of the Pact.

"Right. So you have the stone, possibly slumbering, possibly in some sort of stasis. I don't know, I'm not an expert in it either. And now here it is, on the open ocean. Did it wake earlier, going to Bombay or Alexandria? Or was it waking then, but now we are out in the midst of a great ocean, and that is sufficiently different?"

"Also not my realm, and I know it." He shook his head. "Will you hold it? See if you get anything from it that I don't? You have..." He waved a hand, a little uncertain now. "You have a better touch with such things than I do."

Part of her wanted to hold the stone very much, the kind of feeling she had learned to be deeply suspicious of. It often indicated some charm or glamour that would get in the way at the best of times, and foul everything up if given the chance. And yet, he was right. She had more of a touch for it than he did.

"Let me go make a few preparations." Gather herself, wash her hands ritually. She had the appropriate eau de toilette in her trunk, just in case. She hadn't expected to need to make offerings, not while they were at sea, but that didn't mean she wasn't prepared.

"Whatever you need." Cyrus sat back, rather wearily, letting his eyes close. She went silently to her own room, pouring fresh water into the basin from the pitcher. She added three precise splashes from the glass vial from her trunk, inhaling the scent of herbs and flowers. It was made precisely to her specifications by her favourite apothecary, a mix of the cleansing herbs and the purifying ones - rosemary, hyssop, lavender, and hints of cypress and lemon. Her mother despaired of it, proclaiming it far too masculine, but Rhoe didn't care.

Drying her hands on clean linen - she'd have to thank the steward - she came back out, sitting down with her skirt cupped to create a broad hammock in case the ship moved or she dropped the stone by accident. 'Good preparation saves lives', as had been drilled into her from the first day of her apprenticeship. "Ready."

Cyrus opened the box, then stood, bringing her the stone and presenting it to her with both hands, formally, with a slight bow. She held up her cupped hands. It wasn't a lightning bolt - she supposed that was Zeus or Jupiter or some such. Instead, there was a clap of thunder, what sounded like the drumbeat gallop of horses, the sound of a drum beating time in a great galley. Rhythmic, measured, a hair faster than her heart beat. She felt it, more than heard it, and she knew, without looking at her brother, that this had not been his experience.

She settled in, to focus on this stone with all her attention. She couldn't know all of how this came to be, but she could feel, like a delicate net, the ways the magics coiled around the stone. More than that, how they braided themselves into the energy of the stone, making something that was neither stone nor net, no longer an inorganic crystal, but something that sang. Or drummed, at least.

Rhoe felt her heart settle into the same rhythm, felt her body respond to the drumbeat drawing her along, the feeling of need. Of loneliness, perhaps, though that might be a figment of her imagination, but of needing something. Wanting something.

When she finally looked away from the stone, Cyrus was standing there, his hand a few inches from her shoulder, as if he'd been thinking about touching her, and afraid to.

"How long?" She kept her voice brisk, comfortable, the tone she used with nurses or patients who needed a little reassurance.

"Twenty minutes." Well, that was a reason for him to be a bit worried, she supposed. "You didn't seem wrong. Hurt. But you kept going." Then, carefully, he asked, "What do you want to tell me?"

The phrasing made her laugh, but then she gathered her wits. "What I want to tell you? As my brother, standing in for the Council, since you're here and they're not."

"That, yes." He had the sense to sound properly scolded.

"No one's asking you to be religious and mean it. But if you are going to hoard a sacred gem like a custos dragon with an obsession, it would be a good idea not to be insulting."

Cyrus blinked at her several times, and then he laughed, without being able to stop himself. He bowed to the stone, and then promptly - reassuringly promptly - asked, "How do I make that right?"

"A propitiatory ritual of some sort. I'm sure you can draft something up by tea-time. It doesn't need to be fancy, but it needs to be done."

"By tea-time? So fast?"

"There's a concert tonight, we should make an appearance there. The ritual. And arranging whatever foods and drink we can from the stores. I'm sure Nerissa could be persuaded to help."

"And you think that will work?" He gestured at the sketches she'd made. "With that?"

She shrugged slightly. "It's the right thing to do, whether or not it helps with that particular need. So we will do it."

Cyrus sucked in a breath then he nodded. "We will. Let me draft something for your review."

TWENTY-TWO
SATURDAY AFTERNOON

Hugh was not sure what he was doing here. Or rather, he was clear on the explanation, but not why he was here, and not someone else.

"Surely there are other options? The Scali men, they do ritual magic regularly." He looked from Rhoe to Cyrus searchingly.

Nerissa leaned over and patted his arm. "The Council Member is the one doing the work here. Healer Rhoe is taking the second's part. All we need to do is stand where we're told and say our parts. Which are nicely written out for us on these cards."

She was settled comfortably in one of the chairs, facing the table, where a small array of cards were spread out. Hugh suspected that they had been intended as invitation cards for some more social purpose. Each was neatly filled with surprisingly legible handwriting in a deep green ink.

Rhoe said briskly, "You both know what's out there. Which seems a thing we might not want to spread around unnecessarily." She had changed, somewhere along the way, from her usual dress. Now she wore what was clearly a ritual robe in the Greek mode, two long flowing rectangles of linen, pinned at the shoulders and belted. Nerissa wore one of her working robes made of silk and wool in much the same design.

Hugh had to admit that was an excellent point. He took a breath and looked at Nerissa. "And you're all right with this?"

"I think an offering may not do much about the Ones Below. But I think it an excellent idea for a number of reasons, and I do not think the proposed ritual will do any harm."

"It is one of the oldest consistent offering rituals. Wine, meat, grain, incense, honey." Cyrus settled in the facing chair, gesturing at the table with a silver platter laid out with the offerings. "There's a place for the stone there in the centre, on a bed of sea salt."

Hugh was not sure he wanted to know but asked. "Sea salt? Did you raid the kitchens?"

Rhoe snorted. "Part of my supplies. A salt-water wash is excellent when dealing with some kinds of infections. It stings, but it cleanses."

Hugh had gone into the ocean after minor cuts on his hands - a danger of being fond of cats - time and time again. He couldn't quite repress a shudder. When he looked up again, Rhoe was grinning at him, amused. He was glad someone was. Something about this still felt wrong to him. Or off, at least. "If this doesn't work?"

"Then we will try something else. In which case, having made a gesture toward mending things with the Lord of Oceans certainly won't hurt."

"But why us?" Hugh tried his hardest not to sound plaintive.

"We are land-dwellers. You both spend your lives on the

ocean. You know the rhythms and the pace, and all the other things that we might need to understand." Rhoe's voice turned softer. "Does something in this feel wrong to you? Close your eyes, take a moment, if you need."

He suspected that was the same tone she used with patients, but he couldn't resent it. She was actually listening, paying attention, to all the small details. So he did as he'd been told, closing his eyes and letting his mind flow, as he'd been taught in school.

When he inhaled deeply and opened his eyes two minutes later, they were looking at him, but everyone had kept silent. "I agree with Nerissa. I don't think it's enough, but I don't think it's wrong. But I can't for the life of me figure out why."

Cyrus cleared his throat. "I don't suppose either of you has a talent for divination in any form?"

Hugh shook his head, and Nerissa said, "Not in this setting, no. I assume neither of you, either?"

Cyrus shook his head. "Scrying, I can do, but I get nonsense, even if someone else is laying the cards. And Rhoe - well. Very specific about particular questions, framed correctly, and otherwise not at all helpful."

Rhoe said amiably, "It makes an interesting parlour trick, but not a pleasant one, so I don't. So. We'll try this ritual, and see what else we need from there. You trust that we can do the thing properly?"

Hugh shrugged. "I take you at your word. The things you've said you're competent with, you have proven so. I don't need an oath on it. Nerissa?"

Nerissa nodded in turn. "Let's get to it, then. No point in dallying."

Rhoe moved to set the silver tray on a small table in the centre of the open space in the sitting room, aligning it just so. She rearranged a few small items that had rolled out of place. Cyrus disappeared to his bedroom, coming out with the ebony box. He set it down on a different table, opening it, and then setting the gem in the centre container.

The whole thing must have been bodged together from whatever items they had in their trunks. Hugh had borrowed a few crystal pieces from the steward, but the whole had a surprisingly pleasing appeal. There were sprigs of rosemary and bay around the edge, a few loose pearls gleaming as decoration, the salt, and of course the incense and food offerings. And a bottle of champagne, along with a proper corkscrew. Decidedly modern, that, but now becoming traditional for blessing ships. Queen Victoria had a number of things to answer for.

"We don't have a silver cup, the more traditional option, that we can throw overboard, so champagne it is. Novelty can be delightful." Rhoe's voice was even, and when he turned to look at her, she was smiling. He supposed she must come up with modifications for ritual on a regular basis, but it made him nervous, to go changing things from the traditional forms.

"Hugh, you take this side, facing me, and Nerissa, you face Cyrus. You just repeat the words as we get to them." Rhoe indicated their places.

They took up their cards and their places. Compass directions had rather little meaning here. But he could see that this was one of the ritual forms that had some sense of alignment to the four directions or the four winds. Four something, at least. He found himself facing Rhoe, as Nerissa settled herself steadily in front of Cyrus.

The ritual, in and of itself, was largely in Greek. Ancient Greek, not modern. Hugh knew enough of the latter to order an excellent meal. He knew the words for chicken and beer, for the wines he liked, for convincing the local taverna that he really did want retsina. Of the ancient version, he knew enough to catch words, phrases.

He caught a bit of what he was sure was the Orphic Hymn, but only a part. It didn't continue in the words he knew. There were words of praise, epithet after epithet. Wielder of the trident, blue haired, sea-resounding, abounding with waves, lord of the sea. He noticed, as much as he was capable, that they were steering well away from those phrases about shaking the earth or roaring waves. He caught some of the more general ones, the ones that applied to any of the great gods: lord, graceful of aspect, august, majestic, mighty.

It was praise after praise, and he and Nerissa echoed those praises, as Cyrus made offering after offering, touching a little of each to the stone, then blessing them. He could see the power building, little sparks of light of the magic moving. This was what they needed him for, to lend his energy. He was out of practice with this. He normally only engaged in the ritual magics for the blessing of a new ship, but he did his best to join his magic with theirs, to lend strength to the offering. Nerissa had an easier time, he thought, like this was something she did more frequently.

And Rhoe, it was like Rhoe was lit up from inside. She had made herself a beacon of brilliant sun, distilling it through her eyes, cupping in her hands, so she could let it flow from her, enchanting everything she touched.

When the words finally came to an end, they were all breathing hard, like they'd run a race, and he could see Cyrus and Rhoe were both damp with sweat. It was everything a proper lady sailing first class should not be, and yet, in that moment, he thought her more beautiful than he'd thought anyone ever. She had given herself fully and freely to the work as she had to her healing days before.

Before she could begin to fold, he managed to tug the chair so she could sit. She offered him a faint smile, as if she were still focused on the offering. "You're right." She spoke directly to him, though in all fairness, Nerissa had said it first. "I don't think it's enough. Where can we make the offerings from?"

"What are we bringing with us?"

Cyrus waved a hand. "The champagne, the five pearls there, the herbs, the incense, the food."

Hugh flicked open his pocket-watch, startled to discover that the ritual had lasted only twenty minutes or so. It had felt like hours, like they were going to miss supper. Instead, it was barely five. "If we go out on this deck, it should be quiet enough. And enough light."

"Then let's." Rhoe made as if to stand. Hugh wondered if he should say something, but Cyrus cleared his throat. "Different clothing, sister-mine. Or at least a properly enveloping cape and a hat."

"Bother." She sounded truly annoyed at it, but pushed herself upright to go and rummage for something from her room. Hugh watched her go, the way the linen draped over her curves, then stopped himself from looking further. It wouldn't do to be rude. Ruder.

When he turned back to the group, Cyrus was watching him, a slight tilt to his head. Hugh flushed, and said, "Drinks, anyone? You must need something, Cyrus."

The older man sounded amused. "A little glass of the brandy, certainly." He didn't seem upset. As Hugh handed him a glass, he was watching the stone. "I admit, I am coming to agree with you that it was not sufficient. And with my sister, that it was necessary. A beginning. I suppose we'll have to look for omens when we make the offerings."

"Birds, or something of the kind?"

"Birds, dolphins, some other sea creature. Less pleasant things, in theory, though I think the offering is acceptable." Cyrus reached for the glass of brandy that Hugh handed him, and took a deep drink from it. "Eat well at supper, you've used a fair bit of energy, especially if you're not used to regular ritual work of that kind. Beef, by preference. Bulls are sacred to Poseidon."

"And if this wasn't enough?" Nerissa's voice was sharper, now, as if the ritual had refined something in her.

"Then we will try again." Cyrus sounded queer. Not tired, but something complicated. Like he had done this many times before, done a thing that should have helped, and it was not enough. Hugh thought that must be a rather exhausting way to live.

Instead of pressing him, Hugh asked. "The pearls?"

"From a necklace Rhoe does not much care for. True ocean pearls, not river. She'll have it reset, she says, when we're in Boston, or something of the kind." Cyrus leaned forward and gathered up the stone, though Hugh noticed that he slipped it into a velvet pouch, then into a deep pocket.

At that moment, she reappeared, now dressed again respectably in a deep green dress with golden embroidery on the cuffs and hems. "Are we ready?"

"I have reminded them to eat well at supper. Do you need a drink?" Hugh thought he detected a bit of shorthand there.

"Drink after. Offerings now. Can you bring the tray, Hugh? You're steadier on a ship than we are, and it occurred to me, you're the best representative of the owners of the ship we have. As much as a ship is a thing that can be owned."

There were implications in that sentence about the nature of ships that Hugh rather wanted to explore. If Nerissa didn't get there first, since he knew Nerissa had similar inclinations. Now was not the time. He simply nodded and picked up the tray. They made a small and awkward procession out to the stern, off to the starboard side. That way, the offerings would not go directly into the churn from the great propellers.

With a small phrase of thanks, each item was ceremonially dropped into the waves. They ended with the pop of the champagne cork, and it being poured down, before the bottle was tossed in besides.

They all waited, barely breathing, when the bottle disappeared beneath the waves. Nothing happened for a moment - nothing good, nothing bad. Then, in the distance, barely visible against the growing twilight and the shadow of the waves, they all saw one tentacle emerge. Then there was another, then another, until four seemed to be reaching out toward them.

"Not enough." Cyrus spoke quietly.

Rhoe hesitated just a moment longer. "I think I have an idea."

TWENTY-THREE
SATURDAY LATE AFTERNOON

Once the four of them had reconvened in their suite, Rhoe settled into the chair. "That was not the best of omens."

"Easy to interpret, but by no means good." Hugh agreed, nodding at her. "Nerissa?"

"Rather unambiguous. Though I do think that the offering was worth doing. You said you had a thought, Rhoe?"

Rhoe nodded. "What if we created something, fed a great deal of energy into it, and then gave that to the - whatever we call it."

"One of the Ones Below." Nerissa said firmly. "Names summon things. You can use the name all you like on dry land, or when you're not talking about one within easy reach of you. At the moment."

"One Less Below Than We'd Like," Hugh offered, but it fell flat immediately. He coughed and tried again. "What sort of object did you have in mind?"

"That depends on what we can get our hands on.

Cyrus, you have books with you, I have seen them on your desk, about which objects might work."

Cyrus leaned back. Rhoe knew that expression, when he was trying to come up with a good reason not to do something. "Most of them are gemstones, and I do not think we have a ready supply of suitable stones. A good size bit of amber might do, but...."

"You have that emerald brooch." Rhoe eyed him thoughtfully. "Which I know you hate."

"Emerald is a poor candidate. Mine in particular, it has inclusions that make it prone to shattering. Who knows what it might hit on the way down, even the force of hitting the water..."

Rhoe raised an eyebrow. "Suggest something, then."

"Quartz. Metal. Fluorite would be ideal, actually, if we had some."

"Metal?" Hugh leaned forward. "What kind of metal?"

"Copper jewellery's gone out of style, unfortunately." Cyrus waved a hand, obviously thinking about something else.

That made Hugh hold up a hand. "We're on a ship. With engineers who need to be able to fix things. Copper or steel or something else?"

Rhoe watched Cyrus shift from reclining back to leaning forward. "That we could use?"

Hugh shrugged. "Captain's word is law. If I go to the Captain and say we need a thing, can he order it, I'm sure he will if it's something like that. Or there are copper mixing bowls in the kitchens. We could get one of those. What do you actually need?"

"Two copper mixing bowls of matched size. Small is fine." He sketched the size with his hands, thinking through things. "Or a length of copper tubing, a hand's width wide, but the bowls would be better."

Rhoe saw it immediately. "You want something in them. Sea water holds a magical charge well. Especially with a few things to seed it. British coin, if we can turn out our pockets or ask a few people to."

"The purser will have some." Hugh stood. "Anything else?"

Rhoe pursed her lips. "I don't suppose your engine room has any hydrofluoric acid? It's rather tricky to have around, even in solution."

"You're thinking a core of coins and whatever else, then seal the container, add a few drops of the acid?"

"Exactly. Take all that energy, add a little more."

"Pardon," Nerissa's voice cut through the discussion. "Can you explain in small words what you have in mind, in case it's a bad idea?"

Rhoe turned to look at her, then glanced over at her brother. Cyrus waved a hand, now deeply lost in thought. She said to Hugh, "Do you want to hear the explanation, or?"

"Let me go fetch things. I can do that much more efficiently than the rest of you. If Nerissa agrees with the plan, I'm likely to. Back in two shakes of a lamb's tail."

They waited, by mutual agreement, until Hugh had closed the door, then Rhoe turned to Nerissa. "The basic idea is that we will take an object and charge it. Then we put it in some sort of container suitable to holding more of a charge, and drop it into the water, for the One Below to find."

"On the theory that if you do that right, it will be more interesting than that stone or this ship?"

"Exactly. How clever is it?" Rhoe wasn't sure how to ask what she wanted to know.

"No one knows. But there is some evidence they like opening things. Ships, usually." She shuddered once. "And you really think this will work?"

Cyrus said, without opening his eyes. "We'll need something to hold the energy, and something to create the energy. What were you thinking, sister mine?"

"There's a concert tonight. We charge the key materials. We bring the portable portion of them with us to the concert, and draw the essence of magic into them, as much as we can. We combine everything, and then we drop the resulting chamber into the ocean."

"You make it sound so simple." Nerissa's voice was dry now, which was at least less fearful.

Cyrus waved a hand. "From my point of view, most of it is straightforward communal ritual work. Entirely within the usual scope of my life."

"Isn't it unethical to take energy from people?" Nerissa stood, going to look out the window.

"We're not drawing it from them - though Rhoe's done that, as a Healer, regularly, I gather."

"It's one of the things nurses are trained in." Rhoe agreed. "Which is helpful here, because Cyrus and I are in fact comfortable doing that kind of ritual magic together. But the four of us aren't enough. A concert." She tried to figure out how to put this in a way that would make sense. "A concert adds a dimension greater than the sum of the participants."

Then it hit her. "The merfolk, the way they were moving about. They were saying things not only by their individual movements, but by the connection of the whole, where each of them was at a given point."

Nerissa whirled around, then held up her hands. "Point made. And you honestly are sure you can, what's the phrase, skim the cream off, and turn that into this device? Whatever we call it."

"Supper." Rhoe and Cyrus spoke as one.

Nerissa looked from one to the other. "Was that what we call it, or something else?"

Rhoe waved a hand. "We'll have to go up, make sure people go along to the concert. Not that there's much other evening entertainment until it's done. See if we can get some nice cheerful pieces in the mix if they aren't. Unless you think the Ones Below prefer some emotion with a long German name and a great deal of distress?"

That made Nerissa smile despite herself. "I don't think it will matter much, the quality of the energy. Or at least, I have no idea if it does, and it seems better to have a ship full of cheerful people than otherwise."

Which made perfect sense. That meant Rhoe was back to the puzzle of what to use as the focus. "We do want something we can focus on. Coins are all well and good, and so is sea water, but it doesn't catch the imagination the same way. Come on. What have you got with you? I'll get my jewellery box, you get whatever men call their thing for fancy pieces."

Cyrus sighed, beleaguered, but nodded. "A moment, Nerissa." At least he was going along with the nagging, which was good. They'd both need their energy for other things.

Thirty minutes later, they had narrowed it down to one of three pieces. One was a piece of quartz Cyrus had had since school and obviously didn't want to give up. A string of fluorite beads from Rhoe's collection was not a particular favourite, but she also didn't think they grabbed the eye much at all, or the heart.

The last piece had turned out to be the sticking point. It was a single large topaz, of a tawny shade that didn't flatter Cyrus at all. She remembered. "That was a wedding present, for Tanith."

"From her favourite aunt. It suited her. And I thought sometime, Gemma..." He shrugged.

"Gemma would prefer you make it to the other side of the ocean safely. I'm quite clear on that." Rhoe kept her voice even, but she was certain about this.

He traced a line along the stone, then looked up at her and nodded. "It's not much of a sacrifice to give up what we do not care for." He looked up from it. "Will you wear it tonight? And do we want to add your beads? I could tuck them inside my shirt."

Rhoe considered. "For a balance of energies. Better, yes. I'm willing." Just as they heard the bell go to change for supper, there was a knock on the door. When Nerissa got it, there was Hugh, with a wooden box. He set it down on the floor. "Everything but the water, and they'll have that after supper. I need to go change. See you up there?"

Then he was gone again, leaving Rhoe somewhat breathless with his efficiency. Nerissa excused herself immediately, to go see how things were in the waves and keep a look out. She was not dining with the passengers. Twenty minutes later, Rhoe had put on a heathered purple gown that suited the gem, with a deep square neckline that made it stand out against her exposed chest. The glow of the topaz would pick up the gold of the trim.

When she came out, Cyrus stood - he was already changed. He held out the necklace. "May I?"

When she nodded, he came behind her, fastening the

necklace, then letting the weight of the stone fall from his hands slowly. He stepped back, coming around her. Silently, he made a single bow before holding out his arm to her. Words would spoil the moment.

As soon as they were in the dining room, they were immediately folded up into all the chatter of what they had missed that afternoon. There had been mishaps in the various small competitions, there had been a bet on one of the duels - all in good fun, of course. The honeymooning couple were thought to be arguing. Not that anyone had heard them, of course. But they had been at opposite ends of the ship nearly all day, and one of the young men from an unknown family had been seen bringing her something.

Rhoe smiled and nodded, as best she could, but it felt even more cloying and unreal than usual. It would do no good - and possibly a great deal of harm - for people to panic. Most of them could do nothing to aid the work they had in mind, not directly, that they would not already be participating in.

But their various demands and delights seemed so small, all of a sudden. Rhoe had had this happen before, when she had worked too long without a break. She knew all the signs as well as any attentive Healer did, and she did not like them. There was no quick way out, however; she could not beg off with a headache and then be at the concert later. Instead, she let Lady Jenifry snub her, and Miss Lytton ignore her, both in a particularly active and tiresome way. She fielded questions from several others about what she'd spent her afternoon doing, saying she'd got caught up in some professional tasks.

She was sure more than one caught the queerness, but it was unlikely they'd hit on the correct reason she'd been busy if the plan worked. And if it did not, they would all be very busy with other things, probably. More likely, they'd assume that she had been doing something she didn't want to talk about. She wondered if they thought she'd had an assignation, and if so, with whom they thought she'd been occupied.

When the supper finally broke up for everyone to get some air before the concert, she excused herself, took her brother's arm, and they went off in search of Hugh. As they approached, he was in the midst of what seemed to be an exhaustive discussion of the port of Bombay and its particular available luxuries. It was as if he were a guide from Thomas Cook, ready on demand. They could not pull him away without being obvious, so Cyrus drew her out on deck, silently, where they could wait for him.

Hugh did not manage to extract himself from conversation until the first sounds of the music were starting up. He'd hoped to find Cyrus and Rhoe, but they had disappeared. He'd just have to figure out how to help things along himself. He encouraged a couple of others lingering on deck into the concert, cheerfully talking it up. As he came in through the doors, one of the last, he glanced from left to right.

Rhoe was in the back right, a chair angled slightly so she was tucked into the back corner. As he looked left again, he saw Cyrus had taken up a similar position. His eyes, though, were drawn back to Rhoe. Her dress and necklace tonight were not conventionally beautiful, not following the current mode as Lady Jenifry and her little band of hangers-on did. There was no corset to shape the figure, no plunging decolletage that was just this side of scandalous. Frankly, he thought that sort of thing a sign of poor judgement, on a ship on a northern ocean in November.

Rhoe, though, wore her dress like it was a robe of state. The necklace picked up the glint of colour of the embroidery, the whole effect being entirely Pre-Raphaelite in the most appealing senses. Someone who was wholly at home in herself, and with beauty, but who followed her own road. Cyrus, now he thought about it, was doing much the same thing, as if they were deliberately matching each other in mode. He glanced to the left again, and realised their positions were almost exactly the same. Outwardly, they looked relaxed as if they were enjoying the first song. But he could see a slight tension of the arm and one foot tapping slightly, as if they were both internalising the beat of the music.

They had implied, both of them, that they had done this sort of work together before, one of them feeding the other. He wasn't sure how this was going to go, now. The first ritual, the offering, that had been a well-worn pattern. What they were attempting next was something different. From the way Cyrus and Rhoe had talked about it, it was a mode of ritual that was fitting pieces together, somewhat tenuously.

He could only hope it would work. That he wouldn't foul it up somehow, not knowing better. He envied them, for a moment, for their much greater knowledge of how to put a thing like this together. Dunwich had taught him many things, but the focus of his school years had been solidly on practical work. He had found himself on more or less familiar footing with the offerings to Poseidon. Not how he would have done it, or his family, but an entirely acceptable offering, done properly. The ritual later, though, that was a whole new topography, and he had no idea how the rivers ran to the sea.

The music pulled him out of his thoughts, and he moved to settle, leaning against a pillar, a little past the line between Rhoe and Cyrus. They barely looked at each other, but they stayed in sync, with each other, with the music. It was only when things halted for the intermission that he moved, going first to Rhoe's side. "May I fetch a drink?" He kept his voice low and quiet, the kind of thing that should not shake her out of a trance if she needed to stay in one.

She smiled up at him. "Wine, please. And for my brother. Reds, both." Hugh nodded, and went to find both of those. When he brought them back, he got identical nods, each in turn, without any other conversation.

As the concert ended, he was caught up in conversation again, briefly, finding an excuse that would keep him away from an invitation to a card game. Then he'd had to duck Heloise Adams asking for his company after the concert. For this evening, he had more important places to be. By the time he freed himself again, brother and sister had disappeared.

Hugh made his way down to their suite, and knocked on the door. Nerissa opened it, and he slipped inside, to find a small table in the centre of the open space, by the windows, freshly arranged with new items. The two copper mixing bowls, the beads, the coins. He had not been able to get the acid, it was far too dangerous to transport without the proper container or precautions. A bucket of sea water stood under the table.

Rhoe was moving around the table, her hands carefully placing each thing in its proper place. Hugh was too far away to see exactly how she had things arranged, but Cyrus was handing them to her, one by one, as if aiding a surgeon. Despite how nervous Hugh felt, she seemed steady as a rock, not rushing, not fumbling.

Finally, she turned to her brother, and he unlatched the necklace from around her neck. She removed the chain, and handed it back to him. As he slipped it into a pocket she placed the gem inside one of the mixing bowls. Cyrus looked down into the bowl for a long moment, then closed his eyes, and turned away, while Rhoe laid out the final few items. Then she looked up, and her voice was as clear and firm as any captain Hugh had ever heard, utterly in control.

"Hugh, you here at my right, then Nerissa, then Cyrus. We'll be joining hands, except for my right. Hugh, you focus on making things flow to Nerissa, Nerissa to Cyrus, and so on. If you don't manage anything else, that."

Nerissa had been quiet through the setup. "Is there a focus?"

Rhoe nodded. "There will be a chant. Harmony is welcome, whatever works to make us act together. Cyrus will handle the ritual language. If you need a word to focus on, use fiat. Let it be done."

"And we do that until you tell us to stop?"

"You ate well, yes? You'll be using that energy and more, probably. Try not to faint, it would disrupt things." Hugh realised, with a sudden certainty, that this was not as simple as she was making it seem. But they needed to do this thing, and do it well. He had obligations, promises. So did Nerissa. And if this worked, it might be a terribly useful technique to disseminate to the other ships of the line.

He refused to ask more questions now. It wasn't the time for it. Instead, he simply reached out his hand, letting Nerissa take it when she was ready. Rhoe somehow focused all the attention on herself, like a conductor picking up a baton, that moment of anticipation, and then she began chanting. She began with vowels, long ohs, without cutting the words up further.

Nerissa picked up the pitch first, and then Cyrus, who had an obligingly clear bass, leaving Hugh to fit himself into that. He was not a confident singer. He was fine with a sea shanty, but that required volume, not subtlety or even precision of pitch.

Somehow, though, it began to come together. He couldn't entirely focus on what was going on, not and keep singing, but Hugh had the clear sense that they were swirling things together, like moving water in a great tub. He could decidedly feel something moving from Rhoe through him, to Nerissa, like a pulse. It warmed him, making his hands sweat. It was about getting it all going in the same direction. Cyrus and Rhoe between them were doing something to funnel it into the gem, and into the gem, and into the gem.

It should have been like bailing the ocean with a bucket, but instead it seemed more like scooping up a lake and pouring it into the ocean. Enough to make a noticeable difference, perhaps. This just might work.

Not too long after that, he was greatly impressed at Rhoe's stamina. He was only singing - well, and lending his magic to the work - and he could feel the sweat beginning to pool at his back. Rhoe just forged on, her voice clear. Cyrus had settled into a chant, something long and complex, but clearly memorised, with phrases that repeated regularly. He stood with his eyes closed, hands at waist height.

The magic built and built. The music didn't get louder or faster, not exactly, but it got more, like there were octaves below where they were singing, the depths of the ocean. And there were resonances there. Someone had explained how overtones worked on a fiddle, once. You played a note, but there were pitches created by all the smaller movements of the strings, like the roar of the engines, down in the heart of the ship, that were felt as much as heard.

Finally, there was something that moved toward a conclusion. If it had been simply music, he'd have expected a musician to begin talking about a restatement of the theme, about modulation of the harmonies. All he knew was that after all the building of anticipation, things were finally resolving. When Rhoe hummed one final pitch, he and Nerissa joined her, immediately, while Cyrus intoned one last phrase in resonant, rolling Latin rather than the Greek they had been using.

Without being told, they all dropped their hands at the same moment, and took a breath. The stone glowed, and when Hugh shifted his hand, slightly, he could feel heat coming from it, much like how a fire would warm a grate nearby. Rhoe nodded once, and then set about doing what must be the final steps, silently. Cyrus handed her first one thing, then another. He held up the bucket for Rhoe to ladle in the sea water, which began to glow, faintly but visibly.

When the mixing bowl was almost full, Cyrus set down the bucket. He carefully held the other mixing bowl over the base, as Rhoe cupped her hands and sang a much faster syncopated chant in some language he couldn't even begin to guess at.

When Cyrus released the top half, it stayed put, balancing steadily. Rhoe nodded, and said. "The deck." Hugh could only open the door and check to make sure no one was in the passageway. It seemed early, yet, comparatively, for the rest of first class to be coming back to their cabins. As he flicked his pocket watch open, he realised it had only been forty-five minutes. It wasn't yet midnight.

They got up onto the deck without being spotted, with Cyrus carrying the copper globe, carefully and reverently. When they were in position, Rhoe lifted her hand, and said three sharp precise syllables.

A tiny shiver went through the globe, then Cyrus took a

deep breath. He let out the kind of bellow that summoned inhuman strength in the oldest legends. It was the sort of thing one let out before charging into a battle you knew would kill you. Then he took the globe and hurled it as far behind the ship as he could.

It flew through the air as if it were being pushed along on the winds. It had an utter wrongness to it, as if it were hanging in air far longer than it should. They all waited, not breathing, until it finally landed, a good hundred yards or more behind the ship now. There was just enough light from the waning moon - and the glow of the globe itself - that they could see it bob on the surface. It bobbed once, twice, then it suddenly disappeared beneath the waves.

None of them moved, none of them breathed. Hugh wasn't even sure if his heart kept beating.

Then, like frost creeping out on a window on a cold day, crystallising into beauty, the sea began to light up. It had that same uneven beauty that held pattern after pattern, creeping in endless variations on a theme. Hugh both wanted to capture it forever, and felt like he never wanted to see something so terrifying ever again. There was tremendous power there, the kind that would wipe away civilisations if it were used selfishly or stupidly.

One solitary tentacle appeared above the water, gleaming darkly in the reflected light. It was visible mostly because of the dark streak it left against the light of the ocean, the bioluminescence. Then it lowered again, and something changed. No longer threatening, looming. As much as anything under the water could loom at something on the surface.

They stood in silence for another ten seconds, before Nerissa nodded. "It is retreating." She let out a long breath. "I need to sit down. Tomorrow." She turned abruptly, just as Rhoe finally wavered. Hugh and Cyrus reached for her arms from either side, simultaneously.

When she was steady again, Rhoe shook her head. "I should do the same. Cyrus?"

"I need a drink. Something to even out the tremors. Do you want me to walk you back?" Cyrus's voice had a sharp edge to it. Not aimed at anyone in particular, but suddenly present.

Hugh found himself saying, "I would be honoured." It was true, just he had not expected to say that. Not with Cyrus there.

Instead of arguing, Cyrus nodded once. "Appreciated." Gruff, but Hugh could tell he was pleased, somehow. "Rhoe, eat something. You too, Hugh." Then he turned, making a beeline for the smoking room and bar.

Hugh immediately offered his arm properly to Rhoe, and she tucked her arm through his. Taking their time, they walked back to Rhoe's suite, and Hugh made sure she was sitting down comfortably before he asked. "May I send the steward by with food? Help you clean up?"

Rhoe let out a long breath. "Steak, please. And something for sides, vegetables. I'll see to the rest of the cleaning when I've eaten." She then hesitated. "Or possibly in the morning. It will keep, now."

Hugh hesitated. "Thank you. For - for doing it. But also for letting me be part of it." He felt like a stammering schoolboy, now, like he had been permitted to see some mystery of adult magic he had not earned.

Rather than mock him, Rhoe smiled. "We can talk in the morning. Right now, though, I think I'd babble. Very bad for explaining things, babble. You should eat something too. Healer says so. I'm not your Healer, but still, it's sensible advice." She then blinked and held her hand to her mouth, before laughing.

If he hadn't known better, he'd have been sure she was drunk. Delightfully drunk, with giggles and babble, but drunk. Instead of risking her saying something she might regret in the morning, he made a deep bow. "I will go find a steward to fetch you a proper meal, and then go find my own. Tomorrow, I will have questions."

She beamed at him before toppling over into the side of the couch. Taking his cue to withdraw, he let himself out and went in search of steward, red meat, and a drink.

TWENTY-FIVE
SUNDAY MORNING

The next morning, Rhoe woke up with a splitting headache. No matter how sensible she was after that kind of magical work, the hangover tended to be horrible. She levered herself up, rummaged in her trunk for a headache potion, and then another one.

Padding across the sitting room, she saw her brother's door was ajar. He'd set the wards on the suite - she could feel them from here, to keep any of the staff out - but not on his own bedroom. Sensible man. Nudging his door open with her hip, she glanced around. He was sprawled face down on the bed, still fully dressed, but he'd managed to at least kick his shoes off. He was doing his best to snore, despite the position. She set the potion down on his desk, where he'd see it first thing he was upright, and went out, casting a silencing charm before she pulled the door shut.

Once her own potion kicked in, she spent a good half hour cleaning away all the signs of the ritual working. It wasn't that the magic itself would be startling to the staff on this ship, but one didn't want to advertise what one was up to. For all sorts of reasons.

When she was finally done, she went and drew herself a bath, then rang the bell to call for a steward once she was dressed again. By the time Cyrus appeared, an hour later, she had eaten a grand breakfast. She'd made sure plenty of tea and fresh ice water were waiting for him.

He grunted blearily at her and disappeared into the bathroom. She heard the taps turn on, and then the faint noises of splashing. When he emerged, it was nearly luncheon. Rhoe raised an eyebrow when Cyrus sat down heavily opposite her.

"Thanks. The potion."

"Food?"

He grimaced, and she diagnosed nausea. As well as the headache. "I'll get out of your hair. Tea there, water there, your ritual tools are locked up safely in my trunk, you can have them back when you're in better shape. I'll wander off so you can have the place to yourself. I'll get one of the stewards to bring you something light and leave it."

That got another grunt, but the wave that came with it was amiable enough. It had been a hard night for him and not only the ritual work. Being excellent at it didn't make it less demandingly gruelling on the magical side. Letting go of that topaz, and one more piece of Tanith, that was a thing that he would have to grieve.

On the other hand, offering sympathy wouldn't go well, and she knew it. She had her own losses, her own things she mourned, but she didn't understand that one, not bone deep. Part of her was sure she never would, and she'd made peace with that long ago.

Her duty done, she ducked out of the suite and went up to investigate what Sunday morning looked like on the *Moonstone*. By the time she made it to the main deck, she could see people in the main salon. It was perhaps half full, and she was sure some of the people there were from the second class cabins, wearing their best frocks and suits.

As she got closer, she could hear there was a Christian service going. She hesitated by the doors and heard a prayer she had only heard once before. "Thou hast shewed us terrible things, and wonders in the deep, that we might see how powerful and gracious a God thou art; how able and ready to help them that trust in thee...."

She was blinking at the implications, when she felt a hand on her upper arm, tentatively, as if ready to pull away. She turned, quickly, to find Hugh taking a step back. He held a finger to his lips as he guided her off to the reading room, and cast a privacy charm around their chairs.

That only led her to blink more, but before she could figure out how to ask anything sensible, he cleared his throat. "I gather the light on the water was rather obvious last night. Eventually."

The way he said it, amused and apologetic, made her smile. "No particular touch of the divine, in this one. Just solid human work." However Nerissa defined herself, Rhoe was fairly certain it included 'human'. "Are you all right, this morning?"

"Isn't that my line?" Hugh then flushed, and looked away, as if certain he'd overstepped. "I came by this morning, and you were - the door was locked."

"I had a frightful but anticipated headache until I got a potion into me, and Cyrus the same. Though he had rather more alcohol on top of the magic. I got the steward to bring round breakfast, but I admit I'm starving again."

"You said that being hungry was to be expected. I am too. Will your brother be joining us?"

Rhoe shook her head. "I suspect he'll wait until after. This was," she thought about how to put it. "The magic was a lot of effort. Skills we both have, and he uses them far more than I do, but that doesn't make it easy. Simply a challenge we are very familiar with."

Hugh cocked his head, considering that. "Like coming through a storm on a ship?"

"Not quite. Storms vary, don't they? More like, oh, climbing a mountain. The weather might vary a bit, but the basic shape of the mountain, the distance one must go is known, or at least stable. The degree of challenge, relatively speaking."

"And was last night some new first ascent, like what was it, Mount Assiniboine, this summer." When she blinked at him, he added, "Tallest point in the Canadian Rockies, summited this past summer. Someone on the last trip I made was fanatical about climbing news, and spent an evening explaining why it was so interesting. To him."

That made Rhoe smile. "More like something in the Alps where we know how the mountain goes, more or less. Not that there can't be a sudden storm or avalanche. No magic is entirely safe, that's what we learned. Some is simply more domesticated than others."

Hugh leaned back. "And yet you're a Healer. Calling it to your hands every day."

"Calling it from somewhere to somewhere, yes, I suppose."

Hugh leaned forward. "May I ask a question?" Someone starting like that rarely suggested that an easy question was coming. She didn't think it would be wilfully offensive, which made the request rather easy to deal with.

"You've more than earned that much." Rhoe felt that was true and honest. "Please, go ahead."

"There's a ship that's supposed to be ahead of us, but - the more we go west, the more various of the crew feel something's off. Not just the One Below. I did make a report to the Captain. I think he'd like to talk to your brother in more detail, when he's up for it, but that's not urgent. Nerissa is very clear the One Below is no longer near and we've seen signs of the fish returning to normal."

"And there's no way to communicate with the ship." Rhoe tried to think through this, though her brain was a bit more like molasses than ideal.

"Some new forms of telegraphy show promise for shipboard use, but they are not yet developed enough. Semaphore flags in the day, lanterns or flares at night. It's clear, we should see something perhaps four or five miles away."

Rhoe frowned. "Not my area of specialty, you understand. But there are location charms. All the ones I can think of would be more difficult to do from a moving ship, I admit. But I am sure there must be some variations I don't know. If there's some way to link to the other ship." Then, much more carefully, she asked, "Is there a particular reason for the concern?"

"The first officer's wife and children are on board. With a non-magical aunt, I believe, and cousins. He's doing his best not to worry, but he has that sort of lurking dread still."

"Ah, poor man. And no way to resolve it." Rhoe looked away, out over the water. "When Cyrus is more himself again, we can ask him. The Scali brothers might also have an idea, if you don't have someone on board who does already. It might look better to check on that, specifically, before Cyrus sticks his nose in."

Hugh let out a long breath. "Probably, yes."

"So. You go have a chat with whoever there is to have a chat about that. I will, I will something."

"You've been more than generous with your time. And

your thoughts. You're a passenger, after all, not responsible for the ship. Never mind an entirely different ship."

"I am, you realise, in the line of work that tends to care about people. People I'm not actually responsible to, for, or about?" Rhoe was amused now, more than anything else. Hugh was so earnest about not wanting to presume. "Besides, I consider the working last night to be entirely enlightened self-interest. Not particularly wanting to find myself in the water, never mind anything else."

Hugh smiled, his eyes crinkling up. "There is that. But you were, you must have had other plans for the trip."

"They involved reading, and I have done a fair bit of it. Honestly, the rituals have been a delightful excuse to avoid the social obligations I dislike. My parents would despair if they knew."

"You're a grown woman, and independent, surely?"

Rhoe raised an eyebrow. "Only in Albion. In the United Kingdom, they still could control quite a lot of my life, if they chose. Oh, Cyrus would argue with them, and he'd probably wear them down eventually. But I am very aware of the narrow line that protects me."

Hugh considered that for a long moment, as if he were redoing a series of navigational calculations. "Even though you're a Healer. Skilled. Not just at the healing, but all the parts that go with it. Convincing someone to trust you. Speaking with authority."

"Encouraging people like you to go along with rather outrageous requests like last night." Rhoe pointed out, settling back. "Cyrus and I can talk many people into many things, if there's call for it."

Hugh tilted his head. Rhoe would have expected most men - even older men, trained to delay their first reaction - to say something. To come back with something that either defended themselves, or said they'd been willing to go along with it, anyway. Hugh did none of that, just considering her evenly. "You did it for the good of the ship. You did pull me along. Efficiently. So much so that arguing would have been a great deal of work."

Rhoe nodded. That much was true. Once she'd seen the need, nothing would have kept her from doing the work. It had been done better because of Nerissa's gifts with the sea, and Hugh's knowledge of the ship and ability to get what she and Cyrus needed. She wouldn't apologise for doing what had to be done.

"Do you do it at other times?" That wasn't a question she'd expected at all.

"When someone needs care and is too stubborn to see it. Or when their family is terrified, and won't consider a treatment that could help. There's a line, I won't - change someone's mind for them. And honestly, I can't, unless they're already inclined that way. It's more like cloaking myself in magic, and waving a flag, and charging off, and hoping people follow. It doesn't work if I'm not full-on wanting the thing."

"How is that different from any other form of persuasion? A golden tongue, or a bit of a bribe, or an order from a superior in the hierarchy, or whatever other form it takes?"

Rhoe had to laugh at that. "Well, some people think magic must have all sorts of different rules. I think that's silly. One set of rules, which also applies to magic. Mine are that I don't do it except to save a life. Anything else can be sorted out later. Though I admit to being somewhat generous with my definitions. Surgery has quite a few risks, even at the Temple of Healing, so - a few times, I've persuaded people to do the thing that avoids the surgeon's tools."

"That strikes me as largely sensible, so long as it worked." Hugh leaned forward. Then they both noticed the room beginning to fill again.

Rhoe shook her head. "I am definitely not up for luncheon with company. I should go back to the suite, and see what the steward can round up."

"May I escort you?" Hugh stood, promptly, offering his arm, as he dismissed the privacy charms again.

TWENTY-SIX
SUNDAY MORNING

Rhoe nudged the door open carefully. Hugh had escorted her to the suite, then stepped back. Not intruding, not asking to come in. Admittedly, she'd been clear that Cyrus was not currently his best self. She turned to smile at him over her shoulder before opening the door wide enough.

Cyrus was draped over half the sofa, his head just visible off the left end, and she was sure his feet were up on it. She closed the door behind her and came around. "Just me."

"How are things upstairs?"

"Fine. Relatively speaking." She peered at the remains of the breakfast tray and poured herself some tea. She could ring for another meal in a few minutes. Something still felt unsettled.

"Hugh? Nerissa?"

"She'd been up and about, and says the ocean is returning to normal, but I didn't speak to her. Hugh walked me back down. We talked for a bit." Rhoe shrugged again.

"The stone, the Sailor's Jewel. Aquamarine's good for scrying, isn't it?"

Cyrus pushed himself upright, then looked like he regretted it. "Yes. Why?" He didn't exactly sound accusatory, but there was sharpness there. She poured him another cup of tea, and handed it over silently.

"There's a non-magical ship, a day or so ahead of us. The first officer's wife and children and a non-magical aunt and cousins are on it. Hugh didn't precisely say this outright, but I gather a lot of the officers have a bad feeling about it. Without having any clear way to sort out why."

"Did you tell him about the jewel?" He was leaning forward a little now, his hands cupped around the tea cup.

Rhoe drew herself up with some dignity. "I came to ask you first."

That got her a wave of the hand. "Sit. While I think about it."

"I am already sitting." Feeling contrary, she got up and looked out the window, letting Cyrus sort through his thoughts in his own time.

When he spoke again, it wasn't about the jewel. "What was the gossip upstairs?" He, of course, knew there would be gossip. He swam in gossip, in the eddies and waves of it, the way dolphins did. Or the merfolk. Rhoe, on the other hand, had next to no patience with with it.

"Well, the clergyman doing the Sunday service was doing one of the Collects for Thanksgiving for safety on the sea. The bit about 'Thou hast shewed us terrible things, and wonders in the deep'. Which rather implies we were not exactly subtle."

Cyrus snorted, almost inhaling his tea. "How much of it did you hear? Or did they see, to ask the actual question I'm curious about."

"Well, there's a choice of Collects of Thanksgiving, and it wasn't the one about storms. You take your guess." She turned to face him. "Mind, I'm not an expert."

"You know a fair bit more than I do about the practicalities of it. I'd have vaguely wondered if it was out of the Book of Common Prayer. 'Hast shewed' is a bit of a giveaway, linguistically, these days. But I'd not have known which bit. How do you?"

"I never met a detail I didn't find fascinating?" She grinned at him, and he spread his hands in mock submission. "I had a patient a few years ago who'd been a sailor for decades, also a devout Anglican. We had quite an enjoyable time chatting about the nature of prayer, and the different types."

Cyrus let out a sigh. "I am not in the mood for theological discussions, sister mine."

"You so rarely are. Anyway, we were comparing the structure of prayers of thanksgiving in different traditions, I grabbed one of the nurses, who was Jewish, they have some excellent ones. Which led to a lot of quoting, as you do. It was an exceedingly well-blessed room by the time we were done." The memory made her smile, it had been one of those rare moments of sheer pleasure in the middle of a gruelling month of an influenza outbreak.

"You're impossible." He then looked her up and down, before saying, without warning, "Do you intend to break Hugh's heart?"

It made her take a step back. "What?"

"You heard me." Cyrus pushed himself to sit on the edge of the couch, now watching her as intensely as a falcon. "Mother and Father would quite definitely approve, but don't let that put you off."

"He has not so much as suggested any interest like that."

Rhoe thought back, hurriedly, through all of the conversations she'd had with Hugh. They'd been rather pleasant. But she had thought them collegial, not whatever it was Cyrus was implying.

"He thinks you are a terrifying angel of healing and mercy, far beyond his ken. Not knowing you as I do, of course, and how you have quite a few foibles. And eccentricities. Can I get my ritual tools back, by the by? I promise not to go summoning things out of the depths."

Rhoe had to shake her head, then she stuck her tongue out, and went to go unlock her trunk. And gather her thoughts. By the time she came back two minutes later, Cyrus was lounging on the sofa, looking entirely at ease. A little too much like a Roman emperor for her comfort.

She presented him with the leather case holding his ritual tools, and he nodded, setting it on the table. When he spoke, his voice was even. That just made her more suspicious. "You've spent quite a lot of the trip talking to him, one way and another."

"Professionally!" Rhoe did not approve of how her voice squeaked at the end of the word, and swallowed. "He's intelligent, thoughtful."

"And he keeps watching you."

"He keeps watching you, too." Rhoe felt it was important to point this out.

"He sees in me something he'd like to become. He sees in you someone he wants to be with. Quite a different matter." He hesitated for a moment, then added, "I remember looking like that. Seeing myself in a window or a mirror, watching Tanith."

That was not playing fair at all. She had nothing to say to that which was both accurate and kind. Rhoe swallowed.

"Look. Lunch. Both of us. Before I say anything more about that."

He waved a hand. "As long as there's plenty of it, I don't care what it is." He stood smoothly enough, and snagged his ritual tools, taking them back to his room. He stayed in there until the sandwiches and other tidbits she ordered arrived, a quarter of an hour later.

"Food's here." Rhoe called out, settling herself in one of the solitary chairs. The pause had not actually helped her gather her thoughts at all, which was even more annoying. She was going to have to talk it out - with Cyrus - to figure out what she thought. And felt. If she felt anything in particular.

Once they had both had half a sandwich, she cleared her throat. "Like you felt about Tanith?"

Cyrus nodded, once. "Especially early on. When I had no idea what she thought about me, outside of classwork."

"At which, I remember, you were being aggressively competent, at the time. Showing off, even, one might say."

"And I seem to remember you were aggressively competent with that patient in second class. And then doing the ritual work. Hugh's a man who appreciates competence. As he should." He swallowed a bite of sandwich. "Not that I can argue with the general taste. Throwing stones in glass houses, and all."

Tanith had been the sort of woman to excel at any skill she took a serious interest in. In other people, it might have been annoying, but Tanith had always been so delighted to share what she knew, her skills. Rhoe had taken that as a model for her own work, and especially how to deal with junior Healers and nurses who needed a little practice or self-confidence.

Rhoe took a deep breath, and another for good measure.

"What do you think of him, then?" Emphasis firmly on 'you'.

"If I didn't approve, I could just not have told you. Or discouraged him. I am your big brother, I do know the proper technique. We talk about it, in our secret gatherings of men in billiard rooms."

That obviously ridiculous last sentence made her laugh, despite the tumult of her thoughts. "True, true. That's not an answer, though."

Cyrus leaned back again, snagging a small plate to nibble from now he'd got more solid food into him. "First, I like the man. He's a bit young, still, in some ways. Finding his feet. I'm fairly sure there were some complexities with his father and his training, and that he and his brother are sorting that out nicely."

"How on earth did you get that sense?"

"The Scali." Cyrus waved his hand. "They like him, and that is quite a recommendation, mind. Not that they've told me details, but I gather they're willing to open up greater negotiations with his brother, after seeing him this trip."

Rhoe had to agree that they were likely a good judge of character, at least those points they cared about. The fact Cyrus liked him, that also meant something. "Second?"

"Second, I think he's a good man. And I don't think he would want to pin you down. That's what you've been afraid of." It wasn't a question, for all they'd never actually talked about this.

"It isn't something I want, no." Rhoe fiddled with one of the crumbs from a scone. "But people get different, when you start talking romance. Or marriage."

Cyrus tilted his head, peering at her now. "With you?"

"With me." She didn't like to talk about it. No one

sensible would, the way their heart had been bruised. Not badly in her case, or at least not nearly as badly as it could have been. She'd always held some part of herself back, fixed on her commitments and her vocation as a Healer.

"Is that why you've been so resistant?"

Rhoe shrugged again. "One of the reasons." Most of all, she couldn't abide the idea of someone getting between her and the healing. The thing she knew she could do that improved the world, in bigger ways and smaller ones. She'd never met anyone she was interested in who she thought would understand.

She still wasn't sure, but she had to admit Hugh had come nearer that mark than anyone else. On the other hand, it was an exceedingly short acquaintance, for all the intensity of the voyage so far. He had been kind, and he had been thoughtful, but this was the sort of trip where he was also entirely on his best behaviour. She had the wits to know that.

"You could -" Then Cyrus stopped.

"I could what?" She leaned forward, peering at him.

"If you were most other people, I'd say you could have a fling, see what you thought of him. But you're as single-hearted as I am."

"We are, as I keep saying, more alike than we are different, for all the differences. It's why we get on so well. But." She let out a breath. "I'll think about it. Him. And I'll be kind. Not lead him on."

"Sister, dear sister. I'm quite sure he'd be most willing to go where you lead. At least at the moment. When he finds his feet, he might surprise you, though." That said, he shrugged, and said, "Tell him about the stone. The scrying. In private. See what he says."

"You wouldn't rather?"

That got her an arched eyebrow. "Darling, if I tell him, we can't have a little intimate heart to heart about it. That's no good at all."

Rhoe sighed. "You are awful. So we're clear on that. What are your plans for the afternoon, then?"

"Now I'm fed, and the potion's worked its usual magic - thank you, for that - I was thinking I should show my face in public. Shall I send Hugh down with some excuse, then?"

Rhoe knew perfectly well she was being managed. She wasn't going to fight it. Whatever else she thought, Hugh was pleasant. And kind. And really quite clever. There were far worse ways to spend the afternoon than talking to him a bit more.

"You get your way. For the moment."

TWENTY-SEVEN

SUNDAY AT SUPPER

Hugh found his afternoon taken up in one thing after another. He came back to the main deck after walking Rhoe downstairs to find himself drawn into one conversation, then something else. He was required to judge a fashion contest of hats decorated with whatever the competitors could scrounge up. There was a three-legged race that followed, and then a game of deck tennis, until all the balls had flown off the deck, ending the game.

Halfway through the afternoon, he looked up to see Cyrus attempt to get his attention, but by the time he got free again, ten minutes later, Cyrus had disappeared.

When Hugh reappeared, ready for supper, he found Rhoe standing by herself, near the entrance to the dining room. Her brother was not visible anywhere, and he offered his arm, immediately. She hesitated for a moment before taking it. It was the sort of hesitation that made him wonder if he'd done something wrong.

"Cyrus mentioned you were rather busy all afternoon." Rhoe's voice was quiet. "Do you have a moment?"

"I was. All trivial, of course. Was there something you needed?" He drew her aside, into one of the little seating nooks.

Again, she hesitated, and he was now sure there was some undercurrent he wasn't adequately compensating for at all. "Cyrus said he didn't get a chance to talk to you."

Hugh shook his head. "I'm afraid not. Is there a problem?" He almost reached out a hand, then dropped it in his lap, helplessly.

He could see her glance at it, then back up at him. "Can you come to the cabin for a bit tonight? Cyrus is willing to try scrying with the stone. For the other ship."

It took a moment for Hugh to fit the words together. Then he beamed broadly. "You mean it? Really?" He took a deeper breath, trying not to be ridiculous about it. "That means a lot. To me, and to Atherton. The First Officer. Can I tell him we're trying?"

Rhoe tilted her head, chewing on that for a moment. She was wearing a rather dark dress tonight, in a deep purple, but not the Council purple. It suited her, as much as her dress had last night. But where that had been regal splendour, this felt more approachable, calling to mind sun-warmed berries from a country hedgerow. Then she shook her head. "Let's see if we get anything first. If we do, you can tell him the good news. If we don't, you can tell him we tried something and it didn't work, but not get his hopes up."

There was a great deal of sense in that. Hugh knew how crushing that kind of shift could be, and it wouldn't do anyone much good to go through that without any purpose. "Do you think it will work?"

Rhoe shrugged "The stone's attuned for that kind of thing. Cyrus is not a bad scryer, but not among the best we know, and I am rather less good than that. We both do a bit." She wriggled her hand. "You?"

"Not something I've been trained in, but I gather that's not always necessary? Nerissa won't try, for the record, though if you need someone to keep watch on the rest of us, she might be talked into it. She's up on watch again, though, for the moment."

Rhoe nodded. "After supper, then, if you can get away."

"I'll be most grateful for the excuse, actually." He almost said more, but then Cyrus swept in, in trailing robes that were rather more showy than he'd worn the past few nights. "I believe they're ready, Rhoe. Evening, Hugh, did Rhoe have a word?"

"About your generous offer, yes. After supper?"

"Promptly, if you don't mind." Cyrus held out a hand to Rhoe, who took it, and Hugh trailed after them, trying not to feel entirely like a third wheel. They read each other so well, trusting each other's reactions, and he envied that more every time he saw it. That they had that with each other, at least.

The supper itself had the usual combination of interesting conversation and tedium. Lady Jenifry was focusing her attentions on Cyrus, which left Hugh feeling a little less under attack.

Cyrus kept making it clear he was not at all interested in whatever she was offering, without once suggesting so much as an insult. It was a masterclass in conversation management, and Hugh could not concentrate on it at all. Instead, he found himself alternately watching Rhoe - who was largely quiet this meal - and staring off into space. So often that he had to be called back to attention to the table several times.

When they could finally make their escape, Hugh a few

minutes after the siblings disappeared, it was rather a great relief. By the time he got down to their suite, they had rearranged the space. Someone had drawn the curtains and turned off all the lights except for a charm light set in a lantern.

Rhoe had changed into the ritual robes she'd worn before, with her hair down her back. He hadn't seen it loose before, and he thought it most striking. He knew a number of women used all manner of decorative pieces to make their hair puff and billow properly. But from what he could tell, Rhoe's hair was all her own, with a full wave that gave it body, falling full down to her waist in a dark sheet, with a few threads of silver.

That too was a distraction. After a moment's consideration, he took off his jacket and carefully undid his cuffs so he could roll up his shirt sleeves neatly. Cyrus glanced up from where he was arranging a tray on the floor, as Rhoe set out several pillows from the furniture for them to sit on. "Getting comfortable is good. I'll just change, and bring the stone out. Rhoe, explain what we're doing?"

Rhoe nodded, and settled herself gracefully on one of the pillows, gesturing for Hugh to take the one next to her. "The stone will go here, a little raised, and be the reflective surface we need. There's a chant - isn't there always a chant? That should help bring the images forth, if they're going to come. You should pay attention to anything you see, because we may see different details, or there may be something that makes sense to you that doesn't make sense to us. There's paper, here, and pencils, if you need to make any notes or sketches."

"Do you, do you think it will work?" In the dim light, he could barely see her face.

"It's worth trying. I try to go into this sort of thing with, let's say, a spirit of hope. Seeing how it goes, without assuming in advance of the experience." It wasn't quite an instruction, but Hugh figured he'd heard far worse instructions.

Cyrus came out at that point, wearing a loose tunic and trousers, similar to Rhoe's. His hair was loose, past his shoulders, rather than the pulled back queue he kept it in normally. He was carrying the stone, carefully. "It will stay in the box - I have that warded, now, to absorb the energy, to avoid..." He waved a hand at the ocean behind them. "But this is what it does, so I do not think the ripples will be particularly noticeable. They might even be beneficial."

He settled on his own cushion, then carefully set the box on the tray between them, before intoning a low-voice prayer of some kind. It seemed to be a standard one, because Rhoe echoed a line along with it, here or there. But it wasn't one that Hugh knew, or even a language he could muddle through. Then Cyrus settled into a chant, and Rhoe took up a melody above it. It moved slowly, like the unfurling of a flower in the sunshine over the course of the day.

There was a moment where nothing happened, despite all the chanting, and then Hugh saw it, a play of light in the depths of the stone. It was undeniably real, not some figment of the lantern light. They were shades of that pure blue-green, but somehow different from each other, each one darker or lighter, building up in layers.

It was just shapes, moving like a ship's wake, the way nothing stayed still, for quite a while. How long, Hugh wasn't sure, it was as if time had stopped working, or at least, that all the markers he used for time didn't make sense. He still had a pulse, but the light was too compelling to get him to stop and feel for it. It wasn't as if the time mattered, anyway.

Then, just as slowly and deliberately, those shapes began to build up new patterns. Or not the shapes, Hugh realised, but the gaps between them. In those spaces, he began to see things. A ship, anchored, somewhere. A long flat island, barely rising above sea level. A few creatures - horses, he thought, by the proportions, but too far away and too small to be more than moving shadows.

He focused on the ship, as much as he could, trying to get a sense of any identifying details. He noted the propellers, the funnels, but he couldn't read whatever numbers or name were on her bow. The colours, though, he got some sense of them. Especially as his view shifted a little, as if he were on some smaller boat circling the greater one, bobbing up and down in the waves.

Hugh made notes, then, on his paper, scribbling in the dark, hoping it would all be sufficiently readable later. He could hear, in between the scratches of his pencil, the other two both writing, that the chanting had faded away at some point, all of them concentrating.

After some amount of time - it could have been three minutes or three dozen - all of their pencils fell quiet. Hugh had fallen into just watching the scene, to see if any new detail would catch his attention. Suddenly, he realised that whatever time of day it was, he could see the angles of the shadows of a setting sun, and where the sun was setting, roughly.

He sketched that out, trying to use one of the funnels for a sense of proportion. Once that was done he set his pencil down. Some time later, there was a gentle chant that started up again. Rhoe's voice, first, then Cyrus joining her. It was as if they were bringing them all home, scooping Hugh up in a coracle, safely drifting along the ocean back to shore.

When they stopped again, Rhoe did something to bring the light up, a wave at the lantern. It was almost too bright at first, leaving Hugh to blink owlishly at it. Then his eyes adjusted, and he found Rhoe leaning toward him, peering at him.

He nodded once, and she smiled, leaning back again. "There we go. Take a few breaths, have something to sip on. A bit more light?"

"Please. If you're ready, Hugh? I want to look at my notes."

"Certainly." Rhoe lit another lantern, handing it over to her brother, who first closed up the gem with several little ritual gestures, before peering closely at his notes.

"Did you - I mean." Hugh didn't know how to ask.

"You wrote quite a bit down." Rhoe's voice was careful. "Do you want to start?"

Hugh glanced at his notes. "I'd need to check a map. Angles. Do the calculations. But I got a strong sense of a ship - I think the right size and build - at anchor near a small island. I think..." He paused. "I'm not sure, but the shape makes me think that maybe it's Sable Island."

"Sable Island?" Cyrus's voice cut across the space, rather like an arrow.

"It's almost a sandbar, a little over a hundred miles off Nova Scotia. Notorious for shipwrecks, but this one didn't look wrecked, exactly. Not in obvious distress, or taking on water. At anchor, in shallow water, and I saw what might be horses on the island."

"Are there horses on the island?" Cyrus asked.

"A fair few. Couple of hundred, I think? I don't know a lot about it."

"So." Rhoe cleared her throat. "I didn't get anything near that clear, but I got a sense there's a concern. Not life or death, not right now? But a concern, that tugs like that. And things that are like an island. I mean, an island doesn't surprise me."

Immediately, Cyrus followed on. "I got rather a lot of heraldic black. Sable, as it were. I couldn't figure out why it came out like that. I often get symbols, rather than the clarity of shape. You might want to see about getting some proper training in scrying. It could be quite a handy skill, out here, in particular."

That bit of praise made Hugh look up, and blink. Then Cyrus was brushing his hands. "I'd take that to the Captain, as soon as you've a chance. I assume we're still some way out from there?"

Hugh nodded. "But we could aim that direction, see if they need aid. It's far enough from the coast they might not have got word back to the mainland yet, if they need help."

"I should - I should go tell the captain." Hugh stood up, awkwardly.

Cyrus nodded. "And I should go make a pass around and be social. One of us should."

Hugh blinked at him. "I was expecting..." His voice trailed off, and he glanced back at Rhoe.

"You have done yeoman's work. Or whatever the proper nautical term is. How about you go up and pass along whatever they need to know to aim - carefully - for Sable Island? Rhoe can rummage out some drinks or whatever. She's much better positioned to talk about what you might want to learn if you want to improve magical skills than I am. She's seen far more apprentices go through."

Hugh was dithering when he heard Rhoe say, "You are not at your most subtle, brother. Shoo. Go find the smoking room or whatever it is you have your eye on."

Cyrus turned, made a full flourishing bow, and then opened the door for Hugh. "Leave me something for a snack, how's that. I'll send a steward along."

Rhoe rolled her eyes and waved him off, leaving Hugh

to go through the door, entirely awkward. When they were in the passageway, Cyrus said, amiably. "Come back down, please. You really should get a chance to talk without some new doom looming."

Hugh felt that he was being managed. No, he was sure of it. And he had duties elsewhere on the ship, surely. On the other hand, the last few days had more than a bit of chaos and complication. Part of his duties were to make sure that their most prestigious passengers had what they needed.

All right, coming back down would be skiving off his duties, he wasn't going to lie about that, even to himself. But he also knew he was going to do it. "Council Member." He made a slight bow.

"Brother, in this case. Come down once you've passed along the essentials. Have a bit more to eat. Chat. My sister could use a chat, I'm quite sure. You'd be doing the both of us a favour." That said, Cyrus smiled, a mysterious but amiable sort of smile, and went striding off to the stairs to the main deck.

Hugh saw nothing for it but to do as had been suggested. Fortunately for him, the Captain and First Officer were both still awake and handy when he got up to the bridge. Hugh was able to give Atherton the good news directly.

The Captain was not entirely happy about diverting to Sable Island, but he was willing enough to do it, so long as they didn't stop for long. Just enough to check and see how things were and bring a message along to Halifax or whatever other point made sense about what was needed. It took longer to pull out the charts and estimate the arrival time than it did to come to a decision.

Which meant that twenty-five minutes later, he found himself knocking on Rhoe's door. Again.

Thirty seconds later, the door opened. She was settled on the sofa, he could smell that there was some sort of food. He cleared his throat. "It's Hugh."

"Come in. If you want, of course. If it's just because my brother was being presumptuous, you don't actually have to do what he says."

Hugh coughed, and said, "Um." That sounded awful. He did take a step in, carefully closing the door behind him. "Captain Melcott and First Officer Atherton are both very grateful. For your help and his."

Rhoe craned her neck around and waved a hand at the other end of the sofa. "Come, sit. Eat. If you're not starving yet, you should be soon. And you're the one who did most of the work."

He wanted to argue with that, and mostly couldn't. "If I saw more, it was because you and your brother made it possible." As he sat, he realised she was looking at him with her head slightly cocked, studying his expression. "Is there something wrong?"

"No?" She hesitated. "Is Cyrus being difficult at you?"

Hugh had no idea how to answer that. "I'm not sure what being difficult would look like, in this context. He's been direct, but..." He waved a hand at the food. "About my coming back here."

"Cyrus has some theories. And he does like testing his theories." Her voice was even, but there was a slight wobble in it, as if there were things she was still sorting out. herself.

"How accurate is he with his theories?"

That made Rhoe laugh. "Annoyingly often. If he were right less frequently, he'd be much easier to live with. But arguably less useful, so there we are."

"You strike me, as a family, as given to high standards?" Hugh wasn't sure how she'd take that.

It made her laugh again, longer this time. "Cyrus and I are not what our parents expected. Either of us."

"You both," Hugh stopped, and tried again. "You both seem very secure in yourselves. Your skills, your talents, and the space between them."

That made her lean forward, peering at him for a moment. "You're most observant. Most people wouldn't put it that way." Then she reached over for a petits four, and settled back. "We're not much like our parents. Our parents are conventional, and conventional by Victorian standards. Do the proper thing, the proper way, in the proper time. A life rolling like clockwork. Tea and toast at breakfast with a freshly ironed newspaper, and so on through the day. Until you close with some dinner party or some family evening then repeat it all over the next day, and the next."

Hugh shook his head. "I'd hate that. And - that's not either of you, is it?"

Rhoe grinned at him, eyes crinkling up in a way that made her entire face change. And that made him want her to do that and again. "No. And they can't exactly complain about how we ended up, but oh, they'd like to."

"Why on earth would they complain? You're both, I mean, he's Council. And you're, you are." He couldn't begin to come up with words for what she was.

There was a gleam in her eyes now, almost as if she'd found a target for a hunt. There was an intensity, all of a sudden. But when she spoke, it was entirely about her brother. "We haven't had a Council Member in our family in generations. Our great-great-grandmother. They didn't expect him to go for it, and they didn't expect me to back him. And now they have no idea what to do with him."

"Back him? I don't know - I mean, I know what everyone knows about the Council, but that's not very much."

Rhoe laughed again. "Which is how they like it. When it comes to backing him, I helped him practice. They're allowed to bring whatever items they want for the trials, and I know a few excellent apothecaries. I traded favours, a few of which I've only just paid off. He can't tell me what he used, or why, he's oathsworn not to. But," she shrugged. "He's here, and he came through in one piece, and victorious, and that's a fine thing. What he wanted. What he needed."

"Needed?" That seemed baffling. "He doesn't seem - I mean. That kind of need to have power."

Rhoe settled back, peering at him again. "I suppose you'd have seen quite a range sailing. The people who have power, and the people grasping for it."

Hugh nodded. "Not that I'll gossip, but both. And most of them don't hold it as lightly as your brother does. For all I'm clear he has it."

"He does." Rhoe made a decision. There was a flashing change in her expression. "He nearly lost his mind, when Tanith died. His wife. Bearing their daughter. Nothing anyone could do, even me. She'd been my friend, too. Sharp and bright - like a meteor shower on a winter night. Intense, sparkling, moving."

"You loved her." Hugh could hear it all through her voice. And how Rhoe missed her.

She nodded, just once. "It broke Cyrus open. He had Gemma, but she was a baby, and that was a future he didn't know if he deserved. Should have. He threw himself into training for the Council trials, except for the time he spent with her. Like it was knitting something back together in him, letting it slowly heal, scar over. And then all the work to keep the scar tissue flexible."

Hugh tilted his head, thinking about that image. "You'd think about it like that. That things don't heal back the same way."

"They don't." Rhoe's voice was flat now. "You can go on, or not. But it's never the same." She then shrugged. "When it's bones, sometimes they're stronger, after, if they heal a certain way."

That made Hugh watch her for a long moment, before he said, "And how did you end up as you are, then?"

Rhoe tilted her head, as if she were trying to decide something. "My parents don't understand me because I believe things. And act on that belief." She laid it out as if were a line in the sand, like she'd had to draw it for nearly everyone, over and over.

"Like Nerissa. Though, well. It's not like you believe in the merfolk. They're there. And the selkies. And whatever else."

Rhoe's lips twitched up. "Something like that will do, yes." She waved a hand. "I need to be healing. I've known it since I was eight or so. For certain since my school years. I can't not. And my parents ask me, again and again, if I wouldn't be happier doing something simpler. That I don't need to work, I don't need the money."

"They're not very fond of logic, are they?" It was the first thing out of Hugh's mouth, and then he flushed. "And not very observant, either."

That made Rhoe throw her head back, laughing, somehow entirely free. "Well, no. They think I should marry, settle down, have children. If I wanted to be a Healer, I could do something settled. Children's healing, perhaps. Which is anything but settled, but of course they assume they know what it's like better than I do."

"And now you are moving to something a little more settled, but not what they expect." Hugh wanted to know. "Why are you choosing that, of all the things you could choose?" He was clear that she had choices, even if he couldn't sort out all of what they were.

"Because I want to tend the healing waters. And I've been figuring out how to reach that for a decade or more. Step by step." She waved a hand, vaguely, toward Cyrus's bedroom. "Cyrus is direct, much of the time. Not that he tells you things, but he sets a straight course. Me, I wander. He's a waterfall, I'm an ancient river, all the curves and bows."

Hugh snorted. "That's a fair way to put it. But winding your way to what, then? The ocean?"

She shrugged. "The light. I am going to swear to Belisama. Light and water and the space between them." She said it simply, as if it were crystal clear to her why someone would do that.

Hugh took a breath and let it out. "I am not - not particularly religious. But I've made my offering to Merope, and I've a proper respect for the gods and powers of the ocean." He gestured vaguely off the stern. "Even the ones I'd rather not see. Not the same. And easier for me, I think, than for you?"

"For all we're a temple of healing, plenty of Healers make a bow and a nod and an oath. Whatever they feel, whatever they believe, they keep to themselves. I'm not like that. Not that I think what I believe is the one true way. Just a way. I think people should find their way, that gives them a light to lead them." She looked him up and down. "Merope, hmm?"

Hugh was about to say something, when there was a careful knock on the door, and a "Sir? Master Pelagius? Captain's requesting you on the bridge," from the other side.

Rhoe waved him off, immediately. "Go, go. Let me know if I can be of help."

Hugh stood and made a small bow. "A pleasure, and we'll talk again, of course." Then he tugged his clothing tidy, all the quick automatic gestures, as he headed for the door.

Rhoe didn't see Hugh again that night, nor was he around at breakfast the next morning. She had felt the ship seem to shift and slow slightly as she sat in the reading room after breakfast, not managing to read at all.

When she next looked up, Hugh was there, breathless, but looking very smart in a jacket and freshly pressed shirt and cravat. "Pardon, but might I prevail on your time today?"

She almost said yes without pausing to wonder what the question was. She knew, for certain, that he wouldn't be asking unless she could be of help. And it would certainly give her a way to avoid the shipboard games and people not being sure what to make of her. Then she swallowed, and said, "What's involved?"

Hugh gestured. "We're getting close enough to signal with the ship. We'll be taking a message on to Halifax, but there are a couple of passengers doing poorly who may need to come with us. Or who need medication. Would you be, it's rather a big favour?"

"You know they won't respect me as a Healer. And I don't have a doctor's credentials."

"I won't ask you to pretend to be a nurse. I mean. That's an insult, to you and to nurses. But could you, could you come be sensible? Doctor Northton's coming across, of course, and their ship has a doctor. I don't know, as someone who's been involved with hospital administration, a women's board or ladies' auxiliary or something?"

Rhoe considered. "I'll have to change. But I can do the right sort of thing and be soothing and supportive." She waved a hand. Then she hesitated. "Non-magical ship."

"Non-magical. Is that all right?"

Rhoe nodded. "Bugger." she said, having picked up the useful word from a patient early in her training. "I really should pull out a corset. Can you find one of the stewardesses who can help with that?"

"I did not realise I was asking you to go to such extremes." He took a step back, looking unsure.

She waved a hand at him. "Send someone along, and I should be ready in say, twenty minutes?" It would take that long to do the corset, change shoes, put on a dress that went with the corset, and pin a hat firmly into her hair.

"Bless." He said it softly, like it was a prayer. "We've at least half an hour before we can disembark. So long as you're on deck by then."

Twenty-three minutes later, she was back on deck, in a tailored green women's suit and shirtwaist. She had on proper buttoned boots that made her ankles too stiff, and she was trying not to fidget with the corset that pressed her into the proper shape. She hadn't had one on in months. The last time she'd worn one was a necessary meeting in London, that business about supplies for the Temple.

The look on Hugh's face when he turned around, though, that was worth something. He was, she thought, simultaneously impressed, and also quite clear this was not a thing she normally did. He came over, and bowed, one of the little precise bows. "You have a delightful sense of costuming, madam Healer. How should I be referring to you?"

"Miss Alexandra Smythe-Clive, if you would." She waved a hand. "That's the name that connects to the sort of person who wears this sort of thing, if anyone mentions me."

"I will do my best to avoid calling you Rhoe, then. Though, of course, that wouldn't be proper. Your brother?"

"My brother has had a good laugh at my expense, and put his feet up to read the newspaper." Which was only fair, really. There wasn't much he could do here. He was far less deft at the necessary circumlocutions necessary in non-magical circles. "How do we do this?"

Half an hour later, they had navigated getting into one of the small rowboats, rowing across to the other great ship, and being hauled up the side of the *Memory*. First Officer Atherton was in charge of the party, appropriately, and he was almost immediately swarmed by three tow-headed children, ranging from about ten years old down to five. His wife, who was looking very relieved, hung back for a moment, until he gave up on all attempts at dignity and held out a hand to her.

Rhoe whispered to Hugh, "There's a close family. And glad it's him, here, obviously." There was something that made her wistful in that, how eager they were to see each other. When she looked up at Hugh, she caught something similar in his expression.

They waited their turn, and after a few other

pleasantries, First Officer Atherton turned, introducing them to the group. "Our ship's doctor, Doctor Northton, Mister Hugh Pelagius, brother to the owner of our line, here to see how we might help. And ..."

Hugh picked up smoothly. "Miss Alexandra Smythe-Clive, who is kind enough to lend us her expertise organising material support and assistance. She's served on the boards for that sort of thing at more than one hospital." All true enough, if a tad misleading. First Officer Atherton managed to turn his smile into a little nod.

Rhoe made it easier for him. "I gathered that you had a few passengers who might not be comfortable waiting for relief from Halifax? I thought I might help sort out what they'd need to be transferred. The practical concerns, rather than the medical, Doctor Northton is quite competent at that, of course."

The captain let out a visible sigh of relief. "We do have a couple who - well. We'd prefer them seen into port sooner than later. One woman expecting, she's been having trouble keeping much down while at sea." He glanced at Rhoe, as if he weren't sure what she'd do with that indelicacy. Rhoe just nodded. "An older woman with some heart trouble. And a girl of about ten, who's had some bad fevers, we'd prefer to get her somewhere she could be properly seen to and we have some limits on bathing water now."

"May I ask what happened with the ship, that you found yourself here?" She was curious and it might well help her be more persuasive.

"One of our engines went out, our engineer is still investigating why. We thought it safer to put in and anchor here, and get help from Halifax than push on." His tone suggested they'd had a harder time of that than he was willing to put into words.

Rhoe made a sympathetic noise, tutting slightly. "I'm sure you had every care for all on board, Captain." It seemed true enough, and it was a kindness to reassure him that taking care was the best thing. "And pardon, that meant that you had fewer amenities than otherwise, being focused on finding somewhere safe to anchor?"

The captain nodded. "Exactly. There will be help from Halifax, but it will be a day or two more, depending on what's in port and available there. Getting those three passengers somewhere they can get better care would ease my concerns a fair bit."

That sounded manageable enough, and Rhoe wondered if they could share any fresh food or fruit or something of the kind. She'd have to ask Hugh later. Doctor Northton nodded. "Perhaps if someone might escort us, we could see about that."

Hugh nodded. "I'll join you." He leaned to say in Rhoe's ear. "We've permission to bring a handful back with us, but we'll need to take appropriate care."

Rhoe nodded. One of the officers led their little party of three off to examine those concerned. Some things about the ship were entirely the same as the *Moonstone*. A number of the passengers in first class sat around, peering down noses at these goings on, not approving. She fully expected that by the time they came back, one of them would have worked up a fury that he or she wasn't being given priority.

Once they were down on the lower decks, she smelled the smell of people packed into rooms without a chance to wash properly, and wrinkled her nose. "They've not had the ventilation going, since they're anchored. It's not usually quite so much." Hugh spoke over his shoulder.

In the end, they agreed to take all three of the possible

patients. There was a brief consultation in the hallway about how many cabins they had that could be properly isolated from the rest of the ship - and the magic inherent in the *Moonstone's* design. "We've three cabins we can free up, all in the non-magical area. Currently being used for storage." Hugh said.

"And they could eat there?"

"Quarantine. Just to be on the safe side. We can make sure one of the stewardesses visits them regularly." Doctor Northon was decisive. "But I'd like to take all three of them, and the girl's mother and brother, of course."

Hugh nodded. "Let's do that. Can you explain to them what it will be like, Rhoe?"

She nodded. That was the kind of thing she had excellent skills at, laying out a temporary restriction in exchange for something better down the road. The poor girl with the fevers wasn't hard to convince - or her mother. Rhoe actually had suspicions it might be malaria, given that the mother mentioned they'd been in Africa, with her husband. He'd been reposted to America, with them following along after a visit to her family. But someone in Halifax could sort that out, and they could try some treatments in the meantime.

The old dowager was more difficult to convince, enthroned in her room as she was. Rhoe knelt down and asked some questions about how she was feeling, and tutted gently. She referenced an aunt who had been lucky enough to be seen to promptly and went on to live another decade in full health. The older woman clearly knew she was being coddled, but eventually she waved her hand and said, "I'll not argue further. But you'd best be right that the beds are better over there."

Rhoe had laughed, and said, "Very comfortable, and we have excellent cooks, too."

The last, the poor woman who was pregnant, was somewhere in the middle. She desperately wanted to be off the ship, but she didn't see that being on a different ship was any better. Rhoe, in the end, simply resorted to practicalities. If Agnes came along now, they'd be in Halifax tomorrow, and she could do the rest of the trip by train at her convenience.

All of that done, she retreated to the hallway as the stewards swarmed to help their three new sets of passengers pack up. Hugh offered his arm, as they made their way up to the main deck again.

"I say, you, you there." That was one of the first-class passengers, a man in a sharp business suit. "You're someone respectable."

Hugh inclined his head. "Hugh Pelagius. My family owns the *Moonstone*."

"You'll understand the needs of business then. Look, I simply must come with you, I've a business deal in Philadelphia."

"I'm afraid that's not possible, sir." Hugh kept his voice even. "We've only space for a few, and we're only taking those most urgently in need of medical attention."

"Pah. I'm sure you've people who'd share, so I could have a cabin. I gather your cabins aren't bad, never sailed on you myself, but I suppose there's a first time, and needs must, and so on."

"Again, sir, I'm sorry, that won't be possible."

"Do you know who I am? I'm meeting with Weightman, I simply must get to Philadelphia. A new drug that could save lives."

Rhoe, of course, did not recognise the name. Hugh

made the sort of polite and non-committal nod. "I'm sure he understands the exigencies of ocean travel, sir. There should be a ship along to take you tomorrow." Then he glanced up, as if hearing something. "Do pardon us, I see that our First Officer's wanting my time."

Rhoe promptly set her hand through his arm again. Once they were well away, Hugh murmured, "Pharmaceutical man, that's Weightman. Made a lot of money on a quinine alternative, during the American Civil War. Regardless, I was sure he was going to try and bribe me."

"Americans are rather presumptuous at times." Rhoe glanced around. "I thought you handled that well."

Hugh smiled at her, lighting up. "Thank you. Do you have any questions you need answered, before we turn things over? Are you all right?" He was suddenly solicitous and Rhoe wasn't entirely sure what to do with it.,

Rhoe waved her free hand. "Nothing unexpected. And no particular difficulties, as long as they can stay isolated for the day it will take for Halifax."

"It will put us a bit behind, but no help for it, really." Then First Officer Atherton was motioning them over, to introduce his wife and family. Not too long after they were tucked into a rowboat to go back across to the *Moonstone*.

Rhoe kept quiet, on the trip, a little nervous of saying something that would be out of character for her assumed role. Either of them. Both the non-magical part, or the well-bred woman with causes who wore corsets. She suspected that came across a little oddly, but none of the new passengers seemed overly inclined to talk.

Thankfully, someone had thought ahead, and cleared the way between where they brought the rowboat up on deck and the stairs and passengers. Rhoe went along to see all three into their cabins, but then turned the entire mess over to the entirely competent stewardesses and Doctor Northton. Hugh had disappeared by the time she made it out to the passageway again. Rhoe shrugged and went back to her suite to get her brother to undo her corset and change into something decidedly less fitted.

THIRTY

MONDAY EVENING

By the end of supper, Hugh felt exhausted. It wasn't just the trip over to Sable Island, but all of the questions before, during, and after. Supper had been round after round of questions from other passengers. About why they'd brought 'those people' on board, was it safe, were they going to be allowed out.

Lady Jenifry had, of course, been disapproving. She'd been clear that she wasn't going to change anything she did because of others on board. She was consistent, at least, but unpleasant.

Heloise and Elaine Adams had tutted about the delay in the voyage. It had at least given Hugh a chance to explain the code of the sea. So many things could go wrong on the ocean, it was their bound obligation to lend aid if they could. It was what decent people did, whether they had magic or not.

Amadeo Scali had, at least, backed that up. He'd even had a story or two about non-magical ships coming to help. He'd steered the conversation in a better direction, talking about the nobility of the human spirit in a crisis.

For Hugh, who routinely sailed on mixed ships, the assumptions were just one more thing to cap off an exhausting day. He explained over and over. And he knew he had to keep his voice kind and calm, because letting his irritation show wouldn't help anything at all. Rhoe and Cyrus were seated somewhere else - with the Professor and his wife, he thought, from the few glances he'd got.

It made him wonder, though, what she'd thought. Rhoe obviously lived most of her life firmly in the magical community. She worked - and lived - in the heart of Trellech, a city cloaked by illusion and warding so as to be effectively invisible to people without their sort of magic. She wore clothing that was certainly worn in the larger world, artistic dress wasn't solely the province of magical women who hated corsets. But she'd had a suitable tailored outfit in her trunk, even for a voyage that was supposed to be a pleasure trip for her.

After supper, he had to put in an appearance in the smoking room, chatting here and there as he made his way through the space. And again, once the various social card games got set up. Tomorrow night, there would be dancing, and that would be an entirely different social puzzle to navigate.

He made his first pass of the night through the public rooms. That done, he stepped outside to clear his head, taking a brandy from one of the stewards with a nod. Hugh circled the deck, carefully avoiding peering into corners too closely. They were well into the period in a voyage where flirting turned to other things. If the parties in question couldn't make use of their own quarters, up on deck was one of the options. So long as no one sounded distressed, or was doing something unsafe, the policy of the line was to quietly ignore it. They were a shipping line, not nursemaids.

Coming up to the bow, he caught sight of someone in the solarium, which was largely empty at this point in the evening. There, he saw Rhoe's familiar shape, and it startled him how quickly he recognised her from just a glimpse of her back. Pushing the door open, he ducked his head as she turned toward him, then visibly relaxed.

"The people a bit much for you?" Hugh asked. "Can I fetch you a drink?"

"Oh, no, no. Don't throw yourself back in that on my account. But yes. The chattering, after supper, about ..." Rhoe waved a hand. "I don't understand what it's like, not having magic. Living without it. But I understand that people do, that they have lives full of things I can't imagine, that are wonderful and fascinating. Also troubles, but we have troubles too."

Hugh grinned. "You sound like Nerissa's sister. She has an entire speech about it. Mind, she's known for being opinionated."

"I suppose someone from her family would be. About all of it. And with good reason." Rhoe tilted her head. "You have more in common with Nerissa than just the schooling."

It wasn't a question, and Hugh flushed. He'd wondered if she'd notice. If she noticed, if she'd ask. "You might understand this better than most." Hugh wasn't sure how to go on from there, other than to add, weakly, "Given your own commitments."

"I wondered, when I mentioned them, if you might have slightly more of your own than you were admitting to." Hugh tried not to squirm. There was something wonderful about being seen so clearly, and yet something utterly terrifying about it. He wondered for a moment if he were brave enough to keep offering himself up for that clarity, before he had to admit to himself that he'd been doing it all trip.

"You have secret societies at Schola. We talked about that. There's a group devoted to Merope."

"One of the Seven Sisters, that line of the Fatae." Rhoe rocked back on her heels a little. "Huh." Then, grinning, she said, "Thank you for your trust. I'd assumed there must be something of the kind. That no one ever talks about."

"You wouldn't." Despite his nerves, Hugh was smiling now. It wasn't just her reaction. He had that rush of warmth that signalled he'd done the right thing, navigating on the open ocean of his life and choices a little more elegantly than normal.

Rhoe smiled back, and now her expression was a little more shy as she leaned into her curiosity. "Is there anything you can share?"

Hugh considered that and then gestured out at the ocean. "She's the one sailors turn to, for safe voyages, for protection on the open ocean. Some part of it seems to help. There's a shrine, down below, by the engine room. Tucked into the wall, in a nook."

"She's long been seen as the one with the most ties to mortals. Fondness. There's the myth about a mortal husband, about having children." She tilted her head, as if thinking through something, before she went on. "But she's not a goddess, not exactly, by how some reckon it."

"How does one define a goddess?" Hugh didn't mean it to come out as a profound statement, but that was what it was. "How do you measure an ocean?" He waved his hand at the waves, stretching to the horizon. "We ask for her grace and her knowledge and her love of the waves, and she lends her hand to our work, and brings us home safely. Most of the time."

"Blessings and thanks on all such works." Rhoe said it like it was a phrase she said often, but it didn't sound rote, coming from her, but entirely heartfelt. "Have you felt her touch more directly? Have you needed to?"

The way she put it made Hugh duck his chin, now left speechless. He nodded, gathering his thoughts for a good minute before he went on. "There was a terrible storm, going out to India, a few years ago. Right around when Father died, it turned out. I couldn't do much with the ship, but I could pray for mercy, for safety, that we'd come through it in one piece. It was..." He had to close his eyes tight, then forced himself to open them. "We came across another ship, the day after, that was floating, on her side. There'd been survivors, but none had outlasted the waves. Or the sharks."

Rhoe shivered once and then reached for his hand, threading her fingers through it. "But you kept going to sea." It wasn't judging him. Her tone was again that engaged gentle interest.

"I'd die if I didn't." It came out of him in a rush. "When I was little, it was all I wanted. And now, it's what I know. What I'm good at."

She looked up at him, taking her time, like she was reading something in his face. She took his hand, and turned it over, her fingertips tracing lightly over his palm. "Not the heavy work, though you've done some."

"It's hard to be captain on a line your family owns." Hugh said, softly. It was the first time he'd talked to anyone about this since his father had made it crystal clear he was to put the idea from his mind forever. "But I can make sure things run as smooth as silk, that we're prepared for storms and sudden needs. That our people are trained and provisioned. More than anything, that they're listened to, about the things they're expert in."

"That's the thing, isn't it? Watching people be foolish, small-minded, stubborn. Putting their pride before the greater good. And anyone responsible for the ship, you've hundreds of people relying on you."

Hugh tilted his head, watching the way she leaned into that, earnestly. "You know that, too. The weight of it. That your choices change all sorts of things, for all sorts of people, some of whom you don't know, and never will. I think about that a lot, the nights I can't sleep."

Rhoe nodded. "I think about the ones I couldn't save."

Hugh twisted his hand, taking her hand in both of those. "Yet we both keep doing those things. Facing the ocean."

When she looked up at him, it was with something he couldn't begin to name in her eyes. He suddenly wasn't at all sure where this was going, never mind where he wanted it to go. If he wanted to go anywhere with it. If there was anywhere to go that wasn't entirely a figment of his imagination - or his fear. Hugh didn't quite pull his hand away, but some indefinable quality changed.

"That's the thing I've never been able to explain to my parents." Rhoe's voice was quiet now. "Cyrus doesn't fully understand, but he understands enough. He has his burning desire to do whatever it is the Council does. But that need to be doing a specific thing, and how it makes you distant from everyone who doesn't understand it."

Hugh swallowed hard. He thought for a moment, then offered, carefully. "Father was travelling a great deal. And it destroyed both his marriages. His first wife died alone, and bitter, by all I've heard."

He felt her squeeze his hand before he could look at her clearly. "And your mother?"

"It broke her heart. She'd tried to go into it clear-headed, she said. Knowing that he'd be gone. That he had children already, who deserved his time. Though they were almost out of school by that point, about to apprentice." Hugh shrugged. "She didn't blame him, but she wasn't happy."

Rhoe hesitated. Then apparently her curiosity got the better of her. "Did she have something she cared about like that?"

"Oh, no. Nothing that burned in her, like the ocean does in me. Or - or healing in you?"

"Burned is a fair enough term for me, yes." Rhoe clucked her tongue, just once. "I've always thought the only way to make a decent match like that is to both have things you feel like that about. Knowing it will take you away from each other, but also back together, as things ebb and flow. There's a couple Cyrus knows socially, he's working his way up the Army ranks, she consults for the Ministry and some others. Protection magics, ritual magics. Sharp as a whip, and he's the sort of steadily ambitious and competent that will sneak up on you."

Hugh sucked in a breath. "It works for them?" He hadn't ever really had a model where it could. Oh, plenty of the captains and officers he'd sailed with had families, but he'd never seen anyone where it was a proper match, passion with passion. They'd so often seemed fond, loving - but as if one had to give up their dreams for the other.

"I haven't asked dozens of details? But it seems to. Mind, they have an excellent nanny, household staff, that sort of thing. Which would be a help." She wrinkled her nose. "There's an excellent woman who does for our set of flats, but that's entirely different."

"Rather." Mind, Hugh had no idea how to arrange things domestically, even at that level. Before he could ask anything further, there was a sound from the other end of the room. The doors nearer the rest of the public spaces opened and a small knot of half-drunk men pushed their way in.

"Pardon. I think I'm going to be needed to smooth things over shortly. Tomorrow?"

"Tomorrow." Rhoe hesitated, then added, "The dance, if I may save a few for you?"

Hugh flushed, suddenly, then bowed once, over her hand, before releasing it. "It would be my pleasure."

THIRTY-ONE

L ate Wednesday morning, Rhoe was stretched out on the sofa, reading. Or rather attempting to read, the book was currently face down on her stomach. Cyrus had finished in the bathing room, after rising very late indeed. Now, he came out of his bedroom dressed for luncheon, running his hands through still-damp hair. "Ah, you're still here."

"I wasn't up for making polite small talk. Luncheon is soon enough." She had, in fact, been feeling slightly irritable all morning, for reasons she wasn't at all sure about.

Cyrus settled down with a thump in the chair, leaning forward to peer at her. "Distracted, then?" He gestured at the book. "You've not read much since yesterday."

"You," Rhoe said, "Are annoyingly observant."

"Normally, you appreciate my observations. What's different now?" Cyrus leaned back now, looking entirely at ease. "Did you have an argument?"

"No! No." Rhoe felt that came out far too energetically. She didn't know what to call her conversations with Hugh. They weren't exactly flirtations. Though to be fair, saving him dances, never mind telling him she'd save him dances, plural, was certainly a step toward something like a conventional courtship. Or at least not fleeing in the opposite direction from one.

"But you did talk to him last night." Curse him, her brother wasn't even asking questions.

She narrowed her eyes, peering at him. "Briefly, yes. Someone pulled him away and I came down to read. How much did you win at cards?"

"Rather more than Ignatius Longfellow had to lose. I took it all last night, so he'd save face, but I returned most of it to him first thing this morning. Except for enough to take you out for a modestly extravagant supper somewhere. Assuming you don't have other plans while we're in Boston?"

Rhoe hesitated, then went with honesty. It wasn't like Cyrus wouldn't figure it out shortly. And he might, in fact, have either good advice or useful intelligence. "We talked a little last night. Around various topics."

"Should I tell our par...." Then he must have caught something in her expression, and stopped dead, leaving an echoing silence, before he coughed. "I won't tease, sister mine. It's too tender a thing."

She nodded, minutely. That put the proper label on it, at least. "You know how I've felt. That I keep abysmal hours. I'm near enough married to my work. It wouldn't be fair to someone who wasn't just as single-minded. And why would someone so single-minded about their work, their passion, want me?"

"The last part is a logical fallacy, and you know it. But the base logic of the rest of it is sound enough. You could not love someone who only loved you."

"Or who didn't understand." She lifted her hand, one of

the gestures of reverence she'd learned during her initial apprenticeship. She knew Cyrus would read it as what it was, praise and affection and awe and mystery, all woven together. There were times when his fluency with ritual - the way he lived and breathed it, even if he wasn't a theist - was very helpful.

"And he does?" That had a note of question in it.

"Not mine to tell, but - I do not think that would be a difficulty." Rhoe considered. "We didn't talk about my commitments directly."

"Should you? Are there things he ought to know, to make whatever decisions he wants to make?"

"Probably." Rhoe let out a long breath. "But when. I mean, we have tonight, probably. Today, I'm sure he's busy with the unexpected stop in Halifax, and now we're trying to make up speed down to Boston. And then getting ready to disembark."

"Except for tonight. When you should wear your loveliest frock - the blue one - and your best jewellery, and your brightest smile. And outshine everyone there."

Rhoe snorted. "That doesn't actually solve anything, and you know it."

Cyrus waved a hand, amiably. "No, but it will annoy Lady Jenifry. And half a dozen others."

"I thought it was your job not to cause needless discord amongst the best and brightest." Rhoe pushed herself slightly more upright, rummaging for a bookmark for her book.

"You dressing appropriately for the occasion and having a good time is not sowing discord. If they insist on discord, it's their own damn fault." He stood, suddenly.

"More of a problem than you'd mentioned?" Rhoe

watched as he went to the window, looking out over the stern. "You've been keeping it close."

"We have been a trifle busy, you realise." It sounded sharper than she was sure he meant, and an instant later he turned around, looking over his shoulder. "Sorry. It's not your doing."

Rhoe nodded and considered. "What can I do to help? Besides dancing with you some? I didn't promise Hugh all my dances. Just more than one." She shrugged, a little twitch of her shoulder. "Besides, he couldn't, even if he wanted to. Dance with just me."

"Which brings us back to your plans for Boston. Do you know when he's sailing back?"

"On the *Moonstone*, but she's not leaving for a fortnight after the *Citrine*. Something about a particular cargo that needs the hold's precautions."

"So he'll be at something of loose ends?"

Rhoe shrugged. "I didn't ask. I mean, asking implies things, and we haven't exactly had time to figure out if implications are welcome on both fronts."

Cyrus turned more fully to face her now. "Do you want those implications?" His voice was much gentler. "You know I think he's a good man. And that he'd be good for you, and with you. I'd certainly be glad to see more of him."

"And as you said, Father and Mother would approve. Enough." She half-laughed. "I'm fairly sure they'd approve of anyone male, magical, and from one of the Five Schools, at this point."

"You're not wrong. They want you happy, it's not entirely their fault that they can only see one way to get there. And to be fair, they've been quite happy with each other, in their way. They want us to be happy, they've been foiled with me, and - I suppose daughters are different." Cyrus grimaced at that.

"This was not one of your more silver-tongued moments, for your calibration." Rhoe shook her head. "I barely know the man. For all that a shipboard acquaintanceship has a certain amount of intensity to it."

"For all several complex rituals have a certain amount of intensity." Cyrus pointed out. "You've always said you could read someone, what sort of person they were, once you'd done one of the greater healing workings with them. What we've done this week is certainly comparable. Isn't it?"

Rhoe sucked in a breath, wanting to argue with that. Or rather, figuring out how she was going to argue with it, because she was about to do that. "It's not the same."

Cyrus turned to face her more directly, leaning forward. "Lay out your reasoning, then."

They'd both grown up with this. Their father's love of reason and rationality. The tutoring house, which had put a deliberate emphasis on demonstrating one's work. It had suited them well enough for different reasons. "Ritual is a thing of the mind, and of the will - air dancing with fire, each of them feeding each other. Healing - healing is water."

"Your healing is water, certainly."

"In general. Water and earth. Cleansing and growing. It's an entirely different feel." Rhoe spread her hands, then turned and retreated to the couch again, sitting down with a slight thump.

"So, what did you learn from him from the ritual work that we have done, which, I note, involved rather a lot of water, both physical and metaphysical." Cyrus followed her, taking up a place on the other end of the sofa, and crossing one leg over his knee, entirely at ease.

"That he's steady. Reliable. That he means what he says, and does what he promises. That his inside is like his outside, there's integrity between them. Harmony. That's not true for a lot of people. People lie to themselves, or they don't know things about themselves. For all he's cautious, he runs deep, and he knows how to handle the depths."

"And is he what you might want in a partner?" Cyrus's voice was quiet now, with that little edge of intense focus that was flattering. And terrifying, to have all of his attention in one single place, on one particular question.

She took a breath, feeling it in her body as a Healer had to, before she nodded, just once. Never mind that she hadn't talked about so many things with Hugh. Whether he wanted children. What he thought his life should be like, what he wanted. Whether he could stand to live in Trellech when he wasn't on the ocean, how often he'd be away. All of which were, to be fair, important questions. But the others, about whether she liked him, whether she wanted to match him, in all the ways she might match someone. Those were easy to answer in the end.

"So. You have a lovely time with him tonight, whatever anyone else thinks. And you arrange to see him in Boston."

"How much am I obligated to in Boston?" They'd talked vaguely about plans, but she had no idea how many of them were firm.

"I have my ritual work. I should do a quick trip to New York - you'd enjoy that if you want to come, but you needn't if you'd rather not. Supper out once to be sociable, but other than that..." He shrugged. "Mother and Father said you should enjoy yourself. I'm not going to decide what you enjoy. Or tell them what you may or may not have got up to when I wasn't looking."

His slightly prudish phrasing made her snort. "It's good to know where the lines are." Rhoe let out a long breath. "Assuming there is anything. I got the impression he's - none too sure about things of his own. Do you know anything about his parents?"

"Not beyond the most general. Mother would know." Cyrus spread his hands. "But we can scarcely ask her. For one thing, she's not here, and for the other, she'd get the bit in her teeth and start planning a wedding."

"Neither of which is helpful." Rhoe agreed with that. "All right. I'll - I'll dance with him, and talk with him, and we'll see how that goes. And I'll let you know about Boston when I have the slightest idea what I want to be doing with myself."

Cyrus grinned at her. "Oh, you always have things to be doing with yourself. It's just a question of whether you're willing to try a duet."

Rhoe tugged a decorative pillow from under her arm, and threw it at Cyrus, who of course caught it easily. "I'm going to change for luncheon. Ten minutes?"

"Ten minutes. You keep Lady Jenifry off me, and I'll get the topic on something interesting. Fair?"

"More than fair." Rhoe got up, and went to the door to her room, before looking over her shoulder. "Brother mine?"

"Yes?"

"Thank you. For being not only decent, but helpful."

He waved a hand. "I want to see you not just successful but happy. However that happens."

Hugh had been working straight through from dawn on Tuesday until halfway through supper on Wednesday. First, they'd needed to navigate the various formalities at Halifax. Getting in through the long narrow harbour had taken both more time than anyone wanted, and a great deal more fussing. There had been a tugboat and various calls for one person or another to come and ask about a thing. Then there had been the unloading of their unexpected passengers, into the hands of waiting staff from one of the hospitals. There'd been messages to pass along.

When all of that was done, Captain Melcott had turned to Hugh. He had strongly suggested - not quite an order - that Hugh could make himself useful writing it all up for the log and reports. Hugh blessed the training that had drilled into him to take notes, even if he didn't think he'd need them. The reports had, however, taken near all afternoon to sort out. Then the purser had several matters to resolve, questions of debts to the bar that needed to be resolved before disembarkation.

In the end, he'd asked for a sandwich in his cabin, and made his way up to the public spaces just as supper was finishing. He caught sight of the captain's table, on what was likely to be their last night. Everyone was in their best finery, but he couldn't stop looking at Rhoe. Her hair was done up in loose puffs, and her dress was a gorgeous eye-catching shimmering silk, something that had all the blue-green depths of the middle of the ocean. Over it was a sleeveless gown of soft cream velvet that drew the eye, with lines of delicate embroidery in silver along the edges.

She was resplendent and regal, and Hugh couldn't stop looking at her. Even though he tried. Eventually, he felt someone elbow him, gently in the side, and he looked over to see Amadeo Scali grinning at him. "You have taste. If she's half as clever and kind as her brother, that's a fine thing."

Hugh coughed and tried not to scrunch up his face or flush in embarrassment. "Her brother?"

"He did a kind thing, this morning. A man lost a great deal at cards, last night. And got most of it back this morning."

Hugh considered. "Did he intend for you to know that?"

Amadeo shrugged, amiably. "We don't pay much attention to whether people want us to know things. Ah, they are setting up for the dancing." He withdrew, which at least meant Hugh could do the same, to take up a position by the door, to welcome people in. Everything was laid out and ready - punch and wine, little pastries, chairs for those who needed a rest from the dancing.

As the various first-class passengers came through the double doors, Hugh smiled and welcomed them, letting his mind roll along, offering some phrase or comment, complimenting them. Then, all of a sudden, Rhoe was standing in front of him, and he found himself entirely speechless.

She stood for a moment, without saying anything, before she offered her hand, the back up. Instinctively, he took it and made his bow over it, offering a kiss just above the skin. When he met her eyes again, she was smiling, the corners of her eyes crinkling with amusement. "My dance card awaits, Hugh. When you've a chance."

He grinned, suddenly. "Of course. Next dance?"

Rhoe nodded an instant before her brother swept her off into the swirling line of dancers, doing the polka in a circle. She must have expected it, because she spun, her skirt billowing up as Cyrus swung her around. Here, even more than at supper, it was as if she were shining. It had something of the same gleam as the magic they'd done.

By the time the song ended, Cyrus had brought Rhoe to the edge of the circle, and genially handed her off. "Hugh." Just the one word, which somehow conveyed his approval of whatever it was they might do. How he could put so much meaning into a single syllable, Hugh had no idea.

"Did he just...." Hugh didn't know how to end that sentence. Did he just give his blessing? Did he signal his approval? There were layers Hugh didn't know how to interpret.

Rhoe simply beamed at him, and he offered his hand, waiting for her to position herself. He'd held her hand, helping her here and there, and of course during the ritual, but this was rather closer, suddenly, than he'd been before. She was shorter than he realised - somehow, her sense of self and her presence made her seem taller. Her shoulder was soft under his hand, comfortable, not edged. He adjusted his position slightly, wanting to make it more comfortable for her as the music started up.

They danced well together. More than well. Hugh was a competent dancer, it had been considered a requirement for his training, as much as navigation or a sense of how an engine worked. Many of the women he danced with were just as competent. This, though.

He'd heard about Healer's hands. There were the old jokes about how bedding a Healer had quite a few benefits. In this case, she seemed to almost read his mind, responding to this shift or that in a way that seemed completely natural. By the end of the dance, he was taking more liberties, letting her spread her wings and show off her skills.

By the end of the next waltz, people were making sure they had plenty of space to spin and curve and twirl. Standing back to watch them. At the end of the third waltz - with several other dances between, for both of them, with other partners - they had a ring watching them. Some sour-faced, but most honestly happy, realising they were watching something taking shape that went far beyond this moment.

When the musicians fell silent, Hugh bowed slightly. "May I fetch a drink?"

"Please. And then perhaps a little fresh air, if you would be so kind to escort me?"

This was another kind of dance. And if he did not know the steps to this one quite so well, he certainly knew how it went. "Of course." The drink was easy. One of the stewards had a tray at the ready, with two glasses of champagne. He offered her his arm. It was still chilly, out in the cold, but she was, at least, wearing a layer of velvet. Once out on the deck, he looked for a space where they could be quiet, and found himself leading her up toward the bow.

"Rhoe..." "Hugh."

They both spoke at once, and then she laughed. "Please."

"Ladies first, is how it goes, yes?" They found a spot on the starboard side of the bow. He didn't want to suggest she climb a ladder in her current dress, and risk rust or oil. Or her dancing slippers. But from here, they could look out - a few distant lights, almost out of view, of the land to the east. Or at least the lighthouses.

She nodded, then cleared her throat. "Do you have some time at leisure, next week? You mentioned you'd be waiting for the *Moonstone's* return voyage." All of a sudden, she sounded less than certain.

"For you, yes. For others who would ask for my time, unlikely."

Rhoe laughed at that, looking delighted. "We're staying at the Wheel." The best of the magical hotels. "Please, do call."

He wanted, more than anything, just to say yes. Instead, he found himself asking, "What does it mean to you, then?"

She let out a long breath. He loved that she didn't have some pat and easy answer. There were things they needed to talk about. Dozens of them, he suspected. And for all he'd been thinking about list after list, all of that flew out of his head. Then, quietly, she said, "I don't know, exactly. Except that I'd like more time with you. To talk about things that aren't the Ones Below, or some ritual magic."

"And your brother?" Hugh coughed. "The ritual magic does bring him to mind."

"I am fairly sure I can convince him to go out and not

loom about being imposing. I do know how to bribe him if required."

"That would be appreciated." Hugh grinned up at her for a moment. "I - I can't promise anything."

He wanted to. Some part of him wanted to promise her the moon and the stars and the pearls of the ocean. The treasure lost beneath the waves, whatever form it might take. And part of him was terrified. He'd seen his mother pine away after his father left on voyage after voyage. He'd heard the stories about others in the family. Whatever promises he made, the sea might well break for him. He didn't know how to put any of that into words. He'd never tried before. Never wanted to try, honestly.

Right now, it left him feeling horribly unprepared.

While he was thinking, she reached out and took his hand, carefully. "We don't need to decide anything. Not tonight. Not this coming week. I'm going to be going back to a nice settled schedule, barring the occasional emergency, with a flat and a cat. And you can do what you need and want to, but I suspect I'll be inviting you to come see me, when you get a chance. And are on dry land that side of the ocean."

Hugh had to smile at that and ducked his head. "Fair. More than fair." He watched her for a long moment. There was something steady and certain in her, a steadiness he wanted to understand better. She was so sure who she was, what she was doing with herself. Her brother was the same way.

He was trying to decide what to do with himself, when she set one hand on his shoulder, and asked, her voice clear, "May I kiss you?"

Hugh blinked, but nodded, not quite able to scramble words together.

Rhoe stood on her tiptoes, her left hand coming up to settle on his shoulder to help her balance. It made him realise he could make this easier for her, and he bent. The kiss was not like their dancing. It wasn't nearly so smooth or easy, but it had an insistent earthiness to it that he liked far better than that smoothness. It was real, honest, and all the little moments of clumsiness made it seem much more solid.

When she pulled back, settling on her heels again, he wanted to take in every bit of her expression and reaction. "You've some experience, then?"

Hugh laughed. "A bit. Nothing lasting." Which just made his heart ache. "You?"

"A bit. Nothing recent. No one I'd tell my parents about."

"Or your brother?" Hugh managed to recover his wits enough to tease.

Rhoe laughed, throwing her head back. "I do not, in fact, kiss and tell. Not even to him. Though I have to warn you, he'll probably figure some of it out."

Hugh was about to say something else when he heard a shift in the water along the bow. He held up his hand, and leaned on the railing, peering down. Then he laughed and pointed. "See, there's a good omen for you."

Down at the waterline, there was enough light to see dolphins leaping and darting over each other. There were perhaps a dozen he could see, cavorting and shifting. He settled an arm around Rhoe to let her see more securely. "See, there? And there?"

"Oh, they're grand. Is that because we're closer in to land?"

"It is. We might see whales, tomorrow, as we come down along their feeding grounds. That's a good sign, it is, that all is well in the ocean. And there will be more coastal birds. You might have heard, as we came into Halifax harbour, how the sound was different."

They stayed out there, watching the dolphins, until both of them could feel the chill. Finally they had to retreat inside again to warmth and other people, trying to avoid attracting too much gossip.

THIRTY-THREE
THURSDAY

Rhoe was coming from a nook in the dining room through the sitting area. She'd nearly turned the corner into the main passage back to the central stairs when she heard several women talking, and hesitated.

"Well, I can't imagine why he was paying her so much attention. It isn't like she's anyone important." The voice sounded, possibly, like Lady Jenifry.

"Her brother is." That was the first voice. Miss Lytton, maybe. It had that slight drawl to it. And Rhoe rather thought Elaine and Heloise Adams would not challenge Lady Jenifry like that.

Eavesdroppers never heard anything good about themselves, as the saying went. On the other hand, the women were between her and the stairs down to her rooms, and there was another ridiculous round of shipboard games behind her. She would, at the least, have to wait a few minutes until she was unlikely to be dragged into something.

Rhoe pressed herself into an alcove and took a breath. Nothing would be gained by rushing or pressing onward.

"Oh, her brother would be a fine catch." Definitely Lady Jenifry. There was a purr in her voice that made Rhoe exceedingly glad Cyrus had kept out of her way much of last night. Her brother had spent the evening amiably squiring every unattached lady over the age of forty-five, and a fair number of others, particularly the Scali wives. He had been all charm and grace, smiling and chatting agreeably. He made an excellent show of the thing, Rhoe had to grant him that. It had been some time since she'd seen him among the general social whirl, rather than at a Council event, where the patterns were different.

Hugh, besides the dances with her, had been paying attendance to the younger women who were travelling for the first time. Thessaly Wallace had been glowing with the joy of it, for one. He'd woven dances with the respectable matrons - their mothers or the widows - in between.

"Did you get any of his time last night., Lady Jenifry?" That was definitely Miss Lytton.

"Oh, more than enough. And a bit in private, too."

"You didn't! Oh, do tell." That was Elaine, she thought.

Rhoe bit her tongue to keep herself from saying anything. She knew perfectly well that was false. Her brother had escorted Nerissa out for a chat, at one point, but the entire rest of the time he had been in public, or down in their suite. He would not invite someone like that round without her permission, and Rhoe was sure she'd have caught the lingering edges of ambergris in her perfume. Lady Jenifry might have gotten a sentence or three out of him, but unlikely any more.

The ambergris was locationally appropriate, mind, given that it came from whales. And it did have quite some use as a fixative in perfume, if you cared for the rather musky, spicy smell. But it was utterly unlike the sharp clean herbal scents Rhoe preferred, or even the floral waters she kept for certain kinds of healing work.

She would have to warn him of what Lady Jenifry was implying and see what he decided to do with it. Quite possibly, he'd just ignore it. He saw no point in making enemies he didn't need to. He got along in the world by being cheerful and easy-going. Most people never saw the steel underneath, brought out only when he cared very much.

"Oh, I couldn't possibly. Besides, we're out in public, aren't we? Anyone might come by." Like her brother, for one. Or theoretically he could. He was in their suite with his books, working out a report about the stone. Rhoe rather wondered what he'd do if he heard that set of implications.

"And his sister?" Hearing them malign her brother was making Rhoe grumpy. She could just edge around the alcove and peer, and see Miss Lytton's shoulder, along with the ridiculously large and feathered hat she preferred.

Lady Jenifry seemed glad to change the subject. "Well, she was up at the dancing for most of it. I suppose everyone was being kind to her. Some people don't have better things to do with their time, I suppose. My, she's frumpy, though. Her brother dresses so well, you think he'd say something."

"I always think women who wear that sort of shapeless thing refuse to make the effort. Doesn't she know men don't care for that at all? A proper man wants a wife who will show well, be an ornament."

Lady Jenifry laughed, and it came out sharp and shrill. "And that is no ornament. Honestly, the woman could at least have a care with her hair. Or her clothing. I gather she didn't even bring a maid, can you imagine?"

"You mean no one at all? Well, it's no wonder she looks like she does. I can't imagine how she has so little self-respect." Rhoe winced. She could do the thing properly when she cared to. She had last night. She knew she'd looked herself, most of all. She'd seen it in Hugh's eyes, as solid and certain a thing as she could possibly wish for. She was just as sure of how the Scali had enjoyed her company, and several of the others on board. That this one group of people didn't have anything better to do, that was surely more about them than about Rhoe.

Even if it was very difficult to remember that right at the moment.

Someone - one of the other women who hung about the edges of that core group - said, "I thought she looked rather grand last night."

The other immediately tittered. "You would think that, Lucy. You always think so well of everyone. The colour wasn't bad, I suppose, but so out of the current mode."

"By decades!" That was Heloise again, and the entire party went off into uproarious laughter. It was at that point that there was a shift, further along the deck. It was far enough back on the other side that Rhoe suspected the knot of women weren't paying much attention. They were all mostly aimed at watching Lady Jenifry, tucked into a throne of a chair in the windows.

As Rhoe watched, there was a billowing skirt in plain black, and then someone else coming forward. "Do just run along and fetch that, Thessaly dear, and come right back, please." Mistress Wallace nodded at the group of women as Thessaly came forward. As she got just in front of where Rhoe was tucked into the alcove, she paused. Gesturing for Rhoe to go ahead, she held her own body in line to block most of the view from the chairs behind her.

It was surprisingly tidily done, and let Rhoe get down to the foyer for the main staircase. She turned to find Thessaly beaming at her. "Mama does not approve of that sort of gossip. And she likes you rather better than she likes them. Will you have tea with us, please say you will?" Thessaly leaned to kiss Rhoe's cheek before she straightened up, being a few inches taller. "I must fetch Mama's handkerchief. Tea, at four."

Rhoe watched her go off, bobbing along. That was a delightful young woman, if a tad impulsive. Rhoe rather expected she'd attract a great deal of attention at her debut, but have the sense to choose someone who would treat her well, not just admire her beauty.

She was still standing there when she felt a hand on her elbow carefully. That was Ilune Merton. "Oh, Rhoe. I feel like we've barely had time to chat the last few days. Will you come and have tea with us?"

Ilune was looking a little worried, and Rhoe immediately said, "Oh, of course." It was almost reflexive. As the older woman led her over to a table in the corner. It had a pleasant view out the window over the deck on the other side. Professor Merton beamed at her.

"There we are, then. I gather you had the pleasure of seeing some of the dolphins last night? And we might yet see whales, later today or tomorrow."

Rhoe smiled back at him. "We did, and I hope we do." She glanced around, trying to figure out who else was close by.

"We're in the corner no one cares for much." Ilune leaned forward conspiratorially. "Though the draughts never bother us, and a charm takes care of the noise from the children playing. And, of course, from unpleasant gossip."

Rhoe knew she didn't hide her reaction well. Ilune leaned over and patted her hand. "We heard them going earlier. You've been rather a target. Of course they're all furious you've caught Hugh's attention and they haven't."

"That is the part I've no idea how to manage, to be honest." Rhoe felt there was nothing for it but honesty.

Ilune considered. "They all think you a bluestocking, of course. And you're not that at all, exactly. You're a professional woman, with respected skills. They don't know what to do with that, not in this context. And especially not with Hugh favouring you over the others." She leaned back. "It happens rather a lot with faculty wives."

"Not husbands?"

That made Ilune squeak with laughter, then grin. "Mostly the professors at the women's colleges don't marry. We're intermingling with the non-magical all the time, of course, at public lectures and the libraries and all that."

Her husband inclined his head. "It helps to have topics to talk about other than magic, of course, which - oh, historians and mathematicians and scientists all do, in spades. Even if our studies are a bit different." His eyes twinkled. "Also, once you get a step or two outside your own field, you often tune out the specifics. There's a man I've been sharing a common room with for a decade, and I don't think we've ever understood each other's work at all. He does something with prisms. I believe."

That made Rhoe smile more. "I suppose that would happen when you have a whole college full of people with their own particular interests."

"Pet obsessions, my dear. Among friends."

Rhoe waved a hand. "I can't complain about people being fixated on a topic. I certainly have my own things like that." She hesitated and then brought things out in the open. "You've been very kind. I remember, when we met, you'd mentioned your daughter had been ill. If I can be of any help, with a referral, or something of the sort, I'd be glad to."

Ilune hesitated, then said, "She's had some challenges with, well. Being a woman. The Healer she saw helped some, but there are ... Goodness, I'm not used to discussing this."

Rhoe nodded. "I'd be glad to write her with some recommendations and check with Healers. I know a few who'd be glad to have a longer conversation. Sometimes talking to a midwife is a help, too, even if a woman isn't expecting. They've rather different training in some areas, and they often see a wider range of needs."

"Goodness, that would be sensible, I suppose. I'd be very glad of it. She's mostly all right now, only she's in pain rather more than anyone would like, and it makes her so unhappy. And limited."

Rhoe nodded. "Of course. And that sort of thing can be so wearing and draining. Of course, I feel obliged to mention the baths. Sometimes that can be of help, even if we can't figure out what else might besides potions for pain or other symptoms. And if nothing else, they so often feel wonderful in the moment."

"There are theories, I gather, about the mineral content being the key to that." That was Ferdinand, now, slipping into professorial mode again. "I've always wondered how solid that was."

"Well, being a temple, we also think the blessings of whatever god you are petitioning might be a help. Or at least might not hurt. But there are quite a lot of people who find relief. Maybe it's simply the hot water. Maybe it's taking time to relax, when you can't be fussing about anything else."

Both the Mertons turned out to be quite interested in

the variations in design of different baths Rhoe had some experience with, and how some encouraged healing or renewal and others pure pleasure. That ensuing conversation them quite contentedly occupied until they ran out of tea.

"You could follow them."

Hugh was leaning against the railings, watching the last of the passengers file off onto the long dock. They'd be bringing the crane in next to unload the cargo. He turned and looked over his shoulder to see Nerissa, now in her mufti, with her carpetbag in her hand and her trunk waiting on the deck behind.

"Cargo." Hugh said, waving at where they'd open the hatch and bring in the crane. "And Captain Melcott asked if I'd supervise the mail getting off in good time."

"Has anyone ever told you that you work too hard, and that you should chase your dreams?" Nerissa came along to join him. She was wearing a dress not unlike Rhoe's preferred style, if with a bit more freedom in the sleeves.

"I am woefully diligent about keeping promises. And I am not yet done with my duties." He looked out across the dock, to see Rhoe's hat bobbing along, and her brother's taller form seeing her into a carriage. He felt a wave of jealousy, all of a sudden, that it wasn't him sorting that out. That they weren't going off somewhere together.

"Are you going to see her?" Nerissa's voice was quiet now. Not abrasive, at least.

Hugh let out a long breath. "Is there any point in it?"

"I saw you last night. And the nights before." Nerissa looked out across the dock, rather than staring at him. Small favours. "She's clever and kind and good-hearted. She didn't ask me all sorts of annoying questions when most people would have. Her magical sense is solid, she thinks about things." There was a tiny shrug. "I like her. I'd be glad to see more of her, honestly, though I doubt that will happen."

"That doesn't mean I should go along and pay a call like a proper courting gentleman."

Nerissa tapped her hands on the railing, the little rolling motion of the fist that Hugh knew meant 'waiting'. Nerissa had a habit of using it when she was thinking about something so hard she couldn't talk at the same time. Finally, carefully, she said, "I think this is one of those cultural things. Why wouldn't you?"

Hugh hadn't been sure she trusted him enough to ask him something like that. There were all sorts of business reasons to be on good terms with Merope's Speakers. Having Nerissa make a good report to her brothers and sisters in that particular guild would mean good things for the line, long term. His brother would certainly be pleased.

But that wasn't the reason he did it. They were a curious set, every one of them he'd met, far more liminal than they looked. Nerissa signed half the time, without thinking about it. She forgot to use spoken language. She noticed different things than anyone else, small movements that gave nuance, while missing things everyone else saw. And she was, she'd mentioned, long ago, often baffled by land-dweller customs. To have her trust him enough to ask, that just made him pleased.

"In the usual way of things, Rhoe would have been married off a decade ago. She said as much, that it is what her parents would like." Hugh began to try and put his thoughts in order then coughed. "Pardon, it might make more sense to me if I explain it, even the obvious parts."

"Explain away." Nerissa shifted to look at him more directly now. "It might be a help all round. She comes from a well-bred family?" She said 'well-bred' cautiously, it was not a phrase her people would have used at all.

Hugh nods. "Not Lords of the land, but the upper crust. Double-barrelled surname usually suggests that. Not always, but the clothes, the manner."

"The fact they were sailing in First Class." Nerissa finished that off tidily, and Hugh grinned back at her.

"That too. I think it's just the two of them, neither of them mentioned other brothers or sisters. Conservative, settled parents. Possibly an arranged match, two children is the usual sort of agreement for that."

Nerissa frowned. "And the Council? What does that mean here?" She waved a hand back towards the bulk of the ship. "People kept treating it as something unusual."

"It's a position you have to earn, there's some sort of trial, ordeal. No one talks about it, I'm fairly sure there's a detailed oath to the Silence that goes with it." Hugh reflected on the pieces he'd picked up. "Cyrus was quite young, comparatively. Very determined. She mentioned she'd helped, with things he could bring with him for the ordeal."

"And the Council does things for the land. The country. Roughly speaking?"

"What the king used to do. Or, occasionally, the queen. Before the Pact, when they had enough magic to do it. And the knowledge to do it. I don't know the whole of it. I do know that anyone on the Council has strong magic, and more to the point knows how to use it. Not just bluntly, but also delicately. Not all of them are kind, or thoughtful or caring. But they're all sharply competent, from everything I've heard and seen."

"Sharply." Nerissa snorted. "That gives an idea. But you like him, as well."

Hugh lifted his chin, then nodded, not bothering to argue. "I do. He's sure of himself, of what he knows, and that might get him in trouble sometime. Though at least this trip, he listened when he realised he was in over his head. Or perhaps when Rhoe yelled at him."

Nerissa chortled at that. "At least he did that much? He's handsome, though. And I suspect he'd be fine in bed, if he could be persuaded to it."

Hugh blinked at her. "I didn't - um." There was absolutely no good way out of this conversation now, and he had the sense to know it. "That wasn't a thing I was thinking about."

"I was." Nerissa grinned again. "Not that he would. But she, now, she's not running away."

"She's not here." Hugh felt it was important to point that out.

Nerissa let out a puff of breath, the kind that would make bubbles rise under water. "She told you exactly where to find her, didn't she? What did she say?"

"The hotel. That she'd be pleased to see me. But half the women tried to say something like that. Encourage me."

Nerissa just raised an eyebrow, waiting without saying anything at all.

"I know, I know. This is different. But I don't know what to expect. What she wants."

"When a selkie courts a walker, there have to be some

discussions." Nerissa said, amiably. "They go better if you actually talk to each other, rather than assume you know what the other person wants or is feeling. Use words. Out loud, if you can't use your hands."

Hugh wanted very much to argue. He also knew how futile it was. He waved a hand in one of the signed gestures of resigned agreement, that he wasn't arguing. Nerissa leaned over to pat his shoulder. "Boston has museums, restaurants, concerts. Find something she'd enjoy."

"Healing baths. And I don't think they have those."

"There's water. An ocean. Rivers. Lakes. I am quite sure she would enjoy other things than water. She strikes me as the sort who prefers her local waters, anyway." Nerissa shrugged, as if baffled by this.

Hugh let out a long breath. "All right. I'll go see her. At the hotel. With a few ideas of what we might do."

"Grand. Now. What are you going to write up about the stone?"

The change of subject hit him hard. "I've a week to come up with something, the report's going back with the *Citrine.*"

"That's not an answer, and you know it. What do you plan to report? And how much do I feature in it?"

Hugh leaned against the railing, shifting to watch Nerissa's face more closely. "I can go either way. Play down your role, or make it clear you were in fact a great help."

"The first, please. I'll be making my own reports, of course."

Hugh nodded. He hadn't expected any differently. "What will you say?"

"That it's a rather brilliant approach to the immediate problem, but it raises troubling questions about the larger systemic effects. If the Ones Below learn to come to the surface until they get a bit of tasty magic, what's to stop them doing that more often?"

Hugh let out a low whistle. "That is a problem, you're right. In the moment, it was the best decision we could have made, but..."

Nerissa nodded. "I had a word with Cyrus. He promises that the stone will be extremely thoroughly warded on the return trip, in a multi-layered box designed to absorb and hold any surplus magical energy. He also thinks the working they have in mind will help drain off a great deal of energy, but he couldn't be sure until the ritual is complete. If so, it may change their plans for the South American port."

"That's something." Hugh hesitated. "Do you think that's sufficient?"

Nerissa spread her hands, shrugging. "I don't think we'll know until they cross again, honestly. The theory seems sound enough, and Cyrus does seem to know what he's doing in that realm."

"Fair enough. New magics, and all." Hugh shook his head. "I was going to report - I'm not going to lie. But say that a magical item, under Council protection, seems to have attracted attention. An overview of what you've shared, about the Ones Below. Signs to watch out for, of a problem. And then a brief summary of the ritual. But of course, not every ship will have people on board with that degree of ritual competence."

Nerissa tilted her head. "Probably not. But given the structure, a competent ritualist could probably make it work. And most voyages have a Healer, or a member of the Guard, or a Lord or Magistrate, or some combination. If you arranged supplemental training for any members of the crew who had sufficient magic, it might do."

"That might not be a bad idea. Rhoe demonstrated how useful it was to have people familiar with drawing magic from others, and using it in an emergency. Any number of things can happen on the ocean." He waved a hand. "Do you think the Ones Below do this often?"

Nerissa shook her head. "I think we'd know, if they did. The merfolk would mention it, at least, the ones we are on good terms with. I think it was something particular about this stone. Perhaps a combination of things. The stone, the season, something else in the cargo hold. But of course, people never do declare all of their magical treasures . Only the ones too obvious to miss."

Hugh laughed despite himself. "There, you have a clear sense of human nature and custom. Right. I'll come up with something. You're heading south, aren't you?"

She nodded. "Picking up a ship down to the Caribbean. Various ports. And then across to Africa." She glanced down at the dock. "Fair winds and safe travels. I'm sure I'll be crossing paths with you again soon. And looking forward to it. My respects to your brother."

Hugh pushed away from the railing to give her a formal bow, respected colleague to respected colleague. "I'll look forward to more voyages with you, certainly. Fair winds to you and vibrant waters."

She grinned, toothily, for just a moment, then turned and gathered her bag. One of the stewards came over immediately to see her trunk safely down the gangway.

Rhoe was settled in a chair in the sitting room of their rather grand suite in the hotel. The Wheel was tucked into what she gathered was Boston's premier magical neighbourhood, a small block of houses not far from the State House. They'd taken a pleasant, if blustery, walk around Boston Common, a large green space a few blocks away, and the Public Garden next door to it. Neither were at their best in November, but must be lovely in warmer weather.

Cyrus had offered to get tickets to some concert or performance that suited, and they had been idly discussing which might be interesting of the available offerings. It was a question of whether they went to something of particular local interest. *Alice of Old Vincennes* was playing, for example. Or they could take in a historical drama, an opera, or a bit of Gilbert and Sullivan. The last seemed more likely better done nearer home. Besides, *Iolanthe* always felt to her like someone who had heard about the Pact while half-drunk. But that didn't narrow things down overmuch.

Now, though, the persistent clouds had turned to an icy

drizzle not long after luncheon. Neither of them were much inclined to go out, or at least not very far. The discussion had turned to what sort of meal could be found without too much trouble, either from the hotel or somewhere nearby. All the charms in the world to keep off the rain didn't quite fix how it made you feel chilled to the bone. They'd come to no useful decision when there was a knock at the door.

Cyrus raised an eyebrow and went to answer it. Rhoe leaned back, contemplating the rather ridiculously ornate decorations of the room, all vibrant brocades and gilt. It was not particularly her style, but she supposed the Bostonians had wanted to show off their best to the visiting Council Member bearing powerful magical gems.

"Oh, good evening. Come in, come in, the weather's frightful."

Rhoe raised an eyebrow, unsure who he'd invite in without checking with her. Or giving her a chance to make an escape to her bedroom with a book and a mythical headache. Then Cyrus stepped back, and Rhoe realised why. There was Hugh, his wool coat beading with damp, taking a hat off his head, and bowing slightly. Cyrus moved to give him a hand with the coat.

Then Hugh stepped forward. He was holding not a bunch of flowers, but a trio of books, tied together with a bit of string. Small volumes, one bound in deep green, one in red, and one in brown. He was watching her, as if he weren't sure what she was going to do, or how she might react.

"Rhoe. Pardon that it's taken me so long to accept your invitation."

She nodded once, now unsure where this was going as well. "Come in. Sit down?" She glanced behind him at her brother, who was hanging Hugh's coat and hat up where they could dry out, and doing a charm to help that along.

Hugh came and sat on the end of the sofa nearest her. "I found these for you. I thought you'd like them?" He pulled the string loose after untying the bow, and then held them out. The green volume was about local plants and their properties, the brown one apparently local folklore, and the red was a handsomely illustrated collection of historical stories. "They were rather short on volumes about deep sea life, unfortunately."

The dry tone in his voice made her look up from the books and snort. "You looked? No, of course you'd look." She smiled down at them. "Thank you. They're clearly chosen with a great deal of thought. But it would be horribly rude to scurry back to my room and read them." She hesitated for just a second. "Have you had supper? We were just trying to decide if it was worth going out."

Hugh ducked his chin. "I'm not sure I could recommend it." he agreed. "May I be so bold as to ask you something?"

Rhoe looked him up and down. He seemed outwardly calm, but the set of his shoulders and a faint quiver in his magic made it clear he was anything but. "Of course."

That certainty baffled him, visibly, for a moment. Then he cleared his throat. "I am most clear that you are a professional woman, with your own vocation and commitments. But I would be most pleased if I might have your permission to pay court to you."

She had not expected it, not like this. Hugh had spoken directly to her. He hadn't so much as looked at Cyrus since sitting down. Just at her, steady and utterly committed to asking her properly. Listening to whatever her answer was. Rhoe found herself leaning forward, reaching out a hand for his. "What does that mean to you, courting me? So we're both clear."

"Arranging my schedule, when I'm on the proper side of the ocean, to have time to see you. With plenty of notice, so you can make your own arrangements. Learning what you enjoy - what food, what music, what outings. Meeting your friends. Introducing you to mine." Hugh gestured with his free hand. "Whatever comes of that."

"I would like that very much. Seeing how things develop." Rhoe hesitated for a moment, trying to find the perfect words for this, and then going with the words she had. "I've come to enjoy your company, Hugh. And I was feeling sad I wouldn't get to see more of you."

He lit up like a sunset, or perhaps even more so a dawn, all glowing and golden. "I'm glad. That's - that's how I feel about you, too. That I want to spend more time with you." He flushed, then added. "Nerissa might also have been blunt with me."

"Well, I'm glad. That you're here, whatever the reasons." She squeezed his hand again. "We could start by figuring out supper?"

He lifted his other hand, finally looking away, to glance over at Cyrus, who was leaning against the side of the fireplace. "Pardon, Cyrus."

"Oh, don't mind me. At all. Though I should probably make the obligatory speech. Don't hurt my sister, etcetera, etcetera. Though honestly, she knows a lot more painful things to do to a body than I do." Cyrus waved his hand, and Rhoe could read him clearly. He was not just pleased, he was crowing inside. He likely would do more of that as soon as they were on their own again, even if that weren't until they boarded the *Citrine*.

Rhoe snorted. "That wasn't a very demanding speech." Cyrus waved a hand, amused.

Hugh looked up. "I promise to do my best to avoid causing any such problems. But I would like your help, if you're willing."

Cyrus raised an eyebrow and came to sprawl in the facing chair. "My help? You seem to be doing well enough on your own." He flicked his fingers. "Besides, you've met my sister. Even on such a short acquaintance, do you think she's going to let you foul your oars at this point? Or however the phrase goes?"

Hugh squeezed her hand again, his focus otherwise on Cyrus. "For one thing, if a man wanted to find a gift for some special occasion, or some surprise, a brother's knowledge might be most useful. It's in my interest to learn the things you know, at least in that regard."

Cyrus laughed evenly and loudly, enjoying it. "That is fair, and I will be glad to consult." Then he leaned forward. "That's not the only matter at hand, though, is it?"

Hugh shook his head. "I would appreciate your help with, shall we say, navigating things with your parents. Are they likely to be pleased? Offended? We are in trade, after all. How I might, at the appropriate time, make the best impression possible."

He was so earnest about it. Rhoe squeezed his hand. He shifted to let his thumb run over hers, a surprisingly intimate gesture. Cyrus nodded once. "I'll think about the best strategy. Though honestly, there's a fair likelihood that they'll be so pleased she's considering romance they'd not mind a number of things they'd have complained about a decade ago." He then tilted his head. "Now, what Gemma's going to think, that's a good question."

Rhoe tsked at him. "You only have to point out that

Hugh is in an excellent position to bring back books from all over the place. If he's willing to do that kind of favour." She added to Hugh, "Cyrus and I are great readers, and Gemma puts us both to shame."

Hugh let out an audible breath. "Well, that's easy enough. I do usually find a good bookshop wherever we put into port." He gestured with his free hand at the books on the table. Then he realised where they were, and what they were doing, and flushed again.

Rhoe thought it was about time to make her own preferences clear. "Cyrus, brother mine. Would you go away and do something, somewhere else? If you happened to find a something else that kept you away all night, I certainly would not complain."

Cyrus flicked his fingers, amused. "I was already considering that particular matter. I do need to do a quick trip to New York, as I mentioned. I could get the train down tonight."

"Or a portal." Rhoe felt obliged to point out. "I gather they work on this side of the Atlantic as well."

"A different underlying schema, I gather, or something of the kind, but that would also be an option. Let me go pack a few things, I'll be back...." He hesitated, counting days. "Monday by mid-day, I'll telegraph or send a note by portal if there's a change. Hugh, could we put you in charge of arranging theatre tickets for Tuesday night? Beside whatever else you might choose between now and then? I'll have the necessary ritual work on the Wednesday."

"Of course." Hugh glanced at her, then back at Cyrus. "Wait. Pardon?"

Cyrus stood up, brushing his hands off. "My sister has made her preferences plain. I am going to head off to New

York for several days. Enjoy yourselves, whatever form that takes. Let me pack, first, though."

He strode off to his bedroom, and Rhoe shook her head, amused. "He likes making an entrance. And an exit. Don't worry. If it were actually a bother, he'd have suggested something else."

Hugh peered after him. "Just like that? Without checking with you?"

Rhoe could tell he was trying to decide what that meant. "He might have opinions about our needing some more time together." She waved a hand. "Without external deadlines. Supper, first, and then we can see from there? Well, talking and then supper, it's still only, what, four? I can barely tell with how dark it is outside."

Hugh let out a breath. "Um. Yes. I'd like that. Do you know a restaurant you like, near here? Not near here? I mean." He was babbling now, and Rhoe found that delightful.

"My hopes are for more talking, less walking around in awful weather. Perhaps a modest amount of warming alcohol. If you don't know what's near, we could consult the hotel concierge?"

Hugh nodded, looking relieved to have that much sorted out. He was still looking at her when Cyrus reappeared, though to be fair Cyrus did reappear exceedingly promptly. He must have taken just enough time to have packed a few things, added three extra books for good measure, and closed up his smaller suitcase.

"I'll be off, then. No advice, sister mine, beyond what I've already said. Pleasure to see you, Hugh, and see you both on Monday." A minute later, he was out the door, leaving Rhoe and Hugh truly alone together.

Hugh had not been sure what to expect when he turned up at the hotel. Whatever expectations he'd had, they had been utterly upended when Rhoe had told her brother to go away. He'd only barely caught up with that when he'd found himself escorting Rhoe downstairs. That had at least been familiar enough, asking the concierge for a suitable restaurant.

The restaurant had been magical, softly lit by charm lights, with plenty of booths set off with privacy charms. It focused on seafood, unsurprisingly for Boston. Hugh had quite enjoyed the clam chowder, followed by scrod, and Rhoe had enjoyed a lobster bisque and cod. They had both, he thought, been nervous of getting too deeply into any more personal matter. Instead, they kept to lighter topics - books, more about Gemma, a few amusing stories from their various colleagues.

It was not until he'd walked her back to her suite that he'd felt uncertain again. Rhoe seemed so sure of what she wanted, what she was doing. She never seemed to hesitate. He felt like he was lagging behind somehow. When she settled down on the sofa and gestured for him to join her, that made sense. When he ventured to take her hand, she slipped her fingers into his rather eagerly. There was no denying that she was encouraging him, but it seemed a great leap from this to anything more intimate. Not just physically, but in what they talked about. How they talked about it.

They had been going back and forth about smaller things again, her years at Schola, his at Dunwich, the way they overlapped, and the many differences. The next thing Hugh knew, he was largely horizontal, with his head on a somewhat lumpy pillow. A moment later he realised his head was in Rhoe's lap. Her left hand was draped over his shoulder and side, while she was reading with the book in her other hand.

As soon as he moved, she patted his arm. "Don't fuss. You must have been exhausted."

"I am horrible company." He tried to sit up, to apologise. He felt like a complete cad. "You must, I should..."

"Stay." Her voice was clear. It wasn't an order, but it was firm. "I rather like you there. If you're comfortable."

Hugh let out a long breath. "Let me, let me wash up?" A moment, several minutes, to gather himself. That would help. Surely. She patted his arm again and gestured. "That door, there."

He managed to push himself upright without further embarrassment before finding his way to the bathroom. He washed his hands, letting the cool water run over them. He was using all the little tricks to centre himself that he'd learned dealing with his father, if deployed here in a very different situation. He wasn't sure what to expect now. He wasn't even sure how to ask about it.

He took about five minutes in the bathing room, enough

time to wash his face, use the facilities, and wash up. He straightened his jacket, and went out to the sitting room again, not at all sure what he would find.

It was empty, but as soon as he stopped walking, unsure, he heard Rhoe's voice from the other bedroom, calling out, "Here, Hugh."

That was suggestive, certainly. But she was doing rather more than simply hint that she wanted him to join her. Hugh took a breath and let it out. When he reached the doorway, he knocked once, and then peered inside.

The room was gently lit, and there were books on half the flat surfaces. Rhoe had changed clothing, into the sort of full and all-encompassing gown and dressing gown that covered everything, and yet were clearly meant for the bedroom and only the bedroom. The silk fell over the curve of her hip as she turned to face him more fully. She'd let her hair down again, and he thought, all of a sudden, that she was not playing fair at all.

Something of that must have been visible on his face, because she held out a hand to him. "Please. What would make you comfortable?"

"I don't..." He hesitated for only a moment. Then he gave into the impulse to dive into the water, come what may, for all that he felt like he was all gangly imprecision. "We haven't talked about what you want, what this means to you. Or what I want, what it means to me. Our histories. I mean, with other people." He managed to lift his chin, to take a breath and stop the impulse to babble. "I don't want to rush this."

"And we won't." Rhoe paused, now carefully precisely where he had rushed forward. "I don't want to sail home, without knowing a great deal more about you. I am used to setting that kind of thing to the side." She made a small snorting noise. "Rather far to the side, most of the time. Tucked into an awkward space in the attic. It has been some time since I've had a lover. Six - no. Eight years."

"All right." That was enough that Hugh could let out the breath he'd been holding, and step forward. He reached to take her hand, bow over it, then bring it to his lips and kiss it. "I know how you dance. A little of how you think, when you're presented with a challenge. What am I to you, then?"

"I've had a lover or three. Only three. But never a partner. Never someone who wanted to walk alongside me, going into the future. Whatever that looked like. I didn't think I wanted one." She turned her hand, taking his fingers and tugging him closer, gently enough he could readily resist. "Only the way we dance together - dance, and solve problems, face challenges - that makes me wonder about other kinds of partnering. You?"

"I've had lovers before. For the better part of ten months, when I was in India. An Anglo-Indian woman. A few others. The people who didn't just see my last name, and what they thought it meant."

"I imagine that's a bit tricky." Her understatement made him laugh and relax even more. She then tugged his hand. "We won't do anything you don't want. But will you come sit on the bed with me? Where we have space? Or is that too much?"

He suddenly had the sense she was watching him with all the intensity of a Healer making a diagnosis. That was not at all wrong. He was overwhelmed by what he felt. Desire, of course. Wonder. Nervousness. He was not at all sure he could perform, adequately, if they did progress to anything like lovemaking. At the same time, he wanted nothing more than to be closer to her, to be invited to touch or hold. Perhaps to run his hands through her hair, or rest a hand on her leg. All the intimacies that were utterly inappropriate in public.

"What will you do, if I join you?" He found the words, somehow, though his voice nearly cracked at the end. He wanted desperately to know, and feared what she'd say, all in one gloriously tangled demanding mess.

She tugged once more, gently, encouraging them both back toward the bed. "I want to touch you. I want to feel your pulse under my fingers. To begin to understand you. I listen with my fingers, at least half the time." Now, she finally ran out of words, just a silent shift of her hand, making it clear that the touch she wanted wasn't simply sexual.

Hugh found himself bumping against the bed, high enough it was almost at his hip. It had come to this place, then, where he had to decide how he was going forward. "Sitting," he agreed. "At least to start with. What is comfortable for you?"

The bed was, in fact, so high she had to give a little hop to get herself onto it. It should have seemed ridiculous, only she was entirely in earnest. He couldn't help but join her, settling next to her, thigh to thigh, feeling the warmth of her against his leg.

"There. That's a start. You can tell a great deal about someone once you get this close."

Hugh was not at all sure what to do with his hands, whether he should settle an arm around her shoulders, or offer to let her hold it again. She kept doing that to him. It wasn't that she was upsetting. If anything, he found himself drawn to her, like she'd become Polaris, the star from which all navigation flowed. "What does it tell you about me?" The words came out before he could stop himself, but they were true and also something he was suddenly extremely curious about.

Rhoe took his hand, cupping it in both of hers, letting it rest there. Then she shifted one of her hands, reaching with two fingers to feel his pulse, then to rest there. "I think you feel like you haven't got your land legs back yet. Things keep swaying you, side to side."

That hit entirely far too close to home. So close he couldn't argue. He just closed his eyes and nodded. She moved again, taking his hand between hers. "And I am not making it easy at all. Will you kiss me?"

It shocked him enough he opened his eyes wide, blinking at her, before managing, "That does not help." Not that he was upset. Wave-tossed, yes, but not upset.

Rhoe looked unsure for just a moment, and then she beamed at him. "It is a straightforward action. The question is whether or not you're willing or interested."

He didn't have words to answer, but he didn't need them for this. Instead, he twisted, one hand on her shoulder, the other at her waist, in a mimicry of their dancing, and then leaned to kiss her. It took a moment, then something slipped into place for them, and the kiss became a shared delight. If, perhaps, a delight they both found themselves overwhelmed by.

He could not bring himself to pull away. He found his hand sliding down to cup her hip, to feel the thin layers of silk and nothing else between his hand and her body. Then her hand tugged him closer, flat against his back, as Rhoe leaned into him, reaching up to help with the difference in their heights.

When she finally pulled away to let them both catch their breath, her eyes were dancing. "You don't need your jacket, surely?"

He was already shrugging it off by the time she got halfway through the sentence. He tossed it to the footstool at the end of the bed. "We should talk. About what we're willing for. Tonight."

Rhoe shrugged slightly. "I've rather made up my mind to enjoy myself. I think it's unlikely you'll suggest something I'm unwilling to discuss." She added after a moment. "Healers hear just about every sexual preference under the sun, and you do not strike me as likely to want the ones I'd refuse immediately. So. We explore. Here be dragons. Here be sea monsters." As she spoke, she let her hands shift along one arm, down his chest, until he laughed.

"You are, perhaps, a siren. Especially with your hair down, and that note in your voice."

He had somehow hit on the perfect thing to say. There was a flash of her magic, something coalescing just an instant, and she shivered in delight. When it had passed, she shifted to get closer to him. "A siren." Rhoe let out a long breath, then took his hand, bringing it to her wrist, moving his fingers so he could feel the demanding beat of her heart. "Feel what you do to me."

"Entirely mutual." Hugh swallowed. "I don't want to rush. But I don't want to wait. It turns out." He almost stammered, feeling his heart pounding.

She drew him down into another kiss, then let herself slowly fall back against the bed, so he could stretch out along her body. They both knew where this dance would take them, sometime this evening. Finally, Hugh gave himself over entirely to that course, and all those desires.

Rhoe tucked her hand through Hugh's arm as soon as they were out on the street. The past two days - and three nights - had been like something out of the best sort of dream. It wasn't that things were perfect. She wouldn't have trusted that, and she was sure Hugh wouldn't have either. There had been enough bumped noses and awkward moments to ground them thoroughly in each other.

It had also been tremendously educational. The more she saw of him, the more he let her see the places he normally protected, the more fascinated she was. He wasn't like her brother, who let all his competence show. Instead, he'd been taught to obscure it. To do as much as was needed, without making a show of it. Best of all, though, was how he listened. How he didn't make assumptions.

Rhoe wondered if that was why she hadn't found a partner who suited. The best Healers had the same knack, for paying attention and rapidly navigating between pieces of information without judging. But most of them - herself included - had a significant sense of self-importance. Or at least their own sense of skill.

She'd watched Hugh several times navigate something he wasn't particularly familiar with, and how he'd ask something, listen to the response, and then change course as needed, fluidly. He might be uncertain in private, but in public he simply flowed forward, changing his route as needed.

He adapted. That was a better description. Pleased with herself, she squeezed his arm, and he glanced down at her. "Yes?"

"Oh, just thinking about your particular forms of excellence, and how to describe them." He had quite a few. She'd woken up this morning to find him leaning on one elbow, just watching her. Most other men would have been touching her, or wanting her to wake up. Hugh had just been waiting, without rushing or jogging her elbow. When she'd stopped blinking at him, he shrugged one shoulder, and said "You need sleep. This is a vacation."

She found that hard to argue with, and besides, she didn't want to argue with him at all. Persuade him of things, certainly. Introduce him to others, definitely. But not argue. Now she settled into walking beside him, glancing at the shop windows.

They were on their way to the portal to meet Cyrus, who was due to come through at half-two, and they had tickets to *Iolanthe* that evening. Hugh had persuaded her that the leads were superb, and worth hearing in whatever they chose to be singing. And he'd offered, up front, to let her complain about the ridiculousness of the plot at the interval.

The man did know how to get what he wanted, in the

best way possible. They were half-way down the block when Hugh spoke again.

"I keep wanting to make arrangements to come back on the *Citrine* with you. I won't. But I thought I should tell you that I am nobly resisting the very great temptation."

The tone in his voice, rather like a very determined ten-year-old, made her smile at him. "Good. You have duties to perform. I need to think about how I'm starting my new work. You would be terribly distracting."

"And you. I suppose we can sort that out eventually." Hugh shrugged. "We have time."

Rhoe craned her neck. "You've decided, then?"

"That I want more of this? Oh, I decided that - um. About the point Cyrus walked out the door, even if I had no idea what it would be like. I still don't, but I find I don't care. We will figure out something that works for us. Whatever that is."

"You were worried about it?"

Hugh hesitated for a moment, then nodded. "Father's marriages were both unhappy. In different ways, I think, but it's not as if anyone told me anything. And I refuse to do something like that." He hurried to add, "Not that we're talking about that, exactly, yet."

"We are and we aren't." Rhoe squeezed his arm. "We're new to each other. We shouldn't be making that kind of decision yet. But I think I'm right when I say both of us - need to know that we're steering there. Is steering the word I want?"

He laughed. "It will do. I've been thinking about that. About how it's setting a course. There may be changes along the way, but - you and I, we're agreeing, then, that we are setting out for a port named Marriage, even if there are other stops? Some far-distant place we've heard stories about, some far more believable than others?"

Rhoe paused so she could kiss him, hand on his shoulder for balance. It was a decorous sort of kiss, by most standards, but she heard someone whistle from across the street. When he pulled back, reluctantly, she said, "Yes."

"Well. All right. So, for now, we are sorting out a number of things. And we'll spend more time - a lot more time, I hope - when I get back to Albion. Around your new duties, of course."

"By the time you're back on the *Citrine*, I should at least have a sense of when I'm likely to be free. Now, whether I'm any sort of good company, that's a different question."

Hugh started walking again after making sure she was coming along with him. "A new position is always exhausting. Remember, I worked my way through two dozen of them. There are new people to meet. You need to learn where everything is. And it's never the same place as the last job, even when it's the same supplies, the same department."

Rhoe snorted. "The Temple of Healing's a bit better than that. Though I agree, it's an entirely new kind of work. And I'll need to make the right noises. Go to supper or tea or whatever. Every department has its own way of making their connections stronger. I don't know about the baths. Not yet."

Hugh nodded. "So, whatever time I can get, I will gladly turn up for, if I'm free. And if we're not, we'll look forward to the next time we can."

"Much better than resenting the fact we have other things we love." Rhoe agreed. "I suppose there are other conversations about this eventual journey we should have sometime. If after marriage, we consider a further trip to the

Children Islands." She said it lightly, but she honestly didn't know what he'd say to that.

Or, for that matter, what she wanted him to say. Between her own vocation to healing and losing Tanith, she'd not been sure she wanted children of her own. Only then she'd look at Gemma and wonder. Besides, it had all been an entirely theoretical question, until now.

Hugh turned toward her. "Not a conversation for the middle of a busy street." He had a point, and Rhoe expected to drop the topic, but then he went on. "I don't want to be like my father was. Gone, a lot of the time. Distracted, for the rest of it. But I gather that's not the only way to manage the business side. And there must be ways for Healers to make things work. At least I assume so. You keep hearing about generations of Healers going through the Temple."

Rhoe grimaced, wrinkling her nose. "Not generally the better ones. The ones who like looking like plump satisfied cats, never getting themselves dirty or taking much risk."

"Well, in that case, we can certainly do better than that." Something about how he said 'we' so smoothly made her heart leap. Before she could say anything else, they rounded the corner, down the alley that led to the tiny front garden that held a portal. There were a few other people, and Hugh nodded pleasantly, then murmured to the attendant. "Waiting for someone coming from New York, he thought at half-two?" The British accent attracted some comment, but the attendant nodded. "Should be just a couple of minutes, sir. Ma'am."

They found a place to stand - it was a paved garden, in front of one of the row houses. While the general layout was not that different from a number of streets in London, or even in Trellech, the overall effect felt distinct. Despite being a port city, her impressions of it were all about air and wind, or perhaps sparks of lightning. That might be an interesting comparison to put to Hugh, who certainly had the chance to visit many different places. Rhoe glanced around, taking in the little details of the houses.

Three minutes later, the portal began to glow, and then Cyrus walked out, poised and graceful as ever. He'd practised that, she knew, so that he looked confident coming and going, with no hitch in his stride at all. It took a certain kind of stubbornness to manage. She always had to take a moment to feel the differences in the ground under her feet. He immediately spotted them, and came over, just as Hugh shifted his hand to her waist. It would have been scandalous in non-magical society, but here in the alley people would make largely correct assumptions.

"Good afternoon! Fine time had by all, then?" Cyrus was beaming. More than that, he had that glow of recently accomplished magical ritual.

Rhoe looked him up and down. "New York was good to you, I see."

"Exceeding, thank you. And staying here agreed with you, I see. You've not looked so fine, sister mine, since, well. In some time."

Rhoe took some pleasure in that slight stumble. "We have tickets for tomorrow evening, and a few suggestions for supper tonight, if you'd like?" Rhoe offered it, then stopped. Cyrus was looking more closely at Hugh now, as if he were deciding something.

When Cyrus spoke again, his voice was far more thoughtful. "Hugh, has anyone ever taught you Theremin's First Resonance? For managing magical energy?"

Hugh said, not unreasonably. "That sounds rather more like a musical instrument than anything else. Why?"

Cyrus waved a hand. "Friday, I wouldn't have thought

you'd have the knack for it. Now I'm fairly sure you might. It allows you to better utilise nearby sources of energy. Such as, say, another person, or an ocean."

Rhoe said, mildly, "The former is something I am actually trained to teach."

Cyrus grinned at her and made a mocking little bow. "Then you should do so. He'd have a use for it. You do agree?"

"About it being a useful skill, yes. What else do you think I'd say, given it's a great use in an emergency. About Hugh - who is standing right here." Hugh snorted, and hugged her against him for a moment. "Now being able to do it, I think it's fair to say I'm a little close to the situation to give a proper evaluation."

That made Hugh laugh, and Cyrus chortled. "That is what you have me for. Shall we? I should at least unpack a few things. And I have more books for you, Rhoe, though I'm sure you won't get to them before we're on board the *Citrine.*"

Rhoe managed an amused, "It seems unlikely. Having other things to do with my time at the moment."

"As it should be, as it should be. Well, come along, then, why are we standing around out here?"

Rhoe shook her head. "You're the one who started talking."

Cyrus led the way off, and once he was a few steps ahead, Hugh leaned to murmur, "It's all right then?"

"Oh, he already approved. But apparently he approves even more now. If you don't mind a thirty-minute lecture with at least three digressions, half a dozen footnotes, and at least five obscure references, we could ask him."

Hugh laughed. "I will say, this promises to be

educational on several fronts. I am glad he seems to approve."

Rhoe shook her head. "I suspect a great deal of the trip back will be strategising how to present it as a fait accompli to our parents. But that's something we can discuss at supper."

It was not at all what she'd expected from this trip. But here, on this foggy back street in a city she barely knew, she could not imagine wanting anything else.

Hugh had to wait for nearly half an hour, but he didn't mind at all. His meetings had finished a bit early, but everything had gone smoothly. Ockham was particularly pleased by the latest efficiency reports - and even more pleased by the increased satisfaction of the crew.

They'd dropped turnover on the line down to single digits, and the people who left generally were leaving off ocean voyages entirely. Since their father's death, the Pelagius line had become the coveted employer among the magical shipping lines - and the envy of many of the non-magical sailors.

That left him with half an hour to enjoy the Healing Temple gardens. After taking the portal back from his brother's office in Southampton, he'd ducked through to the side gate that Rhoe had shown him. There, he produced the pass she'd arranged for him, that let him in to the gardens whenever he wanted.

In the five weeks since he'd last been here, they'd moved from the first blooms of spring into a rambunctious burst of colour and movement. Trees had gone from the hints of green into full bloom of white and pale pink flowers. The garden beds were coming alive with shades of purple and blue and yellow and red, all the colours of the flourishing land.

He rummaged in his bag to find one of the books he'd bought for himself, as opposed to the five he'd got for Rhoe, and settled in to read. His trunk wouldn't catch up to him until sometime tomorrow. But he'd left a few things in Rhoe's flat before this last trip, and he had everything else he needed with him.

The great bells at the top of the Temple's bell tower rang five. There was a procession of people out from the doorway underneath, the one that led to the baths. A dozen people, over the first five minutes. Just as the tower bells chimed the quarter hour, he saw Rhoe's unmistakable shadow, and he stood up, strolling to meet her at the top of the ramp. She was utterly distracted. She didn't notice him until she was about to step around him, instinctively. He'd discovered she did that. The same way someone reading while walking would step around an obstacle, she did while walking and thinking.

"Hey." He kept his voice quiet. The Temple did that to him, it was like the world was blanketed in snow, the way all the sound felt muffled. "Do you have time for supper, perhaps?"

She blinked, and then stepped back, beaming up at him. "I didn't expect you until later."

"We got in half a day early. The currents were in our favour, nothing holding us up. I've had a good chat with Ockham, and I'm entirely free of any duties for a week." Before she could say anything, he added, "I know you aren't, but I'll find some way to amuse myself. Somehow."

Rhoe laughed. "Actually, I was going to ask if you wanted to have supper with Cyrus and Gemma tomorrow. He got permission to get her from Schola for the day, there's a lecture at the museum he wanted her to hear."

"Oh?" Hugh offered his arm.

"Something about a painting from the time of the Pact, and the symbolic depictions of aspects of the ritual magic? She's working on a paper for one of her classes where it's relevant. But it's also a painting from a private collection." Rhoe shrugged. "Owned by another Council Member, but not one he's on very good terms with, so this is much easier."

"When the easier option involves all the fuss of signing someone out. But I suppose they'd be inclined not to be too difficult to Council?"

Rhoe snorted. "Oh, the Schola staff consider themselves entirely equal in rank to the Council. As they point out, when it comes up, who do you think laid the foundation for that learning? The tutoring houses, to some extent, but mostly the fine professors at Schola. They're not wrong, exactly."

Hugh shook his head. "You do realise you live in an entirely baffling world. Here, can I take your bag for you? And supper out, or should we arrange something to have in?"

Rhoe looked him up and down thoughtfully. "In. Ideally something that will keep. I am restraining myself from demonstrating, effusively, that I missed you. Because we are mature and sensible people." She waited a beat and added. "And because I do not need to cause the kind of gossip that I'd cause if I did what I wanted here."

Hugh laughed. "Eating in it is, and we can gather something on the way by. That cafe near you? I like their sandwiches."

"You may want a bit more restorative sustenance than just sandwiches, but that will be a start." Rhoe had something decidedly specific in mind. They were still new enough to each other that he couldn't tell precisely what. Six months was not all that long when he'd been gone for nearly four of them in total. And she'd had her own work even when he was on dry land. Or the family commitments over the holidays. He was sure, however, that he would enjoy it.

He bowed. "Your bag, or would that cause too much stir?"

She considered, then handed her satchel over. It was rather lighter than his own, and he offered his free arm to her. Now they could take their time, settling in to being with each other again, talking over the little stories from the past weeks while they walked along.

He still wasn't sure which part of this he liked best. All of it, really. Their time in bed was delightful - a Healer's hands had proven to be as fine a thing as he had heard. But perhaps even more than that, he found he liked the company. The intelligent questions about what he'd been doing. She seemed to feel the same, the way she'd begun talking through events with him. Never anything that would identify a patient, even tangentially, but more about the politics of the Temple, and how she was learning to navigate them.

Which reminded him to ask something. "Did you ever figure out why that administrator was acting so oddly?"

"You were right. Personal, and for once not Cyrus to blame. Her father had some difficulty with our father, and - grudges carry down the family, don't they? We haven't sorted it out yet, but now I know to take my records to someone else, and she doesn't have to deal with me. It will do for now."

"Until you can figure out some longer healing."

Rhoe looked up at him and smiled. "Just so. Letting that linger doesn't seem good for anyone. Even more so when I'm tangled up in it. But it's not a thing to be rushed, so I won't. Tell me about how the *Moonstone* is doing? And did you catch up with Nerissa in New York City?"

Hugh had, and so they could pass the walk back to her flat in comfort. It was a fine afternoon and promised an excellent night, and the following days to come.

If you enjoyed *Sailor's Jewel* and would like to read more of this series, please sign up for my mailing list to get all the latest news and fun extras. Your reviews (on whatever review site you use) are much appreciated, too!

Read on for more historical details about this book and ocean life. If you'd like to see more of Rhoe later in her life, check out *Carry On*, set in 1915, where she is a secondary character.

AUTHOR'S NOTES

Thank you so much for joining Rhoe, Hugh (and all the others) for a week at sea. I've been joking for a while that anyone writing a series in my time period (the Edwardians through the 1920s) is sort of obligated to do an ocean liner book at some point, but the real reason for this book is it just seemed like so much fun (and it was). My original working tagline for it was "Taking a magical gem across the ocean. Alas, leviathan!". You got a kraken instead, but I feel like the basic core is still there.

As always, I owe particular thanks to a few people. Kiya Nicoll remains my most excellent editor, and had a number of ideas that improved the book and parts of the worldbuilding.

A good friend from college who prefers to remain unnamed was an amazing consultant for many details here, ranging from the pelagic mermaids to the navigational implications of some choices. (It was very helpful to have a friend who has both marine biology experience and experience on the open ocean. All remaining errors are mine.)

For historical notes, let's start with **ocean travel** since it's so much a part of this book. There are some fantastic sites out there talking about the golden age of ocean liners, with many photographs, floor plans, and other details. I found the GG Archives (https://www.gjenvick.com/OceanTravel) particularly helpful for the wealth of details, but there are many other great resources out there.

The *Moonstone* is based on other ships made in the 1890s with a couple of magical considerations. I used other ships of the time for the time of the crossing, which varied due to weather, conditions, and any reason for interruption (as happens in the book). Most commonly it was a 5-7 day trip at this point. The cabins were as you see them here: extravagant and spacious for first class, modest but usually well-designed for second class, and larger cabins for third class. It was common to have unmarried men or women in larger cabins all together.

Magical ships have several advantages, many of which are referred to in the text. They are more pleasant to sail on as a passenger because charms and enchantments can help with comfort - items staying where you put them on a shelf, filtered water for bathing, easier and more efficient ways to heat water or cool a cabin. There are aspects not discussed here, such as making it easier and safer to clean and cook for a number of passengers.

But a key benefit, from the owner's point of view, is that magic can make the massive coal furnaces that run the steam engines both more efficient (charms reduce the amount of heat lost) and safer for the crew. That's true both in general due to better ventilation, less exposure to the furnaces, and so on. But a more efficient ship can carry less coal which is safer and leaves more room for other cargo -

less expensive and greater profit, as well as probably a better safety record.

Clothing is obviously a major factor on ship, especially in first class. Rhoe, practical as she is, favours what's known as both **aesthetic and artistic dress.** If you've seen images from the Pre-Raphaelite artists (or photographs of the women among that community), you've seen plenty of examples: they were designed for ease and comfort, and made of flowing and often richly coloured materials.

Oekology was indeed a field of study at the time, and as soon as I came across the name, I knew I had to include it. It's such a great word. It is apparently coming back into discussion as a field again, since it looks at how communities function, especially when there is overlap to other spaces or systems.

There are few details from the chapter where Rhoe gets to show off her skills and bedside manner. **Thermometers** of the period took the five minutes shown to give a reading. This was better than the 1850s, when it took twenty minutes! Rhoe correctly diagnoses the problem as **sun sensitivity** brought on by contact with some plant that causes that (most likely, as she says, wild parsnip.) If you ever have an unexplained rash and you've been near plants or are taking medications that make you sensitive to sunlight, that might be your explanation.

The art songs sung at the first concert are a particular genre of song, popular in the 19th century and into the 20th for smaller performances. They were generally performed by a solo singer with a pianist accompanying, but they range through much of the Western European musical canon. You might hear a

Schubert lied, a Dowland motet, something from an opera or operetta, and then something French.

As soon as I started thinking about this book, I knew I wanted **pelagic mermaids** to make an appearance. I have mentioned coastal mermaids in the past. (In *Seven Sisters*, they are where Vivian learned sign language. The coastal merfolk sign routinely with land dwellers in a form that takes two hands rather than a pod collaborating together. but some signs are adapted for water resistance.)

I think of the pelagic mermaids as rather like killer whales, especially the ocean-going species: matriarchal, forming close-knit groups and pods, passing along generational knowledge. Whales and humans actually have more anatomy in common than you'd think of at first glance, and I think they took a different evolutionary strand (quite possibly influenced by magic along the way, of course.)

Of course, it takes specific skills to be able to interpret between the pelagic merfolk and land dwelling humans, and that's where **Merope's Speakers** come in. I suspect I'll be revisiting them in some future book. They negotiate between land and water in a variety of ways, and they are a peripatetic wandering lot, and fiercely independent.

Seals do indeed have interesting eyes that would result in what humans consider colour blindness - one that does otherwise occur in humans, tritanopia. It's a blue-green colourblindness that makes it more difficult to see the difference between blue and green, red and purple, and yellow and pink. It also makes colours less bright. (I spent a rather long chunk of time reading about how the rods and cones work in seals, and then figuring out what the human equivalent was. I'd like to thank a presentation about the evolution of the eye in mammals I was at due to a work-related conference for knowing I wanted to do that.)

Gemstones feature heavily in this book. **Aquamarine** is as described at various times: it has been particularly associated with ocean deities, with scrying and visions as well as other more mystically-focused forms of divination, with curing poisons or purifying water, for clarity of thought, and for safety on the ocean. Maxixe, mentioned briefly, is a particular deep blue version.

I could not resist a reference to the famous blue stone of Galveston. If you recognised it, I'm guessing you've also seen that episode of *Black Adder*, a historical comedy from the 1980s starring Rowan Atkinson and Tony Robinson (now perhaps more famous as the host of *Time Team*). The series is set in four different historical time periods: Richard IV (yes, that's fictional), Elizabeth I, the Prince Regent, and World War I. There are also a few specials. The history is surprisingly accurate when it's accurate, though parts of it have not aged as well.

During the first series, there is a point where Percy (a somewhat dim nobleman) is comparing the eyes of the Infanta of Spain to the famous blue stone of Galveston. Asked if the people who told him this have ever seen either the Infanta's eyes or the stone, he has to say no. Comparing one thing you've never seen to another thing you've never seen isn's how that works. (You can find clips of this on YouTube by searching "blue stone of Galveston" if you're really curious.)

One reason for Professor Merton to have the specialty he does was so I could have fun sharing a bit of sea monster lore. There's quite a lot of it. The oceans are vast, and there are still so many things we don't know about it.

We are fairly sure there are giant squid, much larger than we've ever seen alive, that may have given rise to the legends of the kraken. The leviathan is sometimes described like a giant primal serpent (in some lore it's associated with Tiamat, a Mesopotamian goddess of chaos. It's also named in multiple books of the Tanakh (the Hebrew scriptures). The aspidochelone is something else that shows up in lore, and is much as Professor Merton describes. It was so large sailors were thought to land on it and then drown when the creature submerged again.

Some of this lore is obviously an attempt to explain mysterious losses of ships at sea (besides storms). Some may well be an overlap with the natural world - squid, large whales, maybe icebergs that have made it unusually far into more equatorial oceans. And some of it, who knows, maybe we just haven't discovered yet.

Port cities have a long and glorious (and complicated) history. Alexandria and Bombay (now Mumbai) are two of the more ancient, and Cyrus lays out the reasoning for some of the South American options. I chose Boston both because it is one of the oldest and busiest ports on the east coast of the United States, but also where I grew up and now live again. The chance to have some fun with Boston was something I couldn't resist, even though there are a number of other good options.

In the vision from the aquamarine, they note that the **temple** they see is brightly painted. We know now (thanks to science advancing so we could find millennia-old flecks of paint) that the Greek and Roman temples were painted in all sorts of shockingly bright colours, rather than being plain marble. Cyrus and Rhoe don't know that yet, however.

The **Collect for Thanksgiving** that Rhoe overhears is indeed taken from the Church of England Book of Common Prayer of the time (which was rather easy to find online). It has prayers for all sorts of things, but the other ocean one (as Rhoe says) is for storms. When I actually read the text, I couldn't resist using a bit of it.

If you've read my other books - specifically *Carry On* - you'll know that Christianity is one religion among many in Albion. Rhoe describes her coming more formal commitment to **Belisama** fairly clearly, but I had a lot of fun figuring out how Rhoe came to that decision and what experience she had early on that made her certain of her choices.

When it comes to the ship in distress, **telegraphing** between ships didn't quite work yet (Though it would be famously a part of the *Titanic* story decade later, when it was still quite new.) And yet, ships had a strong code of assisting other ships having trouble at sea, in whatever way they could.

Rhoe points out that in the United Kingdom at this time, she would not have any vote or a number of other rights such as being able to have her own bank account. Albion is rather more progressive out of necessity (due to women with strong magic needing to have education training for the good of the community as well as themselves), but she's very aware of how narrow that margin can be.

The **William Weightman** mentioned on the *Memory* is a real person. He was at one time arguably the largest landowner in the United States, and he made a synthetic quinine, much in demand for treating malaria. He died in 1904 at the age of 90, leaving all his property to his daughter, Anne, who also has an interesting history.

Finally, once we reach **Boston**, my thanks to the friend who consulted on best areas for the magical streets of the city. The plays mentioned in the Boston chapters were actually playing that week. Thank you to the Boston Public Library collections I could figure out exactly what was on. I dithered about *Iolanthe*, a Gilbert and Sullivan operetta which is about fairies in a way that is utterly incompatible with the Fatae of my books. But it is, as Rhoe says, pretty much what you might get if you heard those stories tangled up, while drunk. The stars of this particular production were particularly respected, according to the reviews I could find.

Thank you again for reading. You'll be seeing more of Cyrus in a later book (*The Hare and the Oak*, which should be out in February 2022.) Sign up for my email list to hear about all the latest books coming out.

And if you'd like to see more of Rhoe later in her life, check out *Carry On*, set in 1915, where she is a secondary character. (Rhoe and Hugh also appear briefly in *Eclipse*, as does Cyrus.)